FIXED FOREVER

LAURELIN PAIGE

Cover by
Laurelin Paige

Content Editing by
Kayti McGee

Editing by
Nancy Smay at Evident Ink

Interior Design & Formatting by
Christine Borgford, Type A Formatting

FIXED FOREVER

DEDICATION

for Kayti
#times

FOREWORD

Hi! Thanks for picking up my book!

I'm so grateful that I want to give you FREE things:

Sign up for my newsletter where you'll receive a free book every month from bestselling authors, only available to my subscribers, as well as up-to-date information on my latest releases and a free story from me sent a chapter a time (sent May 2018—spring 2019).

Visit *www.laurelinpaige.com* to find out more about me and all my books.

PROLOGUE

Hudson Pierce:

You act so high and mighty, you and your perfect pregnant wife, Alayna. With your perfect child and your perfect home.

You weren't always perfect. Your past is filled with misdeeds.

Does your wife know all your secrets?

Would she stand behind you if she did?

You think because she's on bedrest you can protect her? How sweet.

Sleep tight, you two.

-An Old Friend.

CHAPTER ONE

ALAYNA

The thing about being a person with a history of acting crazy was that I couldn't tell myself if my thoughts and actions were sane.

When I was on the other side of it, completely "normal," whatever that meant, I could see the unreasonableness from before. Just not when I was in it. It almost felt like a different Alayna who had spent days and weeks obsessing over the tiniest things. Someone familiar, but not *me*.

But it was all me. Every Alayna was a part of me.

I stared at myself in the mirror, at the light circles under my eyes—signs of motherhood. I was starting to develop wrinkles when I smiled, but otherwise my face still looked young and cared for, thanks to the best beauty products. My hair was a tangled mess from bed, but it had been recently cut and styled. My pupils weren't dilated. My body wasn't fidgeting. On the outside I looked healthy, in control, normal. Tired and worn out, maybe, but that was to be expected.

I looked exactly like the woman I was—Alayna Reese Withers Pierce. The trouble was, both Alayna's wore this face.

"There you are," Hudson's voice was gravelly with sleep. I met his gaze in the mirror as he came up behind me and placed a kiss on the top of my head. "Rough night?"

I shook my head. "One of them woke up at five. Took the bottle and was right back out." I reached for my eye cream, to have something to do. I wondered how long I'd been staring at myself before he walked in.

Thankfully, Hudson didn't really seem to be awake enough to notice that I'd just been standing there, wondering if I was okay, if my swirling thoughts were normal or symptomatic. He padded into the bathroom and shut the door, but called out, "Which one was it?"

"Whichever one slept in the green and yellow frog pajamas." Was I a bad mother for not being awake enough to realize which twin I had fed in the dark? He didn't think so, at least.

Hudson had dressed them for bed the night before. He liked being part of the evening routine. It made him feel involved with parenting even when he worked all day at the office. And I enjoyed the break. I never knew what a luxury sitting down with a glass of iced tea was until the babies arrived.

"That was Brett," he said coming back from the bathroom. He headed over to his sink and washed his hands. "Should've guessed."

I dabbed the eye cream under one eye as I glanced at my husband. "Are you saying our little girl has an appetite?"

"I'm saying our little girl will do anything to get more time with her mama."

Seven years together, and he was still a charmer. I couldn't help returning his grin.

"You should get back to bed. Get some more sleep before they wake up for good."

I could probably get in another two or three hours before Mina, our four-year-old, woke up. It was anyone's guess with the twins.

But my head was spinning. I couldn't sleep now.

"I'll get there. Eventually." I turned my focus back to the mirror so Hudson wouldn't see the anxiety in my gaze.

Unfortunately, he knew me well enough. He didn't have to see my face to recognize it was there. "You're still thinking about yesterday's news, aren't you?"

I blew out a strangled sigh. Of course I was still thinking about it. The question was, why wasn't he?

The answer could very well be that my crazy was seeping back in.

So I didn't ask. I let my huff be my complete declaration. Whether I was crazy or not, I still had a right to my displeasure.

Out of the corner of my eye, I saw him leaning against the counter, his boxers hanging low on his toned hips. "Alayna," he said in that warning tone of his. "You need to talk to me."

I huffed again, dropping the cream jar on the counter before turning to face him. "She's going to be a member of our family, Hudson. Don't you see why I'm concerned?"

"It's not exactly *close* family. And, really, she's been family all my life." He was using his patient tone with me. The one that was calm and steady and even. The one that made my volume increase and my temper flare.

"Your mother was best friends with her mother. That's not the same as your brother marrying her step-daughter. Now there will be legal ties. There will be Thanksgivings with her, and Christmases and summer vacations and baby showers." I shuddered at the thought of Celia Werner around my babies.

Correction, Celia *Fasbender*.

"It's not like she's ever going to be alone with our children," Hudson said reasonably. "I think you will be surprised how infrequently we really do interact with her. She lives in England, after all. She'll go back there eventually." He pushed off the counter and headed over to the shower, turning the water on and sticking his hand in to check the temperature. "You were the one who told *me* not to overreact when they started dating, as I recall."

That had been true. When Chandler had begun dating Genevieve, Hudson had realized her father was married to our arch nemesis and he'd tried to put his foot down. Told his brother no way. It had been me who saw how much Chandler felt for his girlfriend, and I'd convinced Hudson it was not our place to interfere.

But I hadn't expected him to propose to the girl.

"It was supposed to be a fling!" I said, exasperated all over again. "Chandler was supposed to lose interest when he realized this wasn't a Montague-Capulet situation. This wasn't supposed to be permanent!"

"And now things have changed." Hudson turned to face me, then dropped his boxers to the floor. "She's different now. We don't have anything to be concerned about." He walked into the shower, and even if he didn't mean for it to be, it felt like he intended it to be an end to the conversation.

"But you don't know that she's different now," I shouted after him. "You're just guessing. She didn't do anything to show you that she's different."

"She fell in love," he called through the steam. "That changes people. You know that."

"Or she's playing like she fell in love." Which felt a lot more likely to me. Women like Celia didn't fall in love. They played long games. And this was her longest one yet. I was certain.

Hudson stuck his head out of the shower. "Come here."

I folded my arms across my chest and leaned back against the counter stubbornly. "Why?"

"Just do it."

I never could deny him when he talked to me in that commanding way. With a reluctant frown, I trudged toward him, weighted down by my fears.

When I was close enough, he pulled me into the walk-in shower with him.

"Hudson! I'm in my nightgown!" I shrieked, as the water from the rainfall showerhead poured over me.

"It's covered with spit up."

As if that was the reason he'd brought me in here. To wash my baby-stained clothing.

I glowered at him while he wrestled the nightdress over my head and tossed it to the shower floor behind us. That was better. With the physical weight of the wet clothing gone, it somehow felt like part of the weight of my anxiety had disappeared too.

The hot water beating down on my tense muscles probably helped. And the way Hudson was rubbing the knot at the base of my neck.

I tilted my head to give him better access, even though I knew full well what he was doing. "You're trying to distract me. You think I'm acting crazy. That I'm obsessing over this whole Chandler and Genevieve getting married thing and worrying too much about Celia."

"Are you?"

I thought about it longer than I needed to. It was what I'd been thinking about when he'd walked in on me. What I'd been thinking about all night long. "I don't know. I can't tell."

He circled around behind me and moved his massage to both shoulders. "I'm not worried about it."

I couldn't see his eyes now to see if he was lying. Not that he would lie to me—he didn't do that anymore. The only reason I wondered about his response was because, in my opinion, he *should* be lying. He *should* be worried. I would have been worried if I were him. After what I'd put him through the last six months.

But also, I was grateful that he wasn't concerned. Because until I'd heard the news yesterday about Celia becoming a family member, I was pretty sure myself that I'd gotten better.

And it was pretty fucking amazeballs that my husband still believed in me.

I leaned back into his hands. "If you aren't trying to distract me," I asked, my eyes closed, "then why did you drag me in here?"

"Because I do think you need to give yourself a break. Stop being so hard on yourself. Make time for the things you enjoy—your books, your movies. Your husband." He pressed the full length of his body against mine, and if I hadn't caught his meaning from his words, I certainly didn't miss the familiar ridge of his erection against the base of my spine.

"It's been five days," I laughed, amused at how his tone suggested it had been five months.

"That's even longer than I'd thought." He pulled my hair to one side and nibbled at my ear.

Honestly, he was right—I hadn't made enough time for me. For him. It was hard with three kids under four, but I was on an extended maternity leave from The Sky Launch, and I had nannies. There was no excuse for not being with him more often when we both wanted it. When we met, the idea of going five hours without his hands on me was unthinkable, let alone five days.

Besides, I did tend to obsess less when I was distracted. Especially when I was distracted by him.

The point was further made when his arms curled around me, one snaking down past my once flat stomach to sweep his fingers over the round bud of my clit.

I sighed into his body, instantly becoming aroused. He could do that to me. I was Pavlov. I knew the reward that followed the ding of the bell.

"That's it," he murmured at my ear.

I responded in kind, rubbing my ass along his stiff cock. "I miss you."

"Tell me I'm right," he coaxed. "Tell me you want it. Tell me you deserve it." He stooped behind me so that his crown nudged between my legs. "Tell me you aren't going to forget about taking care of your-self again."

"You're right I want it I deserve it I'll take care of myself now hurry please Hudson please." It came out as one long run-on sentence, my orgasm already beginning to peak just from his nimble fingers.

I didn't have to ask again. Without letting up on his manipulation of my clit, he angled himself and shoved in, filling me completely with one stroke. He'd been inside me so many times now, he could find the way easily, and still, his first thrust always felt like an exquisite invasion. No matter how well I thought I remembered what the pulse of his cock would feel like against my walls, it never failed to be a million times better.

I told him as much with an indecipherable whimper.

"I know," he groaned. "You feel good to me too, precious." He pulled out and pushed in again, fucking me in earnest. "I love it when you let me be good to you."

I turned my head toward him, my lips parted, and he caught me in a fierce kiss. "Why is it we don't do this every day again, H?" I asked when he let go of my mouth to suck my jaw.

"I believe the reason is called children."

"Shh. Don't talk about them. I'm about to come, and I don't want to make it weird."

He took my mouth with his again, ending conversation altogether, and deepened his massage on my clit so that I was exploding a moment later, my knees buckling, rivers of warmth shooting through my limbs.

I was still shuddering when Hudson grunted out his own orgasm.

He held me for several minutes after, letting his breathing settle while I ran my hand along his morning scruff. This felt nice. If I could really have everything I wanted, I'd have him cancel his day and continue holding me just like this.

But Hudson Pierce had an empire to run. Sex in the shower would have to do.

"It's been a while since you've fucked me good morning," I said, turning to face him when he let go of me. "Thank you."

"My pleasure. Though I'm hoping it's not quite good morning for you. Do you think you'll be able to sleep now?" He reached for the body wash and poured a dollop in his palm before gently working it over my breasts and torso.

I bit my lip while I considered. My head did seem quieter. Not silent—I still had worries, thoughts chattering about Celia and my sanity and our children and . . . other things—but all of it came through in a fog now. If I couldn't sleep, it wasn't for Hudson's lack of trying.

Still, I needed more reassuring. "Tell me again I'm not crazy and that you'd never let anything happen to any of us?"

He finished washing between my legs before he pulled me to him and wrapped his arms around my waist. "I'm not going to tell you that you aren't crazy, Alayna. But I love you no matter what you are, with all that I am. And there is no way in hell that I'll let Celia Fasbender, or anyone, for that matter, ever hurt you or our children. I swear on my life."

"Okay. Then I can sleep."

It didn't matter if he was lying. All that mattered was that I believed him.

CHAPTER TWO

HUDSON

I hadn't lied to her.

There was nothing I wouldn't do to ensure the protection of her and the children. Pierce Industries was kept as tight as a federal building. Background checks were double and triple performed for my staff and those we hired in our home. My wife wasn't aware, but we had a security team that looked over us twenty-four hours a day. Additionally, the penthouse had a state-of-the-art alarm system, and I'd paid for an update to both the building we lived in and The Sky Launch when Alayna had been on bedrest with the twins. She might be the one who fixated, but I was a stickler for attention to detail myself.

We were safe. All of us. There was nothing and no one coming after us.

Still, my stomach churned as I rode the elevator up to my office.

Alayna's anxiety didn't often incite my own, but Celia was a dragon from the past. And the past, though a foe long ago defeated, had a way of creeping up behind me out of the blue at times, breathing down my neck, reminding me of the man I once was. The man I'd vowed to never be again.

I *could* be him again, if I had to. To protect what was mine.

Could I pull myself back if I started down that path again? I couldn't be certain.

Today, though, there was no need, and I was a different Hudson Pierce.

"Your schedule is already up on your screen," Patricia said, standing from her desk to open my office door as I stepped out onto my floor. She followed me in, taking my umbrella and coat automatically. "Norma asked to be buzzed when you arrived. Shall I?"

This morning's meeting was set early, and I was arriving just on time. I glanced at my watch. Maybe a little past on time. Unlike me, but considering the cause, I was not regretful. "Yes, buzz her. And coffee?"

"Already brewed." She hung my coat in my closet as she spoke, then turned to Taylor Madison, my public relations lead, and my younger brother Chandler, who was finishing up a call on his cell. Both had been in the lobby waiting and followed me in.

Taylor immediately went to sit on the couch in the spot that Norma usually took for herself.

"Ms. Madison?" Patricia asked, already poised to prepare our mugs.

"Black, please."

"Chandler?"

I smirked, never tiring that my brother was the one person my secretary refused to address formally.

"Cream and sugar, Trish. Thanks." He tucked his cell in his jacket pocket then undid the single button as he sat down next to Taylor.

Cream and sugar. He was such a child.

A child who was marrying into Celia's family. Not for the first time, I wondered if he had what it took.

I finished tucking my briefcase under my desk, glanced at the schedule on my screen—it was a full day—then walked over to take my place in the armchair at the head of the seating area. By that time, Patricia had returned with a tray of mugs. Norma Anders, my financial advisor, followed behind her with a coffee cup already in one hand, a file folder in her other. Prepared. Ready. Unflappable. Now there was someone who could handle Celia.

"Let's get started," I said as soon as she closed the door. "Multiple allegations of sexual harassment at one of our clubs. Let's discuss solutions."

She walked over to the loveseat opposite Chandler and Taylor, and before sitting, nodded at Jordan, my chief security advisor who had slipped in at some point and was seated in the other armchair.

I hadn't noticed him walk in, which was, I supposed, the point. I only hired the best, and that Jordan was.

"*He's* here?" Norma asked, a brow raised. "You must be worried about potential backlash."

A hickey on Patricia's neck distracted me as she bent to hand me my coffee. She'd left her usually-kept-up hair down today. This must have been the reason. I appreciated her attempt at hiding it—if only because I didn't like accidentally imagining her with Nathan Sinclair, the man who most likely put the hickey there. He was part owner of the advertising firm I used, and I hated mixing business with pleasure. Even when it was my secretary's pleasure.

As she moved on to hand mugs to the others, I focused on Norma's question. "I'm not worried about backlash, per se, but I think the situation warrants a look at the security angle." I didn't mention that Jordan had asked to be included on meetings such as this. There were very few people who knew he had cause to be investigating anything at all, and I wanted to keep it that way.

"If you say so," Norma shrugged. She set her coffee on the table then opened up her file and distributed copies from inside before taking a seat, smoothing her hand over her pant-suit clad leg when she did.

"You can never be too prepared. Better security could have prevented a lot of this. I happen to think it's a wise decision on your part, Hudson," Taylor said, always eager to refute Norma when she had the chance.

"Of course you do," Norma said, recognizing the younger woman's ass-kissing for what it was. She circled her gaze around the room. "I've drawn up varying cost estimates based on each potential scenario. Option A is the least expensive, where we attempt to settle out of court with the accusers. You can read on all the way through to option F which includes all of that *plus* a complete overhaul and rebranding of the Adora nightclub. Obviously, this last is the most expensive."

Chandler flipped the page of the handout. "Yikes!"

I lifted the bottom of my top sheet to see the number underneath. "As always, it costs the most to do the right thing."

Since it was the first I'd voiced any opinion at all on which route to take, Taylor saw that as an opportunity to make it her agenda. "It might be the most expensive, Hudson, but, like you said, it is the right thing. In today's social climate, you cannot ignore accusations of sexual assault. Even if you pay these women lump sums and have them sign NDAs, they can come back to haunt you. At the very least, you should go with option C. Fire the current management and put out a statement saying that Pierce Industries believes women."

"You'd lose a few weeks of income, or however long it would take to replace the nightclub's managers," Norma conceded. "It is the second best option, financially speaking, and because social statements can have long-term financial implications, it may actually be the most cost-effective in the long run." She looked directly at me. "If I may ignore my position for a moment, Hudson—"

"Go on." She was going to whether I gave her permission or not.

"As of now, the scandal has only made local news. Do the right thing. Get the managers out. But even if you don't issue a statement, there is potential that people will talk and the truth will come out. You'll risk national headlines, and if you don't come out in front of it, it will seem like you're covering it up, which could—"

"I agree completely," Taylor jumped in, eagerly trying to preach on what was supposed to be her soapbox. "And furthermore—"

Norma narrowed her eyes, unwilling to be interrupted before she was finished. "—which could damage your financial bottom line irreparably. I think your best bet, though most expensive in the short run, would be to be transparent with your firings."

"I agree, but there's also going to be immediate backlash if you try to continue business as usual, even if you've fired the offending managers. There were too many people involved." Taylor pushed a blonde strand of hair behind her ear. "Do the statement, do the firings, but you should also shut down for a while. Say that you're doing a complete investigation, and you won't open again until you're confident the entire problem has been washed clean. Then, do a complete overhaul of the building and the brand. Open again in a year as a higher end club when the whole thing is forgotten."

I sat back in my chair, considering. She made a good point, but the skyrocketing cost she proposed wouldn't just be financial. "If we close the place down and do a rebrand, that's going to be jobs lost for everyone who works there, including the women who have come forward about harassment."

"Severance packages for everyone but the three main managers," Taylor offered, making Norma grimace.

"Who are the managers being accused again?" Chandler asked. He'd brought out his phone once more, and I couldn't be sure if he was taking notes or playing Candy Crush.

It was a fifty-fifty shot either way.

"Steve Wolf, Jeffrey Bannon, and David Lindt," I answered.

"David used to be at The Sky Launch," Norma commented. "Did Alayna have any thoughts about this whole thing?"

"I didn't want to bother her with the scandal," I answered honestly. I had wondered about it though. About David and how he'd once upon a time made moves on my then-girlfriend. If Alayna hadn't been the type of person she'd been, hadn't been so desperate for attention and affection, would she have thought his behavior was inappropriate rather than welcomed? As his boss, did I consider the way he'd behaved toward her inappropriate?

I did, but it was admittedly hard for me to separate my perspective as her husband from that of his boss when reflecting on the matter.

And as her husband, I didn't really want to discuss her former lover with my wife.

But I didn't have to do that in this case. Other women were saying he'd been inappropriate. That his two assistants had also been inappropriate. That all three men had assaulted employees on various occasions at my Atlantic City nightclub.

And that was all I needed to hear.

"Fire the three accused. We'll offer severance packages to everyone who is being laid off, and encourage them to re-apply down the road. It's time to rebrand and put new life into that nightclub anyway. Sales have been sluggish under David's management for some time. This is a good opportunity to regroup. Besides, it will take us a while to find a qualified person to take over."

"I'll prepare a statement," Taylor said excitedly.

I nodded in approval.

"Alrighty," Norma said, but she was smiling. "Expensive, but I'm sure it will pay off. Any leads on who you'd like to hire for the position? The sooner you start looking, the cheaper the transition will be."

"Chandler," I waited until I was sure I had his attention. "I'm putting you in charge of finding someone to take over and rebrand Adora. Start with figuring out a new vision for the place before you search for a manager." If the last year hadn't been what it had, I'd have suggested Alayna. This was exactly up her alley, and I felt a twinge of guilt for not getting her on the phone right then.

But there were ways in which my wife required protection that went beyond security systems and bodyguards.

So I gave Chandler another name. "Try contacting Satcher Rutherford. His family owns a chain of international nightclubs that are doing really well right now. He should have someone for you. He doesn't like me very much, though, so you might want to leave me out of it."

"Do I want to know?" Chandler asked.

I hesitated. Even if it were just my brother and I in the room, Chandler didn't know much about my days of manipulation and scheming. I found I liked it better that way. One person in my family, at least, could look at me without seeing the long shadow my past cast over me. "You don't."

I stood and addressed the room. "Thank you for meeting so early, everyone. You each have tasks. You're dismissed."

Jordan had one too, though I hadn't said it aloud. He would follow up to make sure that no one involved in this incident would become a threat.

Everyone began to disperse.

"Chandler," I called after my brother, gesturing for him to hang back.

I paused until everyone had left before going on. "What happened to waiting a few years?" This was the first chance I'd had to speak to him alone since he'd delivered his wedding news, and, sure, I'd been engaged to Alayna within a few months of meeting her, but Chandler was different. Chandler wasn't me.

He stuck his hands in his pockets and smirked. "What happened to congratulations?"

"I said that yesterday."

"And I said we'd wait last year. Times change, bro. We were ready to settle down sooner than we thought we would be. And no, she's not pregnant, so don't even ask."

I'd been about to ask.

Frankly, I didn't have any problems with his union, save for the distress it was causing my wife. Although I didn't envy my brother the pleasure of Celia's company, I wasn't convinced she was overly involved in their relationship. I tilted my head to study him. "What does Genevieve's father think about this?" The British businessman had given me the impression of being very protective.

"He's oddly supportive. He's even throwing us an engagement party." He toggled his head from side to side. "Well, *Celia* is throwing us an engagement party. But it was Edward's idea."

My skin pricked at the sound of her name, but the information was useful. "Is she, now? How very thoughtful." Perhaps she was more invested than I'd thought. I could feel my jaw tense as I calculated the costs and benefits of getting involved.

"Hudson?"

"Hmm?"

"If you don't need me anymore, I really need to get on the Adora rebrand and tracking down this Satcher Waterford . . ."

"Rutherford," I corrected. "You're free to go." I didn't miss the scowl he shot me. He didn't like it when I treated him like my employee.

I chuckled to myself. Truth was, I enjoyed riling him up. Likely as much as he enjoyed riling me up.

Not that I'd ever tell him.

"Oh, and shut the door on your way out." It was probably the lack of the word *please* that earned me his middle finger. But he did shut the door.

Once he was gone, I circled around to my desk and sat in the chair behind it. My hand hovered over the phone a few seconds before I decided I didn't want to involve Patricia in this call. Instead, I reached for my cell phone from my suit jacket pocket, pulled up the contact I needed, and hit the button to dial the number.

"Hudson, what an unexpected surprise." Celia's warm honey tone filled my ear like sweet poison, sending a shot of familiarity and dread down my spine. "To what do I owe the pleasure?"

I couldn't remember the last time I'd spoken to her privately like this, and because I'd years ago sworn to end all communication with Celia, it was arguably a betrayal to my wife.

I reminded myself I was doing this *for* Alayna.

"I hear you're throwing an engagement party for the kids," I said, my voice steady and in control despite the *tap, tap, tap* of my finger on my armchair.

"Word gets around quick. We haven't even set a date yet." She was moving, walking as she spoke, perhaps comforting her infant daughter. I could hear the baby quietly gurgling in the background. It was a sound I recognized easily these days. "Isn't the news fantastic? I knew those two lovebirds were meant for each other the minute I heard they were dating."

Sure, she did.

While I no longer feared my old friend the way that Alayna did, neither did I trust her. I'd known her far too long for that.

"I can't speak to the wisdom of my brother's romantic notions," I said, carefully, "but he does seem sincere in his intent to marry Genevieve. Therefore, I'm presuming this party of yours will be the first of many occasions that our families will have reason to attend an event together."

"And this concerns you?" Through the receiver I couldn't tell if she sounded bored or if she was two steps ahead of me.

"*Concerned* is putting it a bit harshly." I wasn't about to give her the upper hand. Wasn't about to let on that either Alayna or I was worried about her. "I'm more interested in everyone's *comfort*."

"Ah, I see. I suppose it wouldn't do to have any catfights spoiling the mood. Not fair to *the kids*. I'll be sure to seat you and Laynie, as well as Jack and Sophia, far from me, if that reassures you." She sounded nearly gleeful that she might be the cause of a problem.

Perhaps I'd given her too much credit when I'd said she'd changed.

"That doesn't mean stuffing us in the back, either, Celia. We *are* Chandler's family."

"Oh, Huds, what do you take me for? I would never do that. I want the party to be fabulous. Something everyone talks about. I'm not going to ruin anything on purpose."

Right. On purpose. But I knew what *people talking* meant—drama.

"Then you'll let me see the seating chart beforehand?"

"Definitely. Once we've selected the date and picked out a venue."

She was being awfully amiable, which put me on guard.

It also made me reconsider. Maybe I'd been right the first time. Maybe she *had* changed. It was silly to think that she hadn't. Ridiculous to think that, after all this time, now that she was married and had stepchildren and a baby of her own, that she'd risk all that to destroy my happiness.

Still, there was more than one reason why I could never be too sure where she was concerned.

"I appreciate your cooperation," I said, throwing her a bone.

"Any time. We're family now. Practically," she purred.

Again, my skin pricked. "I have to say, I'm surprised you're still in the States. I'd have thought that you and Edward would've returned to England by now. You said you wanted to raise your child there, and since the merger with Werner Media was denied and the three point alliance has been established between our businesses, there's nothing for you here." The decision to deny the merger had been mine. Instead, I'd agreed to an alliance between Pierce Industries, Werner Media, and Accelecom, the company Celia's husband owned. I still held the controlling interest in Werner Media, the company her father had founded, which gave me the upper hand in the relationship, and I didn't let her forget it.

"Isn't it great that we've decided to stay, though? Or we wouldn't be here for all the celebrating." She knew what I wanted to know. This was a game for her.

I didn't play games anymore. "That wasn't what I was hoping to elicit from my comment."

"You want to know when I'm leaving. Well, I'm not. Not without a bigger piece of Werner."

"Oh, really," I scoffed. She had to be joking. "And why would I give you a bigger piece of Werner Media?"

"I never said that we were looking to get it from you."

My muscles tensed as I sat up in my chair. "Oh?"

"Don't act all casual about it, Huds. We both know this is a big deal between us."

Big deal was an understatement. There were other shareholders with stock in Werner Media. It was possible that they'd found someone who wanted to sell, possible even that they could buy enough shares to overtake my majority. Controlling interest was the one thing I had over her. It ensured my family's freedom from her machinations. It let Alayna sleep at night. If she bought me out, I lost every bit of the power I'd used to keep her in her place for the last six years.

It was possible I didn't need it anymore, but was I ready to risk that?

"We're willing to buy from you, though," she added, spinning the tables again.

"That's not happening. Give control to you and your husband? Why would I do that?"

Was this why she'd been so amiable? Because she wanted something?

"We're not asking for control," Celia answered. "We're asking for equal shares bought at full price. Equal footing in our three-point alliance. We each come to this partnership with a company and stock in Werner, and those shares should be distributed fairly. It's the only way to move on, if we want this feud truly to be over."

She had a point. If she was being honest. If she'd grown and matured and stopped with the schemes.

But if she hadn't . . .

"I'll think about it," I said, genuinely. I'd think about it for my sake, to determine how it could benefit *me*, not *her*. I'd think about Alayna.

"Thank you, Huds. I appreciate your cooperation," she parroted my earlier words.

Considering the betrayal and secrets and dishonesty that ran through the Werner and Pierce lives, I figured it was only appropriate to parrot her back. "Any time. We're *family* now. Practically."

If only it didn't feel like that was exactly what Celia had always wanted.

CHAPTER THREE
ALAYNA

The first words out of Gwen's mouth when she stepped into the foyer of the penthouse were, "I'm sorry."

I didn't have to ask why she was apologizing. The reason was obvious. It was her day off, and she'd come over to brainstorm some ideas with me. I hadn't expected that she would be coming with a baby carrier on one arm and a toddler slung over her other hip.

The look on her face said she hadn't expected to be bringing her children either.

Working mom life was full of these surprises, I'd learned.

"No worries," I said, shifting Holden to my other arm so I could reach for Theo, her squirming three-year-old. "Maya?" I called out to the nanny on duty. "Could you—?"

Before I'd finished the sentence, Maya had peeked her head out of the nursery, her own arms empty. "Oh my goodness. Coming." She hurried toward us. "Brett's just gone down for her nap."

"And Holden is out too, if you want to put him down, and then come back for these two?" I handed my baby over, careful not to wake him.

"Sure thing." She trundled off with my baby in hand.

"I'm sorry," Gwen repeated, setting the carrier on the floor and bending down so she could take Braden out. "JC was going to watch all of them. Since we both have Mondays off, we don't have the nanny, but then Jake got sick, so JC had to take him to the doctor, and here I am, schlepping kids over to your house." She paused, smiling as she gazed downwards. "Hey, look at that. Braden's asleep too."

"I'll put the carrier in the nursery then," Maya said, having quietly returned for a fresh batch of children. "Theo, you want to come help me put together some of Mina's puzzles? She's at day camp right now, but I'm sure she won't mind."

I winked at the caretaker as she lifted the baby carrier and escorted the little boy down the hall.

Then I turned back to Gwen. "We have so many babies," I groaned. "How did this happen?"

"I keep asking myself the same thing," Gwen said with a grin. "But they're so cute."

My mind drifted back to the morning sex in the shower. I was on birth control again, and hadn't gotten pregnant easily either of the times I'd carried to full term. But twice Gwen had gotten pregnant while on some form of birth control. Sometimes just being around her I felt fertile.

"We could've rescheduled, you know," I said, walking with her into the living room. "Today wasn't urgent." I didn't bother offering her anything to eat or drink before plopping down on the couch. We were so comfortable around each other now, I knew she'd help herself if she wanted anything. Besides, having kids meant snacks were easily within reach anywhere in the apartment.

"I know it's not urgent, but I need your advice, and I didn't want to talk about this by text." She sank down on the opposite end of the couch. "And I definitely didn't want to talk about this by phone in case Hudson was around."

I'd been eager for her to come over so we could dive into our project, but now I was one hundred percent sidetracked. "Geez, way to pique my curiosity. Hit me. The doctor is in."

"Okay." She clapped her hands together and put them up to her mouth. "Okay," she said again from behind them.

She was nervous about telling me. Gwen didn't get nervous about telling me anything.

"Oh, fuck, you're not pregnant, are you?" I'd be nervous about telling me that too.

"No! God, no. I'm still breastfeeding Braden." Although with her history, that wasn't necessarily a deterrent.

"Then what is it?" I sat forward, knee bouncing with anticipation.

"Remember how last year Mirabelle told us she'd heard about these sex parties around town? The anonymous, masquerade, private kink parties that required exclusive invites because most of the guests were elite upper class, important people? Famous people? People that don't want their kinks in the gossip columns?"

"Yes, but you know half of what she hears from her clients is bull-shit rumors."

"Right, right." She nodded in agreement, probably remembering the unlikely story passed down from Hudson's sister regarding a prominent figure at the White House and two very famous adult film stars. "But. This time, the rumor isn't so much a rumor anymore. JC got an invite."

"What." It was more of a dumbfounded statement than a question.

"Yep. Exactly what I said." She put her hands in her lap and started rubbing them up and down her legs where they were bare below her romper. "This guy who sometimes co-invests in projects with JC got us the invitation. Honestly, I think he has a thing for my husband—maybe for both of us? And is probably hoping for a threesome, which JC said no way to already. Not that I asked! He doesn't share, and neither do I, but you don't have to have sex if you go to one of these things."

"You mean, you could just go and . . . watch?"

"Yeah. Just watch. Like a live porno." Her face flushed as though she were thinking about it. Or maybe she was simply embarrassed.

I tried to imagine it too—strangers cozying up to one another while I looked on—and sure enough, I felt my body warm. "That's hot." Her face relaxed as though she'd been nervous to hear my response.

"So hot. JC thinks so too."

Now I tried to imagine Hudson with me at a party like that. He'd never last as a voyeur for more than a couple of minutes. And he'd never expose too much of me to anyone else. He'd either find a corner and a smooth, obscure way to get under my skirt or he'd be pulling me out of the room before the stars of the show made it to anything good.

Maybe sex parties weren't for us. We had enough passion on our own. Didn't we?

But from Gwen's stories, my friend and her husband were into more adventurous fornication. It made me wonder if Hudson and I were in a rut.

"Are you going to go?" I asked, hoping like mad she would so she could report back.

"I don't know! That's why I need your advice!"

"Let's talk it through." Usually it was Gwen who was the rational one, but I'd learned a trick or two from her over the years. "Pros and cons. Pros—go."

"It would be fun, an experience, spice up our love life—not that it needs it." She easily rattled off the advantages without even having to think, suggesting she'd already thought a lot about this. "Could learn some new tricks. Make me feel young. Could meet new people."

"Those are great. What are the cons?"

"I hate people. Why would I want to meet more of them?"

I laughed out loud.

Her expression grew serious. "What if JC was attracted to another woman? All those hot naked girls in front of him?"

"He's always dealt with business around naked women, and he's only ever had eyes for you."

"I've popped three babies out. I have a scar from my c-section. Two words: stretch marks."

"Pfft. You know how devoted that man is to you."

"Yeah. I do."

She was quiet a moment, and so I asked the question I should have asked first, "Do you *want* to go to a kinky sex party?"

I could tell from her eyes that the answer was yes. But she mulled it over for a few minutes then threw herself back across the couch arm. "This is stupid, isn't it? I shouldn't even be entertaining the idea."

I frowned. "Why the hell not?"

"I'm a respectable woman. I'm a mother of three. I should be responsible."

"That's right, you are a respectable woman." I almost had to hold myself back, I felt so strongly about this. "And *because* you respect yourself, you should give yourself what you want. You should do something for yourself—and your husband. Something that isn't at all about your identity as a mother. Is that really all you exist for now? To feed and clothe and protect and shuttle around these little humans? Yes, they're important, but if you start acting like the only part of yourself that you're obliged to is your motherly side, you're not going to be any good for them. You need to be a complete person, whole and entire, and, by damn, that means going to a sex party and watching other people kink it up if that's what fills your cup."

She folded her arms over her chest and smiled at me. "Thank you. I knew that, but I needed to hear it."

I shrugged with one shoulder like it was no big deal. "And I need you to go to a party and tell me all the details after."

"I'm still getting up the nerve, but, for sure, if I go, I'll tell you everything." She sat up. "Is that why this project is so important to you? So you'll be whole and entire?"

I thought about it. Was my work that important to me, or was it that I desperately wanted to be seen outside of my role as a family woman? "Maybe? It drives me. Good or bad, I can't ignore it."

"Well, I think it's good. And that's the other reason I needed to see you today—I have news."

My heart started pounding with excitement. "Tell me!"

"Okay. So. I got definite confirmation that Lee Chong is looking to sell all three floors of the space adjacent to The Sky Launch."

My mouth and eyes went wide, and the sound that came out of me bordered on a squeal. This was exactly what we needed.

"He doesn't want to actually sell until January though," Gwen said, cautioning me. "For tax reasons or whatever. But he's willing to do an under-the-table negotiation before that, and let work begin. Maybe do a rent-to-own kind of a thing."

If she still had more to say, I wasn't listening now. I was definitely squeaking. "Oh my God, oh my God! He's really willing to do this? You think he'd really sell to us? We could really expand The Sky Launch?"

"It sounds like it's a pretty good possibility!"

"Holy crapola." I ran my hand through my hair, letting myself acknowledge that I was one step closer to putting my big project into action. "Wait, how do you know this? Did he tell you? Have you spoken to him directly?"

She shook her head. "Liesl. Apparently she's banging his kid."

"Lee Chong has a son?" I didn't know anything about my neighbor. The man owned the property but he'd rented it out for restaurants and event space. It wasn't like he'd ever actually been on the premises.

"No, but he has a daughter," Gwen smiled suggestively.

"Man, Leisl sure has a lot of fun. Did we have that much fun when we were single?" Good for her. Not that I was jealous. But I did miss working the club with her so I could hear her stories.

"I couldn't tell you. It was too long ago now." We sighed, wistfully remembering our younger days. Then she said, "So tell me what you're thinking you want to do with the place. I've been itching to see your plans."

"I've got them right here." I pulled my laptop off the coffee table and flipped open the screen. The drawings I had were already queued up, along with a secret Pinterest board full of different clubs I'd used for inspiration. "It's obviously not very accurate, and it's just in the beginning stages, since we don't have floor plans or specs or anything. But this is what I'm thinking."

I spent the next hour showing her how I wanted to open up a restaurant next door, continuing the DJ theme. The Sky Launch had gotten too crowded with both food service and dancing, and the two needed to be separated. The bubble rooms still remained a high level interest, though, so I imagined a similar design in the new space. Then, for the third floor, a café/bar with a small selection of vinyl records on sale. A more classic, casual vibe, as opposed to the ultra-modern spaces beneath.

"This is all incredible, Laynie. Hudson is going to go bananas for it. Why don't you want to tell him yet?"

I shut my laptop with a sigh and leaned back into the sofa. "Because we both agreed I wasn't going back to work until the twins were at least eighteen months old. And they're not even a year yet."

She shrugged like it was no big deal. "So you changed your mind. He'll understand."

"Not if he doesn't think I'm well enough to go back to work."

The easy air around us grew heavier as I broached the subject of my illness.

"You mean, because of what happened after the twins were born?" she asked carefully.

"You can say it, you know. Because I went crazy." If there was one thing I'd learned in all my years of mental illness, it was that pussyfooting around it didn't make it go away. In fact, it usually did the opposite, as though denying my problems made them even more eager to be noticed.

Gwen crossed her arms and frowned at me. "No, I'm not going to say you went crazy. You had a change of hormones that occurred from being pregnant and then not being pregnant. Which was exacerbated by having twins. A lot of women deal with postpartum depression and OCD. It doesn't make you crazy."

She sounded like my therapist, Dr. Joy. "*Crazy thoughts. Not a crazy person.*"

"Fine," I smiled begrudgingly. "I was being melodramatic. But sometimes it brings levity to the situation. You sound like you've done your homework. Researching up on it." I felt sort of guilty, not having invited Gwen to any of my counseling sessions. My therapist always encouraged me to bring loved ones if needed, to help them understand exactly what I was facing.

But while I knew she was there for me, and I had believed in being head-on with my issues, it was still sometimes hard to imagine my friend seeing me at my worst. It had been enough for me that she knew the basics.

"I wanted to understand," she said, nonchalantly. "And you aren't really sharing. You want to talk about it now? What it was like?"

No, I didn't want to talk about it.

And I did at the same time.

In some ways, talking about it confirmed it was over, a thing of the past, not something I was currently living through anymore. Unless I was wrong. Unless Celia was triggering me again.

I rolled my neck from one side to the other, suddenly aware of how tense my shoulders were. "I guess it was like most of the other times when I got crazy—" I corrected myself. "When I obsessed over someone. Except this time I was fixated on the twins. I worried if they were eating enough. If they were clean enough. I washed their clothes so many times that some onesies fell apart after they'd only worn them a couple of times. Their bottles never seemed clean enough, and I'd buy new ones, and put them in the sterilizer, and then be convinced that the sterilizer wasn't working, and then I'd order a new sterilizer. I don't even know how many sterilizers we bought. Poor Maya, I yelled at her to scrub everything 'better.' Disinfect everything 'better.' Do everything 'better.' I'm lucky she still wants to work for me."

I didn't mention the intrusive thoughts, constant worries that I would hurt them somehow, accidentally. That I'd maybe choke them with my breast while I was nursing. That I'd maybe slip and drop them while I was carrying them. That I might accidentally smother them with their blanket. Those thoughts were nonstop, like movies that played over and over in my head, on the screen even when other people were talking to me, even while performing other tasks, even when I smiled and pretended everything was fine.

Same face, different person underneath. The other Alayna.

"Every mother has a certain amount of those feelings," Gwen said, in that thin voice that indicated she didn't quite know what else to say. I couldn't blame her. This was exactly why I hadn't invited her to counseling. I didn't love the way people looked at me when they knew how my mind worked.

"Right. They do. It's natural, to an extent. But normally, our brains will have the thought, decide it's an incorrect thought, and dispose of it. My brain got stuck there." Fixated to the point of exhaustion. "The breaking point was when I showed up at Hudson's office with both twins strapped to me, my hair a mess, no makeup. No bra. Leaking milk through my T-shirt. Hysterical because I was suddenly convinced that the penthouse wasn't *safe* enough. And we needed to move. Right. Then."

Hudson had seen it then. If he'd been too exhausted himself to not notice before or if he'd been in denial, I wasn't sure, but as soon as it clicked, he acted immediately. He canceled his entire day and arranged for a therapist to meet me in the loft.

He canceled his entire month, actually. He'd done everything for me. He *was* everything for me.

"So now, I have medication and therapy, and a second nanny, and it's like none of that ever happened. I'm much, much better." I *was* much better.

Why didn't I sound more confident when I said it?

Because I worried my fixation had merely changed course.

"You look better, too. And you're obviously thinking pretty clearly to be able to come up with this amazing plan for The Sky Launch." She leaned forward, bracing her elbows on her knees. "Maybe working has been good for you. Maybe the time off was more of a detriment than a help."

"I agree. With all the help around here, I've been bored out of my mind." We both laughed, because it was sort of funny. That any woman with two kids under one could be bored out of her mind. Only another mother could understand the exhaustion of chasing children all day, and the simultaneous tedium of not being intellectually challenged.

"Then Hudson is going to totally understand, Laynie. You just need to tell him. Tell him what you're thinking. Come back to work officially."

I did feel horrible keeping it from my husband, especially when we'd promised no more secrets between us. It was additionally terrible to make Gwen part of the cover-up when her family had dinner with ours every Thursday night. Forcing her to keep my secret was an awful friend move.

And Hudson would support me. He'd always supported me in my work.

If I was truly well.

And there was the sticking point.

"What are you not telling me?" Gwen could read me like a book.

"I do feel better, but there are some things I'm still obsessing over. I guess that's the right term for it. Like . . ." I hesitated before giving voice to my latest thoughts. "Did you hear about Chandler and Genevieve? Their engagement?"

"He proposed? He said when they moved in together that he was going to wait at least a year!" She shook her head. "That boy has it hard, doesn't he?"

I supposed she wasn't to be expected to jump to the same issues that I had at the announcement. She didn't have a past with Celia. She had a past with *Chandler*. Her thoughts weren't even in the same arena as mine.

"I do think they're really in love. I'm not doubting that. Just, a marriage means that now we're going to be tied to Genevieve's family. And Genevieve's father is married to . . ." God, I didn't even want to say her name.

"Oh. Right." Her body sagged as she understood the situation. "And you're worrying about Celia interfering with your life?"

"It seems ridiculous, I know. She has a baby now. I'm sure she's preoccupied with motherhood. And her husband. And probably never thinks about us." My stomach twisted and writhed, like snakes in the bottom of a basket. "But what if I'm wrong? I have more children than her, and I manage to find plenty of time to brood. What if she *is* still obsessed with us? What if we're not safe from her?"

She nodded. "But that doesn't sound necessarily like crazy thinking. That's more just . . . history."

That wasn't exactly comforting.

In my experience, history had a way of repeating itself.

Chapter Four

HUDSON

My phone rang as the limo pulled up to the curb in front of the Bowery. Since I'd had to leave the office early, I hadn't driven to work. We'd be needing the large car later. It didn't make sense to swap out vehicles. Besides, my inner workaholic relished putting in just that much more time handling business before going off-duty. These days, I refused to let much of anything take my evenings away from the kids and my wife, but that meant getting less accomplished in a day than I liked to.

I answered the call. "Jordan, hang on a moment." I put the phone against my chest while I gave instructions to the driver. "Once you're back here with Mirabelle, text me. Alayna and I will be waiting in the lobby. We're already running late."

I grabbed my briefcase, stepped out of the car, and resumed the call as I strode into the building. "Why haven't I heard from you sooner?"

"Because you aren't going to like what I have to say," Jordan answered, point-blank.

"You found something?" My pulse sped up a notch.

"No, just the opposite. I have gone through—"

"Mr. Pierce," the doorman called after me as I rushed past him.

"Hold on again, Jordan." I tried to keep the irritation out of my face, and voice, as I turned back to the doorman. "Yes?"

"Someone left this for you earlier."

I snatched the envelope out of his hand, not bothering to read it before continuing on my way to the elevators. I was eager to hear what my head of security had to tell me, good news or not. "So you've narrowed down the names I've given you," I prompted Jordan.

"And I can't find anything suspicious from any of them. It's going to take some closer investigating than I can do from a distance. I'm going to need to talk to them personally to get a read on their reactions."

I closed my eyes as the elevator doors shut, wishing that the gesture could block out the ring of truth in Jordan's words. I wanted this to be easily handled.

But I knew he was right. "Do you have a plan of action? One that doesn't involve opening old wounds?" The elevator was going up but my stomach felt like it was sinking.

"I have an idea. It probably *will* open old wounds, but it will be safe. I'll tell you more about it on Monday. Enjoy your night at the party. Try to relax this weekend, okay?"

"Relax? What's that?" The doors opened in my penthouse foyer, and I stepped out. "How did Atlantic City go?" He'd been there since Monday's meeting, making sure none of the dismissals caused any problems.

"Everything's good. I don't foresee any problems there."

"Daddy!" Mina, dressed in a yellow ball gown from some Disney show, appeared out of nowhere and wrapped herself around my leg.

"I mean it, Pierce. Take your weekend off from this. I've got it." Without a goodbye, the line clicked, and Jordan was gone. Easier said than done, but I knew Alayna too well to think I could continue to be troubled over this without her noticing.

I also knew myself better than to think I could truly stop trying to solve the problem.

In an attempt to take his advice, I set my briefcase down, threw the envelope onto the foyer table, pocketed my cell phone, and reached down to pick up my little girl into a hug.

"Why, who is this lovely thing? I don't believe I've ever met anyone so breathtakingly beautiful."

"Daddy," Mina giggled. "It's me. It's Mina."

"Couldn't be. Mina's four years old. A little girl. She doesn't wear grown-up ball gowns. She's not a stunningly beautiful woman," I teased her as I carried her into the living room.

"I am too! I'm wearing a costume, Daddy! It's still me! And," she said, tilting her head and giving me an expression that made her look oh-so-very-much like her mother, "you shouldn't tell a girl that she's beautiful all the time."

"I shouldn't?" This one truly did puzzle me. Though, seventy-five percent of what came out of her mouth puzzled me.

And delighted me.

"No. You should tell her she's smart and funny and brave and enough."

I stopped walking and gazed proudly into her chocolate brown eyes. "You are right, smart, brave, funny, more-than-enough Mina. I stand corrected." I kissed her on the forehead, and then set her on the ground. "Is that what you're going to wear on your date tonight?"

She nodded. "Mommy said I could," she added quickly, as though she thought I might object.

"Perfect choice. You'll wow everyone with your smart, funny, brave, enough choice in clothing. Now, go find some shoes." She ran down the hall, and I glanced at my watch. By my estimation, I had just enough time to sneak in on Alayna while she was dressing. It had been a crazy five days, and I'd barely seen her between my schedule and the kids. Rather than go to a dull party in Larchmont, I would much prefer to cancel everything and take Jordan's advice by relaxing, buried inside my wife. More than ever, I wanted her to ground me.

But we had obligations.

So I'd settle for fooling around in her closet.

I started toward our bedroom, when a high-pitched squeal pulled my attention down the hall. Brett was pushing her walker around the corner of the playroom and the piercing happy noise had been her spotting me.

She fell to her knees, abandoned her toy, and crawled fast to reach me.

I bent down to pick up my baby girl. "Hi there, moonbeam." She smacked her hands happily along my jawline, babbling *dadada* and a mixture of other random syllables that had become my favorite sounds in the world. "You know, you are so close to walking. I bet you could've made a couple of steps if you'd tried. All you had to do was let go of that walker. You might have fallen, but it's going to get easier. I promise."

I rubbed my nose along her ear, inhaling her fresh baby shampoo scent before planting a series of kisses along her scalp. Selfishly, I was glad she hadn't taken her first steps yet without me around.

"There she is," Peyton, the evening nanny said, coming out of the toy room. Holden was braced on her hip. "I look away for five minutes to change this guy's diaper, and the other one disappears. I know I need to keep the door shut, but—"

I finished for her. "It gets stuffy in there, I know. I need to have someone come and look at the ventilation in the room. Remind me to do that, please. Are you feeling better?" Part of the reason that week had been crazy was that she had been out with a virus.

"Much. Thanks for asking. If you'll hand her over, it's dinner time."

I passed off Brett, making sure to say hello to my son before the three of them headed to the kitchen. Again, I checked my watch. Still good.

This time I made it to the threshold of our bedroom before the front buzzer sounded.

Shit.

I walked to the intercom and reluctantly told the doorman that he could send our visitors up. When the elevator arrived and Chandler and Genevieve stepped into the foyer, I greeted my brother with a complaint. "You're early. You're never early."

Chandler shrugged. "I'm never early *for work*. This is different, big bro. I'm excited for this." He patted me on the back as I threw him an annoyed scowl.

I turned my attention to Genevieve, pretending Chandler wasn't there. "I hear congratulations are in order." It was the first time I had spoken to her since my brother had popped the question.

She flushed as she grinned. "Thank you. It was unexpected, but I'm truly excited."

Her British dialect was pleasant to listen to. For that alone, I could see why my brother liked her. I glanced down at her left hand, finding it empty.

"No ring?" I addressed the question to my brother.

"It's being resized," Genevieve answered anyway. "I have pictures, though." She opened up the snap on her purse and pulled out her phone. After unlocking her screen and swiping a few times, she handed it over to me.

I took it from her, gesturing for them to follow me into the living room as I examined the image.

"There's a few of them, if you scroll," she advised, walking behind me.

The first picture was from the side and was hard to really see the diamond. I flipped to the next picture—I really was only looking so I could judge my brother. This image made me halt, my eyes wide. "Chandler, really?" The stone was so big it bordered on gaudy, particularly for a sedate young woman like her. "Can you afford this?"

"Har har," he retorted, perching on the arm of my sofa.

His fiancée giggled nervously. She sat on the sofa next to him, properly, like respectable people did. "It's perfect. I love it."

What else could she say? After he'd spent half a million on the thing, she was obliged to love it.

"It's beautiful," I lied, flipping to the next picture. Then the next. I froze.

This image wasn't of her ring, but of Celia. Holding a baby. A little girl in a white christening gown, with deep blue eyes like her mother's. The expression on Celia's face was one I hadn't seen in decades. Genuine emotion. Joy. Pride. Love.

For a handful of seconds—while staring at an image of a woman I thought I had destroyed—something moved in me, something shifted. A door opened that I'd closed long ago. It was only digital pixels, but I was convinced it was proof that something had survived. That I hadn't ruined her completely. That somehow she'd found her way to her own salvation, the way I had through Alayna.

And I was glad.

Genevieve leaned forward to see what I was looking at. "Oh, that's my stepsister. Obviously. And my stepmom." She held her hand out and I placed her phone into her waiting palm. "I guess there weren't as many pictures of the ring as I thought there were."

Part of me wanted to take the opportunity to ask more questions about Celia and her daughter. To find out if the emotion I thought I saw was real. Was she enjoying motherhood? Was it all she'd imagined? What was her daughter's name? I'd never even bothered to ask anyone.

But a bigger part of me only wanted the truth that I had settled on. I shut the door that I'd opened in my mind.

"Where is it that you are taking Mina tonight?" I asked changing the subject abruptly.

"Beauty and the Beast," Chandler answered. That explained the outfit my daughter was wearing. "We should be leaving soon if we're going to make dinner before the show."

"Mina was just getting her shoes on, if you want to help her." I feigned annoyance with my brother a good deal of the time, but I really did admire his close relationship with my oldest child. I offered my family a more tender side of myself, but Chandler was completely unreserved in his affection. Sometimes I envied him that. "She's in her bedroom."

Without another word, he stood and headed toward her room.

"Where is Laynie?" Genevieve asked. "I'd like to show her the ring—or the pictures, anyway."

"I was about to check on her." I turned to leave, then thought to add, "I'd make sure she only sees the ring." Perhaps I was overprotective. I knew my wife was strong, the strongest woman that I knew. But I would still put her in a bubble, seal her off from any possible hurt in the world, if I'd thought she'd let me.

Fortunately Genevieve knew pieces of the history of our families. She nodded in understanding. "Of course."

Back to my mission, I made a beeline for the bedroom, praying that I could catch Alayna just in her bra and panties.

Unfortunately, she walked out of the bedroom as I arrived.

"You're dressed," I stated.

"You sound disappointed. Don't we need to get going?"

I dragged my eyes up her body—up her legs to where they disappeared under the wrap skirt, over the luscious swell of her hips, the indent of her waist, over her full, beautiful breasts. Finally, I met her gaze.

"I was hoping I'd have caught you sooner," I admitted, my cock stirring as I pulled her into my arms. "You look fucking fantastic," I whispered at her ear, "and we have to share the car with Mirabelle so I can't do all the naughty things I wanted to do to you on the ride upstate."

She turned her head so her mouth was inches from mine. "Save it for the ride back when we're alone," she murmured before kissing me.

I pulled her hips closer, rubbing my semi against her pelvis to show her how hard saving it was going to be.

"Uncle Chandler helped me find my shoes!" Mina shouted, running down the hall toward us, waving her black sandals in the air triumphantly.

With a groan, I moved quickly away from my wife. "Then he can help put them on, can't he? You don't want to be late for your musical."

"Uncle Chandler! Come on! The buckle's hard." She pulled him by the pinkie toward the living room.

"Alayna, Genevieve's in there too. She wants to show you her ring."

"I have to see this," she said, scurrying after Mina and Chandler, as I watched her ass.

My phone buzzed in my pocket, distracting me from the view. I read the text that the driver was near, and I shouted out to Alayna to make it fast, then went to the foyer to wait. Spotting the envelope from earlier, I picked it up. It would be a couple of minutes before Alayna wrapped up the ring-talk, and I was suddenly curious about the item left with the doorman.

Most couriers would have delivered either to work, or to Alayna.

Without looking at the front, I ripped open the flap and emptied the contents. There was a slip of paper wrapped around a photo. The paper was blank. The photo was black-and-white.

And it chilled me to my core.

It was an image of Alayna sitting on a park bench, the double stroller next to her while she read her Kindle, seemingly oblivious that the picture was being taken.

The hair stood up on the back of my neck, and I hurriedly reached for the envelope and turned it over. It was addressed simply to the Pierces.

My heart started to race.

I recognized the handwriting.

CHAPTER FIVE

ALAYNA

"Damn, he can fill out a suit. He's still as hot as he was fifteen years ago."

I was sitting on the outdoor sofa, and since I was nosy, I casually turned my head toward the voice to see who was talking. I found two women I'd never met, nursing cocktails next to the water fountain. Following their gaze across the courtyard, my eyes landed on the only guy in that vicinity, his cell phone pressed to his ear, his brows knit in concentration.

He was definitely damn good-looking, and I already had dibs.

The second lady spoke. "Do you think he still—?"

I didn't hear the rest of her question, because Mira, who was sitting at my side, chose that minute to start up a new conversation. "Are you planning anything big for the twin's birth—?"

"Shh," I cut her off. I nodded discreetly toward the women behind us. "I'm listening," I whispered.

Mira's eyes went wide as her head tilted in that direction.

"—walk around all night in just swimming trunks at those parties at Mabel Shores. Remember that? Talk about shower nozzle masturbation material." It was the first woman talking again. She had dark blonde hair with highlights, cut into a very trendy style. Her makeup was perfect, her lips plump. There weren't any circles under her eyes. I felt a pang of envy at her well-rested appearance. "He was every woman's wet dream, that's for sure."

Mira gasped. "Are they talking about Hudson?"

"Yeah. I'm pretty sure they are." Curiosity got the better of me. "Do you know them?"

She snuck another peek over her shoulder. "Shit, I can't tell. They're walking away."

I turned more obviously now, and sure enough, the two were walking toward the bar.

"What dicks. You should've gotten up and told them what was what!" Mira fumed.

I chuckled. "Nah. They can look all they want. It's flattering, in a way."

She narrowed her eyes at me. "It doesn't bother you at all? They have to know he's married—everyone knows he's off the market—and they salivated over your man like he's a piece of meat."

I shook my head. "I salivate over him too. I totally get it. But I'm the one with the ring. So it doesn't bother me." Right? Of course right.

Probably. Those women weren't Celia.

I honestly was really secure in my relationship with Hudson. We'd been through a lot, proven ourselves to each other. He'd definitely proven himself to me. I knew he loved me. He would never leave me, and vice versa.

But did he still *want* me?

With my crazy baggage and my body-after-babies, did I still do it for him? That was a question I wondered sometimes. Sure, he'd wanted to fool around earlier, but that could well have been just to calm me down after a long day before an even longer evening.

"This party is kind of a drag," Gwen complained as she walked up, knocking back the rest of her vodka.

"It's always a drag," I said with a sigh, surveying the surroundings. Nash King's annual birthday party at his house in Larchmont was an outwardly casual event. There were no bands hired, the catering was simple. Yet there were always over two hundred guests filling his backyard and they were the biggest clients of King–Kincaid financial, the richest names on the Who's Who list of New York City. It was a night of schmoozing, bragging, and drinking in evening wear. Perhaps it was someone's idea of fun, but it wasn't mine.

Apparently it wasn't Gwen's, either.

"Well this year it's draggier than usual," she said, shifting her weight from one heel to the other.

JC suddenly appeared behind her, wrapping his arms around her waist. "I'm so glad to hear you say that. Does this mean we can leave now?"

"We just got here," she laughed. "We have to put our time in."

"Can we put our time in alone, in a secluded part of the garden? Just you and me?" JC rubbed his nose along her jawline, and Mira and I groaned in feigned disgust.

"No," she said, though her expression betrayed that she was thinking about it. "I'm having me some girl time here. Go find Adam and have some guy time." She handed him her empty glass. "Oh, and get me another one of these. Please." She batted her lashes, a very un-Gwen-like move.

He rolled his eyes, but we all knew he would do it. The guy was head over heels for his wife.

With the momentary distraction of JC gone, my brain headed right back to where it had left off—my relationship with Hudson.

"Do you guys think I had too many children?" I asked, circling around the real issue.

"You have as many as I do," Gwen said, "and with fewer pregnancies. Better bargain, if you ask me."

"I don't know about that," Mira came to my defense. "You worked until the day you went into labor with all three. Bedrest is hell on earth. I would rather have ten pregnancies than another one with bedrest."

I nodded in agreement. I'd spent nearly four months on my back with the twins. "But do you think I had them too close together? Not the twins, obviously. I mean the pregnancies. Should I have waited longer after Mina?"

Mira put her arm around me, her expression taut with concern. "Are you stressing out, hon? Do you need more help? You need to tell us if you're feeling overloaded."

I bit back the annoyance that crept up at her worry. While I was genuinely asking for my friends' input and I appreciated that they cared, I also hated that everyone around me felt like they had to look out for signs of my anxiety taking over.

That was my cross to bear, though. No one would be concerned at all if I hadn't given them reason to be.

This time, it wasn't my obsession talking. At least, I didn't think it was. "No. I have all that managed, as much as you can manage mommying. It's not like that."

Mira relaxed a bit. "Then where is this coming from?"

I bit my lip, glancing from her to Gwen. "Do you think Hudson's over me?"

Mira nearly dropped her drink. "Oh my God, no! Never. That man is the definition of *only lives for you*."

"He has mad love for you, Laynie," Gwen agreed. "It's gross."

I glared at Gwen. This from the woman who'd just let her husband practically feel her up in front of us? She wasn't fooling anyone.

With a frustrated sigh, I sank back in the sofa. "I know he loves me," I said. "I really do. And I love him. Just . . . can the magic really last forever? Day in and day out. Does it get old after a while? What if there's an expiration on happily ever after?"

My friends stared at me, neither of them speaking for several long seconds.

Finally, Mira broke the silence. "I knew it! Those women *did* bother you."

"What women?" Gwen asked. "Scoot over. I want to sit now."

"These women who were ogling Hudson earlier," Mira replied as she and I moved to make room for Gwen on the other side of me. "It was serious sexual harassment, if you ask me."

"They did not bother me," I protested. "Okay maybe they did. A little." I thought for a second. "But not because they were looking at him. It's just, what if he starts looking at *them*? I would, if I were him."

"Shut the fuck up," Gwen said. "You are hot."

"He would never look at anyone but you. I know my brother," Mira added.

"Mira," I looked her straight in the eye. "You know that this is a size up from what I used to wear." I'd bought the figure-flattering wrap dress at her boutique, so she was definitely aware of the change in my measurements.

"You had twins!" she exclaimed.

"Almost a year ago, and I still haven't gotten my body back. And it's been five days since we had sex."

"Five days. Really? Five whole days." Mira chided me in the same tone I'd chided Hudson when he'd suggested it was too long between rounds.

"I realize that's not long for some people, but it is for us. And it was five days before that, too."

"Because you have babies!" Mira reminded me. Yet again.

"Who aren't little anymore. They sleep through the night pretty well now. I have nannies who help me catch up on sleep during the day. And look—we're out tonight, for the first time in weeks, and Hudson has spent the whole night on his phone. He didn't even try to fool around in the car on the way up."

"Because I drove with you, you sillypants." Mira would defend our relationship to the death.

"He still used to try. No matter *who* was around." Tonight, he'd flirted when I'd first come out of the bedroom, but after that, nada. I might as well have been wearing a sackcloth. To further prove my point, I added, "JC still tried just now with Gwen."

"JC has no class," Gwen stated. Which was a lie, but nice of her to say.

"And Hudson was on his laptop the whole ride, Laynie," Mira continued. "There's probably some work crisis he hasn't told you about, and he's dealing with that. You said he's been on the phone? That proves it. I'm driving home with Adam. You'll be alone with him then. Don't let him work anymore. Give him a little . . . you know. I don't want to think about what the *you know* entails because he's my brother, but make it good, and you'll see it's all as it should be."

I chewed some more on my lip. *Was* I being crazy?

Gwen seemed to read my thoughts. "Every woman has these worries now and then. This isn't weird. It's part of the hormonal cycle, I swear. It pops up somewhere between needing to consume all the chocolate in the world and wanting to hump the first dick that walks in the room."

Mira and I both eyed Gwen.

"Maybe that's just *my* cycle. Point is, it's natural to worry about our marriages. It's a good thing even. It makes us think about our relationships and not take them for granted. That's what keeps them alive."

Somewhat comforted, I managed a reluctant smile. "You're right, you're right. I know you're right."

"Where is Hudson now, anyway?" Gwen asked.

"Over there." I nodded to where he'd been before, but found he wasn't there anymore. I looked around and spotted him not too far off, more in the shadows, farther away from the party.

And he was no longer alone.

Gwen found him too. "Who's that with him?"

I sat up straighter, my skin suddenly feeling tight and itchy. "One of the women who was ogling him."

"Oh, shit," Mira said. "I do know her."

I didn't take my eyes off the woman as she cocked her hip and twirled a strand of her long dark blonde hair. "Who is it?"

"Well," Mira fretted. "You're not going to like this. She's Christina Brooke—or that was her maiden name. She's married. I'm not sure what she goes by now. She used to be Celia's best friend."

My vision went red at the mention of Hudson's old friend. "Fabulous," I said, sarcastically.

"This is probably fine," Gwen said, calmly. "They're probably doing the obligatory catch-up. 'How have you been?' 'How's the wife?' 'How's your mother? I hear she's sober now.'"

"I should go over there." It was a party. Mingling was a party thing.

"You don't need to make a scene, though," Mina cautioned.

Christina Used-To-Be-Brooke took a step closer to my husband, her arms folded across her chest so her tits popped up nice and high.

I knew that move. I used to use that move. Back when I had moves.

The part that had my blood boiling was that Hudson didn't back away.

Mira amended her statement. "Okay. You might need to make a little bit of a scene."

I was out of my seat before anyone said anything else, nearly bumping into JC who had returned with Gwen's drink.

"Where's she off to so fast?" he asked, but I didn't hear anything else, my clipped pace carrying me across the courtyard in record time.

I kept my eyes pinned on Hudson and Christina, neither of them had noticed me coming up to them.

"—know how I feel about fidelity?" Christina was saying in a hushed tone when I got close enough to hear.

"I thought I did, certainly," Hudson responded. "You might've changed your mind." His eyes flicked to the side, and he saw me, so even though I'd considered, for a brief second, just hanging back and listening in, now I had to continue on toward them.

When I got to him, I slipped my arm around his. "Hi, I am Alayna Pierce. I don't believe we've met." I stuck my other hand out in greeting. Pretentious, perhaps. Possessive, definitely.

"Alayna, this is Christina Rodham. We used to run in the same circles. We haven't seen each other for quite some time. Christina, this is my wife."

Christina took my hand and shook it weakly. She likely didn't have much room to give it any force. She hadn't bothered to step back when I'd arrived. Hadn't bothered to wipe the drool off her mouth after slobbering over my husband.

"Nice to meet you, Alayna." She dropped my hand, then turned her focus back to Hudson. "I should get back to Thaddeus. He's here . . . somewhere." She put her hand on his bicep and ran it down the length of his upper arm while I tried not to scream bloody murder. "It was really good to see you again, Hudson. Ta-ta."

She sauntered off, her tight behind swaying much more than it needed to, even walking in heels.

I shot death rays after her.

When I glanced up at Hudson, I discovered he was also watching her walk away, his jaw ticking as though he was deep in thought.

"H, what did she mean when she said that you knew how she felt about fidelity?"

"She was talking about the past," he answered quickly. "Are you ready to go? I'm not in the mood to be here anymore, if that's all right with you." He put his hand at the small of my back and started ushering me toward the house.

"That's fine. But." I stopped walking. "Hudson. Who *was* that woman?"

He spun to face me, his forehead wrinkled in puzzlement. "Christina Brooke. Rodham. I told you. I knew her when we were kids. Let's go." He turned to leave again.

"Hudson."

He stopped.

"You fucked her. Didn't you?" I didn't know how I knew, but I did. Suddenly and certainly.

His eyes searched mine for a moment. "A long time ago. Yes. When we were kids. Now can we go?"

I let him escort me out then, stopping briefly to say goodbye to his sister and her husband, and to Gwen and JC. There was another round of goodbyes to Nash King and his wife and a few other important figures from the financial world. It was hard for me to stay focused on the people in front of me when my head kept thinking about Christina Brooke and her perfect plump lips and her flawless figure and the way she touched my husband and how my husband had once been inside of her.

Of course I knew that Hudson slept with people before me. Hell, I hadn't been a virgin when we'd met. But I'd never been introduced to any of his former lovers. I'd never seen him interact with them. I'd never had to wrestle with this jealousy in the flesh.

It didn't help that Hudson returned immediately to his phone once we got into the back of the limo.

I sat on my side of the seat and tried to figure out why it bothered me so much. Christina. Her fawning. Her history with my husband. Why did any of that matter? I knew he was loyal. I knew he loved me. There was no way he would have an affair.

But did he have regrets? Did I bore him? Was that why he worked so hard, disappeared so much into his job the last couple of years?

Was that why I couldn't be happy sitting at home and wanted so desperately to go back to The Sky Launch?

Maybe the solution was no more kids.

"Hudson?"

"Hmm?" He didn't even look at me.

"I think you should have a vasectomy."

"No," he said with finality.

I crossed my arms over my chest and scowled, trying to decide if I wanted to fight about it. We were definitely done, as far as I was concerned, but maybe the children weren't the actual problem.

Maybe it was as simple as Gwen suggested—it took effort to keep the magic alive.

We just needed to always keep making an effort.

"Crisis at work?" I asked, when I finally decided to act like an adult instead of pouting silently.

He glanced over at me, almost like he'd forgotten I was there. "Yes." Immediately, he looked back at his screen.

I wasn't giving up that easily. "Who do you keep texting? Norma?"

"Right. Norma." His eyes never left the phone. "Who else would be working this late on a Friday?"

I put my palm out toward him. "Hand it over. I want to talk to her." Wanted to tell her to give my husband the night off.

"No." He typed something off quickly.

My temper started to rise. "Why not?"

He didn't say anything as he clicked the button to darken his screen and pocketed his cell. The he swiveled toward me. "Because I'm done playing with my phone. Now I'm going to play with your pussy."

Fury turned to desire, and, slowly, I grinned. "Really?"

"Really. You've been neglected tonight. I have making up to do.

Give me your foot." He held his hand out.

I lifted the leg closest to him and swung it around to put my shoe in his palm, spreading my legs wide at the same time, open for him.

He set my foot on the seat against the back, propping my knee up.

"Good girl," he said, low and husky, eyes piercing mine with greedy lust, even in the dim light of the interior.

I shivered.

Scooting closer, he ran one hand up my bare leg and then farther up my thigh, leaving a trail of goosebumps in its wake. When he reached the top of my leg, he moved to the knot at the waist of my dress and undid the sash, opening the wrap so that I was left in my black panties and matching bra.

He surveyed me with the same hungry gaze he always had. "I've been wanting to get under your dress since the second you walked out of our bedroom," he hissed.

"Sure couldn't tell. All night, the only two things you had eyes for were that phone and Miss Christina Perfect Tits."

He raised a brow before bending to kiss lightly along my inner thigh. "She had perfect tits? I hadn't noticed."

"How could you miss them? If not now, then ten years ago. When you fucked her." Yeah, so I was going there. Sometimes I couldn't stop myself.

He continued kissing up, up, until his kiss pressed along the crotch of my panties. "I wouldn't know. I only fucked her once, and it was from behind."

"Oh my God," I moaned as he dragged his teeth along my clit through the material. After all these years, he knew just how to touch me. How to make me get *there*. How to undo me with a single breath along my skin.

But I wasn't done with this conversation.

"Why would you tell me that?" I asked, breathily. "I don't want to hear that." My comment dissolved into another moan as his tongue took a turn swirling my swollen nub.

"You don't?" he asked, lifting up. "That's not like you. You usually want to know everything."

This time when he put his mouth down there, he sucked, hard, until my fingernails were clawing into the car's upholstery.

"Okay, okay, I want to know," I said when I could speak.

He smirked, sitting up to look me in the eye again. "She might as well have been anyone. She was part of a game. Like every woman was before you." He wrapped his fingers underneath the waistband of my panties and paused. "Are you better?"

"Not yet." I nodded toward the place down between my legs, indicating exactly what would make me all the way better.

He chuckled. "I'm working on it, precious. Patience."

With my help, he maneuvered my panties off. Then he buried his head between my legs and licked and sucked and fingered and made me all the way better. After three orgasms, I climbed onto his lap and rode him until we got home.

There was definitely still magic between us.

But I thought about his strange encounter with Christina as I fell asleep, the fragments of the conversation I'd overheard between them remained a puzzle still unsolved.

And when Hudson slipped out from under the covers in the middle of the night with his phone in hand, I worried again. Even Norma went to bed eventually.

CHAPTER SIX

HUDSON

The first time I received a threatening letter, I was twenty-three and still working with my father at Walden, Inc. When he saw it, he shrugged, patted me on the back, and said, "You've made the big time. Hire a security team. Stop opening your own mail."

I started Pierce Industries soon after that, took his advice and hired a company to handle my security. Besides handling everything in the building, they looked over me personally. While I still opened my own personal mail, they drove me places when needed and monitored my home and computers. Anything that bothered me got flagged and dealt with straightaway.

The agency sent a rotation of men—one was as good as another, as far as I was concerned. I didn't take the whole thing very seriously. What did I have to protect? My money? My life?

Neither meant that much at the time.

It wasn't until Alayna came into the picture, until I finally had someone worth protecting, that I truly got serious about my team. I paid more attention to who was on staff. I required detailed resumes before choosing who would be her driver. There were several with qualifications that fit the bill nicely, but in the end, I chose Jordan Black, a man I'd worked with several times. I didn't choose him because of his skills, though he had them. I chose him because once, when Celia had tried to flirt with him, he'd turned her down, saying he was gay.

I'd been so protective of Alayna, so jealous of any other man in her presence, that even after I was sure Jordan wouldn't come on to her, I thoroughly double-checked his background myself before selecting him.

In the years following, Jordan had proven himself over and over. Eventually I stole him away from his security firm and gave him free rein to start a team of his own. The more time we'd spent working together, the less sure I was of the facts on his resume. It stated he'd been special ops, trained in the Navy, had specific high-level computer coding knowledge—if those items weren't true, he certainly had the skills to fake it. The rest of the details on his resume were what I questioned. That he was given the name Jordan Black at birth. That he had grown up in Omaha, Nebraska. That his parents were named Hannah and George. I wasn't even sure if he was actually gay or he'd just said that to deter Celia.

But I *was* sure I trusted him.

He was the only person outside our family who had access to the penthouse. That meant he didn't have to buzz in when he arrived on Saturday morning, early. He texted when he was on his way up, and I went to the foyer to wait for him.

"I don't need to ask if you got any sleep," he said, looking me over. "If I hadn't been up all night with you on the phone, I'd be able to read it all over your face."

"Hello to you too," I said dryly. "Let's take this to the library." I didn't have to tell him I wanted to hide our meeting from Alayna, if possible.

Unfortunately, we weren't quick enough crossing the hall.

"Good morning, Jordan. It's a little early for company. Should I be concerned?" She pulled the top of her robe closed as she stared into me. Brett, still in pajamas, chattered away in her mother's arms. Behind her, Holden pushed his walker while Mina cheered him on.

"Of course not, precious," I answered swiftly. Smoothly. "Routine security updates. Weekends are the best time to get those things taken care of, and you know Jordan's an early riser."

She glowered. "I suppose this means that we're doing breakfast without Daddy, kids."

I winced. It was eight fifteen, and on Saturdays the nanny didn't come in until ten. Even with the cook taking care of meal prep, the children would be a handful. I felt guilty leaving Alayna alone to deal with them, but reminded myself that I was thinking of her first and foremost, whether she was aware of it or not.

And I saw no reason why it would be helpful for her to know.

"Can we have pancakes?" Mina begged as the crew headed toward the kitchen. "Can I help make them? I can stir!"

"Oh, yes, that won't be messy at all." Alayna's sarcasm was evident. She called back over her shoulder. "I am not getting you coffee, so don't even ask."

"I already brewed some," I called back, glad I'd at least done that. Jordan gave me a disapproving smirk.

But who was he to judge? I was ninety-five percent certain he wasn't married.

Or . . . at least seventy-five percent certain.

We went to the library, and I shut the French doors. As an extra precaution, I locked them too. Silently, we headed past the sofa and the lines of bookcases that housed Alayna's collection, to my desk by the windows. I opened the top drawer and pulled out the envelope and photo I'd received the night before, then carefully handed them to Jordan.

"The handwriting looks like the others," he said, putting on his gloves before he took them from me. I hadn't gloved up before opening the envelope myself, but had only touched the corners as soon as I'd realized what I was looking at. I didn't imagine there would be any prints, but I wanted nothing left to chance. "This is all there was?" he asked.

"The photo was wrapped in a blank sheet of paper. I have that too." I retrieved the blank paper by the corner as well and passed it on.

Jordan pulled a Ziploc bag from his jeans pockets, and secured the items I'd given him inside. He scanned the room, his gaze landing on the shelves. He selected a random book, one with a tall spine and wide cover, then tucked the bag inside.

"Mind if I borrow this?" he asked facetiously.

"By all means." Hopefully, Jordan would slip out without

encountering Alayna again, but in case he didn't, the photograph would now be hidden from her view. Why he was borrowing classics at eight in the morning on a Saturday was a question I'd leave him to answer.

"There won't be any fingerprints. There haven't been on any of them. But I'll see what I can find out," he assured me, confirming my suspicions.

I nodded. "The doorman said for sure that it hadn't been hand delivered?" We'd been over this already, but I wanted to hear it again. I'd texted Jordan on the drive to Larchmont the night before and informed him of the situation, so while I was enduring the tedium of another Nash King birthday party, my head of security was interviewing the man who'd given me the envelope.

"It had been on the counter when Paul Gershwin, the one who gave it to you, arrived. I tracked down Stuart Patton, the doorman on shift before Gershwin, and he swears it came in a bigger envelope addressed to the building. It was enclosed with a menu for a new Ethiopian restaurant and an advertisement for a strip club. Patton threw everything away except the envelope addressed to you, which he left on the door stand counter." Jordan recited the details without any hint of irritation at having to repeat himself for the fourth time.

I liked him as much as I trusted him.

"Damn," I muttered. "I really thought we had him. If it had been personally delivered . . ."

"The cameras in the lobby would have caught him," Jordan finished for me.

"Or her."

"Or her." He waited a polite beat before stating the obvious. "This guy—this person—has proven to know you well enough to know you'd never leave the lobby of your building without eyes."

I hoped that was true. I hoped that this asshole counted on me forming a very tight protective perimeter around my family. I hoped this asshole didn't dare try to invade it.

But if my optimism was in vain, I'd be ready. "How is the surveillance team coming together? Have you managed to fill every position?"

"Remember, you only asked for the increase last night. But I think I've got all the shifts covered for the next couple of days. Long enough to recruit some boys from the old office. How do you want me to handle the team dedicated to your family? Your wife is going to notice she's being followed."

"If they're good enough to have the job, they should be good enough not to be noticed," I snapped.

Jordan stared at me blankly.

"Oh, don't look at me like that." I ran my hand across the back of my neck, trying to relieve the knot that had taken root at the base. "I'm going to tell her. Soon."

I should've told her months ago. I didn't want to tell her at all.

"For now, tell them to do their best to hang back. She's a mother with three kids. She's usually preoccupied with them. She shouldn't be too hard to watch from a distance."

"All right," he acquiesced. "As for the other thing we talked about last night, I'm planning on spending the rest of today setting up as many interviews as I can."

"Good. That's good." I didn't know if I was telling him or myself.

I brought my hand around to rub at my jaw, the prick of morning stubble reminding me I likely looked as ragged as I felt. Reminding me that it was Saturday morning, and I was supposed to be in the dining room eating pancakes with the kids.

I had to hand this off to Jordan, had to trust that he would do his job while I focused on my weekend with my family.

"You know, you have enough cause to bring the FBI in now, if you decide that's the route you want to go." Jordan was always serious, but he managed to sound even more somber by suggesting to give another team a job that he'd usually command.

That was enough to give me pause.

But involving outsiders meant my past would be looked at as scrupulously as my present. That created more problems than it solved.

"No. It's too messy," I said, definitively. "You're as competent as anyone on the FBI's team. More so. We'll keep this between us, if you think you can handle it."

"I can handle it." With that, he took his borrowed book, and slipped out of the penthouse.

I found my wife in the kitchen, and I wrapped my arms around her from behind as she tightened the lid on a baby bottle, hoping she knew that the weak security of my embrace wasn't the extent of the ways I worked to keep her safe.

Hoping she never needed to know that she wasn't.

* * *

"The next one is starting," Jordan called from the couch.

I finished dumping my cold coffee into the sink, put the dirty mug on the counter, then, with a deep breath and the promise of a scotch later, I headed over to take my place sitting next to him.

The setup was simple—a live feed recorded in a hotel room downtown, displayed on my computer screen here in the loft. It worked pretty well for the most part. Sometimes the picture would buffer, and all we'd get was sound for several minutes, but the camera in the conference room recorded it all so we could catch what we'd missed later.

"Thank you so much for coming in," Allison said. She was part of Jordan's security team, usually assigned to computers, but it seemed she had useful acting skills as well.

From the angle of the camera and of the door of the conference room, we weren't able to see the face of the person she was greeting until they sat down at the table, and I hadn't bothered looking ahead to see who was on the list.

There was a certain amount of trepidation waiting for the next interviewee to be unveiled, and for good reason. While I'd always known what I'd done to my victims, it was quite another thing to hear it from their own mouths.

When this one came onto the screen, I knew immediately the story was going to be one of the worst.

"Isaac Zucker," Jordan said next to me. "Do you remember what your engagement with him was?"

Yes, I remembered. In excruciating detail. "He's probably going to be one of the ones you'll want to pay attention to," I confessed.

"As I said over the phone," Allison began, "I'm in the process of writing a tell-all book about Hudson Pierce. I want all the dirt, all the scandals. The worst of the worst." She continued with her spiel about a pretend biography she was writing, creating a safe space for Isaac to speak before asking if he could be videotaped—not disclosing that he was already being filmed.

Isaac was eager to talk. It took him two hours to recite all the details of how I'd picked him out at a Stern symposium years before I'd met Alayna. How I'd invested time and energy and interest in his innovative approach to harnessing solar energy for tech use. He had a multimillion-dollar idea, and I'd courted him, tempting him away from any other offer until it was just him and I on the playing field.

Then I deserted him. Changed my mind. Told him I didn't think his idea was very good after all.

It probably wouldn't have been so bad if I had left it at that, but then I had black-balled him, telling all the biggest names in the business that he was an individual who should never be worked with.

When Isaac had nothing left, no options, no job offers, I'd come back to him and bought up his cutting-edge idea for a measly hundred grand. Then I sat on the patent, and did nothing with it, letting it waste away in a locked file cabinet.

Those were the facts I knew, but in his interview I also learned the constant up-and-down of his career had caused great tribulation in his relationship with his wife. She'd left him, after he found her in bed with another man. He'd developed a cocaine problem. Been through rehab—twice. He was clean now. All of it, everything, he blamed on his lost career. The life he hadn't gotten. The life he'd deserved, stolen by Hudson Pierce.

I hadn't forgotten him over the years, but Isaac had eventually quit bothering me about the patent on his idea, so I'd assumed he was past it, had moved on.

I'd assumed wrong.

"He's definitely angry," Jordan agreed. "I'll see if I can get a better look at his timelines, perhaps I can match up anything to the dates the letters have been sent."

I nodded as I pulled out my phone and texted Norma. -Draw up a $4 million payment to Isaac Zucker. Then contact development, tell them to pull his patent and get you a figure for what it would cost to start working on it.

-Okay.

A second later she texted again. -This is the fourth such request this week—should I be concerned about your psychiatric well-being?

If only she'd thought to ask that fifteen years ago.

-I'll swing by before going home to sign the checks, was all I said in response.

When I looked up again, the interview was over, finally, and Isaac was leaving the room.

Jordan reached forward to turn down the volume on the computer then sat back and looked at his clipboard. "I'm crossing Jeffers off the list," he said, as his pen followed through with the action.

I rubbed my forehead with the palm of one hand, wishing I could erase the interview we'd just watched. Wishing I could erase the need for the interviews in the first place.

But I'd been who I'd been. "Marlene Jeffers spent ninety minutes explaining how I ruined her senior year of college by playing head games with her, and you're convinced she couldn't possibly be the person threatening me?"

He shook his head. "It was in her body language. She had been angry, yes. Hurt, yes. But those are old wounds. She doesn't feel that now. She only showed up to the interview because she's hoping for a free plug of her Instagram lifestyle profile. Didn't you notice how she dropped the name over and over? I stopped counting at mention number nine."

"Hmm." He was right—I could see it now that he'd pointed it out. Usually I was good at reading people, at discerning their ticks and their tells. Was I losing my touch? I had barely slept in days—that could be it.

Most likely my block came from the stakes on the line. When I'd used my skills to predict other people's moves in the past, it had always been for fun or for money. It had never been to protect my family's lives.

It was a good thing I wasn't doing this alone.

"Cross her off, then," I conceded.

It was Thursday, and this was our third day of this. Jordan had set up the feed in the loft, at least, so that I wouldn't have to take it apart when I had a meeting or explain it to anyone who came into my office. It hadn't ended up being an issue since, by Tuesday afternoon, I'd cancelled the rest of my week's schedule. It was too hard to switch gears from this task to any other, and hearing the twisted things I'd said and done to people once upon a time was gruelling. I felt like I was on trial.

Maybe I was, in a way.

Jesus, how much longer could I endure this?

I held my hand out toward Jordan. "Let me see the list."

He handed me the clipboard comprised of all the names I'd given him over the last eighteen months. Every person I could remember who I'd thought might possibly be a suspect. It was a long list. And yet I knew I was still missing so many names.

"What do the highlights mean?" I asked, noting some had been marked in bright colors.

"The green are the people who have interviews scheduled. Yellow haven't called back. Pink declined to meet."

"There's a hell of a lot of pink. How is this going to work if we can't get one of your people in front of them?" I knew the level of my pessimism was related to the level of my discomfort at the process. I'd renounced my past when I'd met Alayna, but for so many other people, it was still present.

Jordan took my mood in stride. "People who don't want to meet are less likely to be our guy. Our guy *wants* to talk. Our guy wants to shit all over you, and if he or she gets the opportunity, our guy isn't going to pass it up."

All of our best leads were based on profiling, and that didn't give me peace of mind. I wanted cold, hard clues.

But this was what we had at the moment, and it hurt like a like a kick to the crotch to admit it.

"Christina Brooke," I said, spotting her name highlighted in yellow. "I saw her the other night." I'd somehow forgotten to mention that.

"And?"

I took a breath before I answered, replaying our conversation in my mind, searching for anything in her words or actions that would tell me her motivations.

"Perhaps this isn't the time to bring it up, but, seeing you, I feel I need to address the way I behaved with you in the past," I'd said. *"It was inappropriate."*

She'd tilted her head and twisted her lips questioningly. *"You mean the night we fucked each other's brains out, and Celia showed up? What was inappropriate about that? We had fun. You weren't with Celia. If she got her feelings hurt, that was on her."*

"It may have appeared that way," I'd kept my voice low and quiet. *"Yet I had indicated to her that there might be something more between her and I. I betrayed that when I went into a bedroom with you."* Even after years of therapy and saying it out loud many times, it had made my stomach churn to have to admit it to someone else.

Christina had pondered then shrugged casually. *"Not my business. I had a good time, like I said. Did you think I'd care if you were unfaithful? Don't you know how I feel about fidelity?"*

"I thought I did, certainly," I'd said. *"You might've changed your mind."*

Had I learned anything from that encounter?

"She wants to fuck me," I said to Jordan, remembering her flirtation, even in front of Alayna, when she'd joined us. "I don't think she's 'our guy.'"

"Are you sure she doesn't want to fuck you enough to resent everyone else who has a piece of you that isn't her?"

I'd only watched *Fatal Attraction* because of Alayna—It wasn't my type of film—but my mind went immediately to the scenario of a woman terrorizing her one-night-stand, ruining his life when he wouldn't give her more.

This was real life, though. Not a movie. And I refused to believe we were dealing with anyone that crazy.

But my skin felt raw and it itched from the inside because the truth was, I couldn't be sure.

For the first time in my life, I was the pawn in someone else's game.

CHAPTER SEVEN

ALAYNA

I paused when I saw the name on the caller ID.

"Do you want to talk to Grandma today?" I asked Holden, who was babbling away while he used the coffee table for support.

"Ba ba ba ba ba," he replied, happily.

"I believe the word you're looking for is *bitch*," I muttered to myself before clicking the talk button on my phone. "Hello, Sophia," I said, with as little enthusiasm as she deserved.

"Good," she said with evident relief. "You answered. I've been trying to reach Hudson all morning, and he won't pick up his phone."

Because he's smarter than me, I thought.

"It must be important then. What can I tell him for you?" She hadn't even begun, and I already planned to forget whatever it was she had to say. Since becoming sober, Hudson's mother had found her favorite hobby to be gossip. Every bit of news was a scandal. Every scandal was immediate.

"It *is* important, thank you. I had lunch with Louise Gunther, and she knew it wasn't her place to tell me this, but she felt it was her *duty*. She's been a very good friend and proved it today by passing on this news."

Very good friend, yet this was the first time I'd heard her name.

"She plays tennis with Joni Sneed who plays bridge with Caroline Dunlow."

My ears perked at the name Caroline Dunlow, and I stopped playing peekaboo with Holden to pay closer attention to where Sophia was going with this.

"Caroline is the director of the New Park Elementary School, as you know. All of the Pierce children and grandchildren have gone there."

I rolled my eyes at that one. Aryn, Mirabelle's daughter, had been the *only* grandchild before Mina.

"Yes, I know who Caroline Dunlow is." We had registered for Mina to attend New Park in the fall but were still waiting for her acceptance letter.

"Well. I'm sorry to be the bearer of bad news." Her tone wasn't the least bit sorry. "But Louise says that Joni says that Caroline says you aren't getting in. I mean, that Mina isn't getting in," Sophia corrected herself. "Obviously, this is a tragedy."

I stood and started pacing the living room. "I wouldn't quite call it a tragedy, but are you *sure* that the New Park School is denying Mina's application? We're perfect candidates, and Mina's a legacy." It was hard not to be a little smug about my smart, confident, talented oldest child. And frankly, with the Pierce name, we had the money to go anywhere we wanted.

"I am certain," Sophia said, annoyed that I would doubt her. "Louise was quite clear."

"That doesn't make any sense. Mina did fabulous on her preliminary tests and interviews. Our references are spotless."

"I'm telling you what I heard. And, again, I'm only the messenger here, but she did give me the reason as well."

There was something a little too excited about Sophia's tone. As though she were delighted to be the one to tell me this terrible thing she was about to say.

I straightened my spine, preparing for the worst. "Out with it."

"Unsatisfactory parentage."

She let the words sink in, though she didn't need to. They hit me like a ton of bricks. Hit me and took me down with them, sinking into the bottom of an ocean.

"Of course we should have expected this. I don't know why we weren't prepared beforehand. Should've made an extra donation or contribution to their foundation in the Pierce name, perhaps a scholarship, but of course it's too late for that now . . ."

Sophia went on, chattering about all the reasons why it was inevitable that I would be the downfall of Mina's education. Of her career. Of her entire destiny. I barely listened to her. The more her voice buzzed in my ear, the more enraged I became. Enraged at *her* for being so gleeful about disappointing news. Enraged at the women who would gossip so casually about our family's social standing.

And most of all, enraged at the New Park School and Carolina Dunlow for only seeing my past history, not the person, the *mother*, I had become. For holding sins against me that had been out of my control, such as my parents' deaths while I was still in high school, my mental illness, my poverty, my lack of good breeding.

It wasn't fair.

And since when did I let people treat me unjustly? Let alone my children.

"... about her in the future, Alayna. How is she going to get anywhere going forward if you can't even get her into the family elementary school?" Sophia meant the question rhetorically, but I jumped in.

"I'll take care of it. Thanks for letting me know. Goodbye."

Before I could hang up, she stopped me. "Wait, wait. What are you planning to do? These people need finesse. They are the kind of—"

"I said I'd take care of it." My rage shot up another notch at the suggestion from my mother-in-law that I wasn't the appropriate one to deal with the situation. I knew she thought Hudson would be the better one to address the New Park School. To approach Caroline Dunlow.

But I could defend my own honor and integrity as easily as he could. And the whole point was that I was worthy, on my own. That I was a satisfactory parent. Not the kind who sent her spouse to fight her battles.

I clicked *End Call* before Sophia could say another word, then threw my phone on the couch in frustration.

Seeing a bright new shiny toy, Holden eagerly began making his way around the coffee table toward my dropped cell. Quickly, I snatched it back up, and exchanged it for a baby toy. He fussed at the substitution.

"Yeah, kid. I feel the same way." So, what was I going to do about it?

I picked up the baby and continued pacing the room. Obviously, I needed to talk to Caroline Dunlow. As soon as possible. Before she sent out the official rejection letter. It probably wouldn't help our situation—once these bureaucratic elites decided what they wanted, their minds were hard to change—but she had a right to know what I thought about her decision. And I had a right to say my piece as well.

With one hand, I did some searching on my phone. The New Park director's office was open until four. It was almost one-thirty. I had time to make it.

Shit.

I swore mentally as Brett started crying over the baby monitor, alerting me she'd woken from her nap. It also reminded me that Maya wasn't here. Mina's day camp had needed extra volunteers for a field trip, and our nanny had elected to be one of those to go.

"Damnit," I cursed again, under my breath, as I trekked down the hall to get the other baby.

She stopped crying the minute she saw me, her face lighting up at my presence. "I'm good enough for you, aren't I?" I bopped her on the nose and she giggled. I looked from one baby to the other, formulating a plan of action.

Finally, knowing neither would respond, I asked, "How would you kids like to go on an outing?"

* * *

It took half an hour to get the babies dressed, changed and ready to go. New Park Elementary was only two blocks from the Bowery, so fortunately it was an easy walk with the double stroller. I packed up the diaper bag and made sure I had enough formula in case one or both of them got hungry, then loaded them into the carriage and headed down the elevator.

As soon as I stepped into the lobby, a bald man wearing dark glasses and a black suit standing by the wall walked toward me. "Do you need me to call your driver, Mrs. Pierce?" he asked.

I blinked at the stranger, having never seen him before. Obviously he knew who I was.

"No, thank you. We're walking today." I eyed him suspiciously as I continued toward the door, and realized he wasn't alone. A second man wearing dark glasses and an earpiece, also in a dark suit, stood near the wall as well.

"Who are your new henchmen?" I asked Stuart, the doorman, as he hurried to open the door for us.

He appeared puzzled, as though I'd asked a strange question. "New security team."

"Oh," was all I said, since it seemed as though I should have already known. And maybe I should have. I'd been so distracted lately, analyzing my marriage, planning my business, having a postpartum breakdown, that I hadn't paid any attention to the mundane details of anything outside the children.

"Enjoy your day, Mrs. Pierce," he called after me when I was outside.

But once I was out the doors and the fresh air hit me, I remembered why it wasn't a good day, remembered my task at hand, and found myself getting riled up all over again.

I walked down the street at a clipped pace, composing what I meant to say in my head. I knew my best shot at redemption was a dignified speech with well-thought-out points demonstrating my strengths, contrition for the past, and ways that I'd contributed to society.

But instead of forming a succinct, humble speech, all I wanted to do by the time I reached the front doors of the fancy school was tell Caroline Dunlow off.

I pushed the handicap button at the entrance and gruffly moved the stroller through the doors of the administration office. The secretary recognized me.

"Good afternoon, Mrs. Pierce. Is there some way I can help you today?"

I took a deep breath that didn't seem to calm me at all. "I need to speak to Ms. Dunlow, please. Right away."

"I'm sorry, but Ms. Dunlow is in a meeting with the board to finalize next year's admissions. Can I take a message and have her get back to you?"

"She's meeting with the board *now*? Deciding final admissions *right this minute*?" If that was the case, then no, I couldn't wait. I needed to talk to her immediately, and if the board was there too, all the better.

The secretary nodded in affirmation."Yes, ma'am."

"And they're meeting in this building?"

"Yes," she said carefully, "they're in the conference center, but—"

I didn't let her finish. The conference center had been where we'd had our interviews for the program. I knew exactly where I was going.

Pushing the stroller forward, I moved hurriedly past her desk and down the long hall.

"Mrs. Pierce, Mrs. Pierce, you can't go back there!" The high-pitch of her panic seemed to indicate that she was unsure whether she should leave her desk unguarded to follow after me or stay put and call for backup. It was summer, so school wasn't in session, which meant there probably wasn't any security on campus. And, honestly, that secretary was a petite little thing. I was a tiger of a mama with a double stroller as a weapon. I would have been afraid of me too.

I kind of *was* afraid of me.

But I didn't have time to think it through. I had one shot. I beelined for my destination, praying that Brett's fussing was only momentary.

The conference center door was shut when I arrived, so it felt extra dramatic when I flung it open and pushed the babies in ahead of me. A handful of faces turned in my direction—seven, I counted quickly. I didn't recognize any of them until the woman who had her back to me turned around, and there she was—Ms. Dunlow.

"Mrs. Pierce," she said, surprised. "Did we have an appointment?" she asked in that condescending way that said she knew full well that we did not have an appointment, but was being polite about *my* mistake. "Denise would be happy to reschedule with you at the front—"

"No, we do not have an appointment. I would not like to make an appointment. I don't want to talk to you at a later time. I need to speak to you right now. Because from what I'm hearing in the upper circles, if I don't speak to you right now, I won't have the opportunity to speak with you at all."

I only paused to take a breath when Ms. Dunlow stood and tried to steer me back toward the door with a nod of her head. "It seems that you're upset, Mrs. Pierce. Alayna. Why don't we take this into another room, and we can—"

Her patronizing tone, her familiar use of my first name, the way she tried to console me while brushing me aside—all of it only fueled my fury.

"I do not want to take this into another room. What I have to say needs to be heard by all of you." I scanned the room, looking deliberately at each face. "All of you. This enrollment system of yours is archaic and downright mean. How can you possibly determine my child's ability to be educated simply by looking at the circumstances under which her mother was born and raised? Obviously you aren't taking into consideration all I have done to rise above my station, the lengths I have gone to in order to overcome my past, and the hurdles and the struggles that have faced me. I have an MBA. I graduated first in my class with a 4.0 grade average. I manage my own business.

"But even if I hadn't done those things, even if I were 'just a housewife,' this determination is classist and pompous and really just terrible-ist. Especially, *especially*, letting other people know that I'm an unsatisfactory parent before you even inform *me* . . . ?" I had to raise my voice then, since Brett's whine had become a real cry. "It's disgusting and intolerable, and I can't believe that we donated funds to this program or that we even wanted to enroll our daughter in the first place. Really. You should all be ashamed of yourselves!"

A woman sitting across the table stood from her chair. "Caroline, I'll handle this," she said smoothly.

I reached down to grab Brett out of the stroller, asking as I undid the buckle, "Who, may I ask, are you?" I didn't like the idea of being passed off, and I certainly didn't like people to think they needed to *handle* me.

I glared at her, waiting for her answer. She was older than me by ten years, maybe even twenty—it was hard to tell with all the Botox and fillers in her face. Her hair was beautifully set, so stiff it didn't move when she turned her neck, and her eyes were sharp behind the Vera Wang readers perched on her nose.

"My name is Judith Cleary," she said. "Caroline is the director here, but I am the head of admissions. I am not sure how you came to the information that you were to be rejected, or who it was that leaked that the reasoning was unsatisfactory parentage, but I am afraid that your facts are not entirely complete."

Bouncing Brett up and down on my hip, I felt my stomach start to sink. "What do you mean?" If Sophia's information had been wrong, so help me God . . .

"It wasn't because of *you* that Mina was given the unsatisfactory parentage enrollment denial, although given *these* circumstances . . ."

I ignored the pointedness of her statement and focused on what she'd said first. "That doesn't make any sense. Why would Hudson be considered unsatisfactory?"

Judith Cleary's smile felt cold and mean, sending a chill down my spine. "That, I'm afraid, you'll have to ask your husband."

I tried to call Hudson's cell four times on the way back to the Bowery with no answer. I called his office directly, and Trish told me he'd put his phone on *do not disturb,* and asked not to be interrupted. Which was fine when it was his mother calling him, but a totally different story when it was me.

"Would you like me to knock anyway?" Trish asked.

If he was going to have to be interrupted, I wouldn't have his full attention. Not over the phone. Maybe it would be better to wait until we could be face to face. That would have to be later because I wasn't dragging Brett and Holden to Midtown. "No, that's okay. I'll see him tonight."

When I got back to the building, Stuart was already holding the door open for Mina and the nanny. With the sudden option of not having to lug the twins around, my plans for the rest of the afternoon could change.

Good. Because I was going to fixate until I talked to Hudson.

"Maya, I need to run an errand," I said after properly greeting my four-year old. "Would you mind taking the twins up with you?"

"Of course not, Mrs. Pierce."

With my children and their caretaker headed up to the penthouse, I strolled over to the security guard from earlier, the one who'd approached me. I noticed he was alone this time.

"*Now* I'd like my driver," I said to him.

Just then the doors opened and the other guard walked in. He seemed almost startled at the sight of me. As though he'd been waiting outside for me to leave and thought I'd be gone by now.

Had he been following me?

"Your driver is right now parking in the garage," security man number one said, pulling my attention back to him. "Would you like to meet him down there, or have him pick you up at the curb?"

"I'll go down there." I suddenly wanted to get out of the lobby and away from the men who not only knew my name and were possibly tailing me, but also seemed to have my private driver on speed dial.

By the time I got to Pierce Industries, though, I'd dismissed my thoughts about the security guards as paranoia and moved back to Judith Cleary and her perplexing statement. Did Hudson know her? He'd never mentioned knowing anyone on the board when we'd applied to the school, but maybe he hadn't been aware she was a member. Or he hadn't wanted to tell me. She seemed to think he'd understand why we'd been rejected when I told him her name, but why?

"His phone is still on *do not disturb,*" Trish said when I walked into Hudson's waiting area. "He's pretty much had his doors closed all week. I'm sure you can go right on in."

I was glad she was sure that I could, because I was going to.

I walked into his office, shutting the door behind me quietly in case he was in the middle of a serious phone call or train of thought. Hudson, however, wasn't in his office at all. If Trish thought he was, though, there was only one place he could be.

I pushed the button, hoping the key was inside. And it was. Which definitely meant he was in the loft. I rode the one level up and walked out into the living room of the apartment above Hudson's office.

I spotted him right away, sitting on the couch in front of his computer screen.

Fast asleep.

I sighed softly. Poor guy. He'd been working like crazy over the last week. Working *too hard*, if anyone asked me. He'd never said what the project was that was preoccupying him. It was strange that, whatever it was, it had taken him out of his office and brought him here, of all places.

Ever curious—okay, snoopy was a better term for what I was—I crept over to him and peeked at the computer monitor. There was an image of a conference room of sorts with a table and some chairs, but the room was empty of people. Remote interviews? Unusual for him to be involved in, but nothing interesting.

I looked instead at the papers spread on the coffee table in front of him. A photograph caught my eye, and I reached for it. It was a picture of me, sitting on a park bench with my e-reader. The babies were in their stroller right next to me. I remembered that day. Mina was on the grass attempting cartwheels in front of me.

But who had taken the picture? There hadn't been anyone with us. Was this Jordan's doing?

I put the photograph back down and picked up the papers. There were several, all covered in handwritten block lettering and blue ink. Very informal in presentation. They certainly didn't give an immediate impression of being business related.

I scanned through them, quickly at first, but slowed down when their meaning began to sink in, the hair on the back of my neck rising as terrifying phrases jumped off the pages.

"*. . . should have counted on your past coming back to haunt you.*"

"*. . . don't deserve your happy life, Hudson Pierce . . .*"

"*The safety of your tower is an illusion.*"

"*. . . you think you can protect her?*"

"*Hold those children tight.*"

"*. . . someone should take it all away.*"

My hands were shaking, my throat strangled and dry as I gasped. "Oh my God, Hudson! What the hell is going on?"

CHAPTER EIGHT

HUDSON

Jordan left in the afternoon to follow up on some leads after the interviews from that morning. The timing was good—I was ready for some quiet time to process the re-emergence of my past. Of the old Hudson.

I leaned back on the sofa in the loft and closed my eyes, waiting for the next victim to show up on the screen and divulge all the terrible things I had done. All the terrible things I used to enjoy were far more painful to relive these days.

I opened my eyes again when I heard the actor portraying our "author" delivering her spiel. "I'm writing a tell-all that will expose Hudson Pierce for the man he is . . . anything you have to contribute . . . completely anonymous . . . extremely helpful . . ." And so on.

Was this whole ruse proof I had never changed? That underneath my family-man persona, I was still the person I had always been? This elaborate set-up to find information on one person who wanted to scare me—was it ironic that I reacted with a manipulative scheme, not unlike the schemes that had put me in this situation in the first place?

Should I be worried I wasn't more concerned about it?

The man being interviewed began to speak, dishing out his opinion before offering any specifics, in a chillingly monotone voice. "Hudson Pierce is a fraud. A pathetic excuse for a human. He deserves his bad karma and ill will for everything he's done to the innocent people who tried to know him and love him."

The voice was familiar, but something was wrong with the camera, and the face was coming in blurry on the screen. I could make out the man's body—he wore a suit, not unlike mine. Perfectly tailored, expensive. Crisp and clean. I fiddled with the computer, trying to adjust the settings while the man continued his rant.

"A liar. A sociopath. A deceitful husband. An inattentive father."

That voice—why did I know that voice? I pushed more buttons in frustration. I turned off the monitor and turned it back on, IT's go-to solution. I even hit it a couple of times, to no avail. I was on the verge of calling Jordan and getting him back to the loft to fix it.

"Unrepentant. His attempts to make amends are shallow and laughable. He hasn't changed."

I found the button to zoom the camera in and the picture suddenly cleared.

"He's exactly the person he's always been—a monster."

The image on the screen was *me*.

I awoke with a jolt to Alayna's frantic cry. "My God, Hudson. What's going on?"

I sat up, blinking, disoriented. I was still in the loft. The screen on the television was clear. No one was being interviewed. It was all in my head.

I looked blearily at my wife. "What are you doing here?"

"No. I asked first." Her voice was tight and high-pitched. She held up a stack of papers, her hands trembling. "What the fuck are these?"

My breath caught, but years of practice allowed me to hide that from Alayna. *The letters. She'd read the letters.*

Fuck!

The adrenaline left over from my dream quickly found a new target. I could only imagine the feelings boiling inside her right now, but more than anything, I knew I had to stay calm.

I couldn't let her panic.

"Give them to me. They're nothing to worry about," I said, reaching for them, fearing it was too late. The bubble I'd tried to seal her in had popped. And I didn't know if she would forgive me for putting her there in the first place.

"Like *hell* there's nothing to worry about," she said, circling around the coffee table and away from me, clutching the papers to her chest. Her expression said she wasn't going to make this easy for me. "I've read them, Hudson. Every word, and every word was frightening."

I leveled her with my gaze, focused on making my tone as casual and dismissive as possible. "Alayna, I'm sure you know we get threatening letters like this from time to time. It's why we have a security team in the first place."

She rolled her eyes. "Yes, of course I know that. I'm not naïve. But those are filled with 'Down with the one percent' and 'Die capitalist pig' sentiments. Those are generic hate letters written toward anyone with the money and good fortune to be included on a Forbes list." She held the letters out toward me in a pointed gesture. "*These* talk about kissing your babies goodnight like it's an episode of My Favorite Murder."

I ran my palm along my thigh, then stopped, afraid she'd see it for the anxious movement that it was. If she knew I was apprehensive, it would only ramp her up even more. I couldn't focus on keeping her safe if she was feeling hysterical. With a concerted effort, I relaxed my entire body.

"It's true that most threats we get are banal and generic in tone, but that doesn't lend any more credibility to these than any others. I assure you Jordan is on top of this, as he is on top of all security risks, and there is nothing to be concerned about."

She stared challengingly at me. "You're telling me you aren't concerned?"

"I am not," I lied.

And I saw her eyes change as she saw right through me.

"Jesus Christ, it's so bad you won't even tell me the truth." She started pacing the room, bringing her free hand up to rub her chest in a soothing circle.

"Don't be ridiculous. Why wouldn't I be telling you the truth?" It didn't sound convincing or comforting, and I knew it. I didn't have the spirit to bullshit her like I needed to. Like I wanted to. This thing was getting to me. I felt like I was losing control. And I *needed* control.

I started to gather the rest of the papers on the coffee table into a pile, in case she hadn't seen them yet. I *hoped* she hadn't seen them yet. The endless lists of suspects only proved we had no idea who was sending us these threats. Proved that I really didn't have any sort of handle on this at all.

"I don't know why you're lying to me. That's the thing. Unless it's so bad you're afraid to tell me. Are you afraid I'd get upset? Which really isn't fair, because of course I would get upset because this shithead is threatening my children!"

"With words, precious. Just with words. It's some angry competitor trying to get under my skin, that's all." *Better. Not perfect.* I piled everything into the manila folder Jordan kept the investigation documents in. If she couldn't see my eyes, perhaps she wouldn't be able to see the lie.

And if I couldn't see hers, I wouldn't have to see her disappointment.

"Like I said," I continued the sham, "I'm not concerned about it, and neither should you be."

"And like *I* said, you're lying. I know you. If you weren't concerned about it, you wouldn't have it all spread out here in front of you. Jordan would be working on this alone. You wouldn't be looking at any of this at all."

She was fishing. She didn't *know* that most threats came in and were taken care of without ever being a blip on my radar. It was a guess, and I took advantage of it. "That's not necessarily true. Jordan was here earlier. He went over some of the details on this particular security threat and assured me it was being dealt with. It was standard protocol, Alayna."

"Yeah, right. You haven't been sleeping. Secret phone calls before dawn. Jordan came to our house on a Saturday morning. Do you really expect me to believe that was protocol?" She stopped her pacing, desperation and anger warring on her beautiful face. "How long has this been going on? How long have you been keeping this from me?"

"I'm not keeping anything from you. There's nothing to keep. It's a few letters that reached an alert level, and we only received them recently."

"One of them mentioned me being on bedrest, Hudson. The twins are almost a year old." Her eyes suddenly went wide as something occurred to her. "That picture of me with the babies—you have someone following us, right? Our guys took it? It wasn't . . . that wasn't someone else, was it?"

Fuck. She'd seen the picture too. No wonder she wasn't buying my calm demeanor. "Listen to me," I said as steadily and reassuringly as I could. "You are safe. The babies are safe."

"Then why is your eye twitching?"

"Alayna . . ." I hated that she could see right through me.

And I loved it too—that she knew me well enough to read my motives and gestures, the tiny tells that went unnoticed by everyone else. No one had ever truly seen me like my wife.

But I sincerely needed to do better than this.

It was bigger than simple reassurance. I had to convince her that she didn't need to worry about this. For her own sake. Not only was I not willing to lose her to the hands of a predator, but I was also not willing to lose her to the anxiety of her own mind.

I stood up, walked over, and put my arm around her. I offered her the comfort I knew she'd always taken in my touch, knowing the strength of my body was there for her alone. With my other hand I took the letters out of her grasp and threw them down on the table. Then I lifted her chin with one finger. "You are overreacting. All of this is Pierce life as usual."

Her brown eyes looked deep into me, and for a moment I thought I had her.

But then her gaze drifted to the left, toward the computer screen. "Do you have suspects? Is that what this is all for?" She pulled out of my arms and walked around the coffee table to look at the screen again. It was still empty, just a room with a table and two chairs. "Do you have the person who's doing this? You know who it is?"

She sounded so hopeful, I almost let her believe it.

But I couldn't let the lie go that far. I wasn't that man anymore. I refused to be the monster I feared I still was. And that was the gift Alayna had given me—that choice.

I needed to give *her* a gift now—one of peace.

"Alayna, I promise you that this is being taken care of, and you don't need to worry about it. Go home."

She whipped her neck sharply toward me. "The fact it needs to be dealt with at all means I need to worry. The fact you're sleeping in the loft means I need to worry. The fact you are lying to me is as good as admitting it."

"I'm not admitting anything. And I'm not discussing this with you any longer. You are safe. Go *home*," I repeated, and gently took her by the elbow to escort her out of the loft.

"I'm safe, meaning you got the guy? Meaning you know who it is?" She wasn't going to let it go. Her tenacity had attracted me to her, but at times like this I could do without it.

"You're safe, meaning I have extra security on you. On all of you. Jordan has bodyguards at the penthouse and at Mina's camp. They'll follow you everywhere you go from now on." I started walking toward the door.

She wrestled out of my grip. "Extra security? Damnit. I *knew* that guy was following me today. Why didn't you just *tell me*?"

"Because there's nothing—"

"If there's nothing to tell, nothing to worry about," she interrupted me. "Then you wouldn't have to up our security team. Stop patronizing me, Hudson. I'm not an idiot. And what about you? Did you increase *your* security team too?"

I set my jaw and looked at her sternly. Why did she have to choose today to come visit, of all days?

"I upped your security as a matter of precaution. And to make you feel safe. My own security is exactly what it always has been because the risk is null and there is no reason to increase it." My blood pressure was rising, I could feel it. Why didn't she understand I was doing this for her? That everything was for her?

"You mean you upped it to make *you* feel safe. You weren't even going to tell *me* about any of this."

I would have. Eventually. Perhaps.

It didn't seem relevant to argue that now.

I needed this fixed. And for that, I needed her gone. "I am telling you there is nothing to worry about, and I mean it. I'm handling it. Trust me."

She shook her head, frustrated tears brimming in her eyes. "You expect me to—"

I settled my hand at her waist, turning her once again toward the door. "I expect you to go home. And I don't want you to fixate on this, either."

I knew as soon as I said it was the wrong thing to say. The tension between us tripled in thickness, growing mean and thistly.

She leaned away from me, her spine straighter, her eyes narrowed. "You didn't tell me because you were worried about my mental health. That's it, isn't it?" She looked ready to spit daggers at me if she could. Daggers I likely deserved, but would take in a heartbeat if it meant I could rewind time and take that back. "Well, fuck you, Hudson."

"Alayna. Precious. That's not what I meant." I reached out for her, but she stepped back.

"Oh, I know what you meant. Thank you. Thank you for validating all my fears of what my husband secretly thinks about me." She stepped back again and headed to the door, walking away from my arms, denying both of us the comfort we'd always found in each other. "If you're stupid enough to come home tonight, plan to sleep on the couch."

"Alayna . . ." Her name tumbled out of my mouth with no plan for what to say next.

She paused, her hand on the door knob. The rise and fall of her shoulders indicating she had to take a deep breath before she turned to face me, but finally she did turn. "What?"

I didn't want her to leave angry. I didn't want her to leave hurt.

But I needed her to leave. I needed her safe.

Only finding the person who was threatening her would give me what I needed, and every moment she was out of security's sight was another worry for me to shoulder. So I didn't apologize. I didn't call her back. Even though I knew the price we were both paying for it.

"Once you get home, don't go anywhere. All right?"

She didn't answer, but I knew she heard me. Heard how serious I was.

It seemed only to fuel her anger. She threw open the door with a huff and stormed out.

"I love you," I shouted after her.

"Fuck you, Hudson," I heard as the door slammed shut behind her.

I deserved it. Every last *fuck you*. From her and everyone else who wanted to give it. All I could do was hope she could find a way to trust me again once this was over. I ran a hand through my hair, and sent a text down to the bodyguard in the lobby to let him know she was on her way down. Once he confirmed he had eyes on her, I called Jordan.

"Alayna knows about the extra security team now," I said when he answered. "No need to continue hanging back."

Jordan was silent for a couple of seconds. "Did you tell her? Or did she find out on her own?"

I wasn't in the mood for his *I-told-you-so*. "Jesus, Jordan, does it matter?"

"I like to have a sense of how cooperative she's going to be. Remember, I've worked with her in the past. But I think I understand now. Good luck." He hung up.

Right now I needed more than luck. I needed a glass of scotch and a goddamn miracle.

* * *

Just before five, I rode down to my office, took my desktop phone off the *do not disturb* function, and pressed the button to check in with my secretary. "Anything pertinent I need to know before you leave for the day?"

"It was relatively quiet, actually," Patricia said. "I hope you were able to get a lot of work done. Did Laynie slip out when I wasn't looking?"

That was one way of putting it, yes. I didn't really want my secretary knowing I'd spent my entire working day up in the loft. The fewer people who were alerted to my unusual patterns as of late, the better.

I definitely didn't want her knowing I'd fought with my wife.

"She needed some time alone, so she slipped out through the loft." It was concerning—disgusting, almost—how easily I fell back into my old patterns of deceit.

"That's probably heaven for her right now. A couple of hours napping in a bed with no kids within earshot." I could hear her smile, and I very nearly felt guilty for lying. Nearly.

"I'm sure it is." God, I was such an asshole. "If there's nothing else—"

"Oh, Lee Chong needs to talk to you urgently. He said call any time tonight. He left you a message with the details on your voicemail. I told him I'd be sure you listened to it and got back to him as soon as possible."

Interesting. Lee Chong owned space near The Sky Launch. We were hardly friends—barely even acquaintances. I'd spoken to him maybe twice in my lifetime. Needless to say, I was curious as to what would prompt an urgent call from the man. "I'll be sure and do that."

I dialed into my voicemail the minute I got off the phone with Patricia. His message was brief. It was also enlightening. In fact, I felt the tiniest bit better. I'd be able to give him what he needed in a simple call.

Seemed I wasn't the only one in my marriage keeping secrets.

CHAPTER NINE
ALAYNA

I enjoyed Hudson's touch so much that I pretended I didn't hear him when he crept up behind me in the kitchen the next morning. I took one long breath with his arms around me, filled my nose with his spicy scent, let myself feel his embrace for the barest of moments.

Then I shrugged him off.

"Don't. Please," I said, sharply, pulling a mug down from the cabinet.

He stepped to my side and leaned against the counter, his aftershave wafting over the aroma of freshly brewed coffee, reminding me what I was missing when I was mad.

But I was still far too mad—too *hurt*—to let it go.

Hudson was my best friend, my anchor. Discovering he was hiding things from his crazy wife was a knife in my gut, one that twisted anew every time I remembered the look in his eyes when he looked right at me and lied.

But in some ways I did understand. I would forgive him. Once he stopped doing what he was doing, and made it up to me properly. Once he admitted that just because I was paranoid, it didn't mean I wasn't under threat.

Until then . . . I stepped away from him again.

"So we're still doing this, are we?" he asked.

"It's not *me* who's doing anything, Hudson. It's you who has all the secrets locked up inside and doesn't want to share the key.'"

"Right," he said, a note of sarcasm in his tone, likely because I *had* been doing something—specifically, I'd been giving him the cold shoulder. He'd come home at dinnertime, ignoring my warning to stay late at the office, but I'd managed to get through the whole entire evening without speaking more than three words to him. And he most certainly had not slept next to me in our bed.

"I see that you didn't sleep on the couch like I specifically asked." I poured the coffee into my mug and ignored his waiting cup.

"I saw no point in sleeping on the couch when there was a perfectly good bed in the guest room."

"The point was that you would be miserable." I handed him the pot with barely a centimeter of liquid at the bottom of it.

"Believe me—I was still miserable," he said in that charming way that he had, moving his gaze up and down my body to leave me in no doubt as to what he was missing. Even after all these years it made my stomach flutter.

But I wouldn't be won over that easily this time.

I grabbed my coffee and headed to the kitchen table, stopping by the fridge to nab the creamer. "Well, until *I* feel less miserable, you can go right ahead and stay in there at night, as far as I'm concerned," I told him, regretting the words as soon as I said them. It had been pretty terrible in the king-size bed without him too, if I were being honest. I never slept well without him by me. I was addicted to him in so many ways.

Was I pushing him even farther away with this?

"I guess I better start working harder." He poured more coffee grounds inside the coffee maker and then took the pot to the sink to fill it with water. "What do you have on your agenda for today?"

I stared at him in his fitted Armani suit. It was light gray, like his eyes, and it brought out all of his best physical features. Once upon a time I would've maybe tried different tactics to get him to open up. Ones that involved me getting into that suit, or rather, getting him out of it. Once upon a time, he wouldn't have been able to keep his hands—or eyes—off of me, especially when I was wearing a skimpy nightgown like I was.

Were we better together now? Or were we boring?

Before yesterday, when I'd been convinced he would share anything with me, even the things that scared him—*especially* the things that scared him—I would've said we were better.

But now, I wasn't as sure.

"Alayna?" he asked again, when I didn't answer his question.

"Things," I said dismissively. "My usual things." He wasn't going to tell me his stuff, and I certainly wasn't going to tell him my stuff. Tit for tat. A secret for a secret.

Okay, so I hadn't planned on telling him what I was doing today *before* I found out about his secret, but that was beside the point. Now more than ever, I felt a desperate desire to lose myself in my business, to drown my fears under an ocean of paperwork.

"You boosted security at The Sky Launch too, didn't you?" I asked, suddenly worried I wasn't being careful enough about this.

"Yes," he said slowly. "Why do you ask?" He eyed me carefully—suspiciously?

No, I was being paranoid.

"Because I don't want anyone to get hurt or threatened there in some crazy douchebag's attempt to get to me." Not exactly a lie.

"How thoughtful." He continued to study me. "I'd like you to stay put today, Alayna. Do you hear me?"

"Jesus, you're kidding me, right?" I stirred my coffee with my finger then took a giant swig. "I can't stay locked in the penthouse like your princess in a tower. Even Mina goes to camp. I have things to do too."

"*Today* you have things? You have to leave the house *today*?" The coffee pot beeped that it was done, but he ignored it, keeping his focus on me. I avoided his eyes as he stared hard.

"Maybe." I knew if I followed this through I would have to name what those things were. A secret for a secret. A lie for a lie. "All right, so there's nothing today. But there *could* be."

I swallowed my guilt down with another sip from my mug.

"Stay put, Alayna." He turned to the cupboard and pulled down a to-go thermos, then poured the coffee inside. When he was done he turned back to me, and added sternly, "And if you do go anywhere, don't give your bodyguards a hard time."

That almost made me smile. Because he knew me well enough to know how hard it was for me to accept an order. Because he knew me well enough to know I would give anyone who got in my space a hard time.

Because he knew me and he put up with me anyway.

* * *

"So do you think it's someone who knows Hudson? Or some rando who's jealous and spiteful?" Gwen asked later that morning at The Sky Launch when I finished telling her everything I knew about the letters and the heightened security.

She had looked shocked while I spilled, but she didn't seem nearly as frantic as I was about it. Was that because it wasn't happening to her? Or was it another sign that I was overreacting?

The answer to that might depend on the answer to *her* question.

Someone who knew my husband might have real cause to wish him harm. Or it could be some unhinged stranger who got wrapped up in Hudson Pierce. A random whoever who could eventually get distracted, or medicated, or arrested, and we'd never hear from him again.

Could.

Or they could be as fixated as I could get.

I crossed my leg and perched on the edge of the loveseat, considering. We had remodeled the office while I'd been on bedrest with the twins, so now instead of two desks there was one large table that Gwen and I sat on either side of while we worked. We figured it was the best use of space since both of us were usually not on duty at the same time, and we liked to look at each other when we did work together, so we could talk and gossip in between running day sheets and balance reports. Of course, I hadn't been back since the new design had been implemented, but the place looked good.

Today, she sat at the desk/table, while I lounged, thinking, in the sitting area on the opposite side of the room since I wasn't officially on the clock.

"I don't know," I answered, finally. "There were some pretty specific things in those letters. Things I didn't even understand, but I don't think they were vague references."

"Someone Hudson used to work with, then? An employee? A business rival?"

"Yeah, maybe something like that." Though I had a feeling our threat didn't have anything to do with Hudson's job or career or how much money he made, but rather the games he used to play. *Games* was the term he always used when he talked to me about the schemes he'd pulled in the past.

Manipulation and bullying were more like it.

I hadn't told Gwen about that part of Hudson's past, and I wasn't about to now. It meant I had to dance around some of her questions, and since she seemed hell-bent on my life being one of those thriller books that she read, she had a lot of them.

Besides, there was no telling where and how the information came from. For all I knew, there were whole internet sites devoted to compiling lists of my husband's misdeeds.

"Are you worried?" she asked now.

I bounced my ankle in the air where it dangled. "A little. Maybe more than a little. I wouldn't be worried if Hudson would give me the status and tell me exactly what was going on, but since he's trying to dismiss it and say it's no big deal, I'm a little more convinced that's not the case." I shrugged.

"Does he not even *know* you? Of course you would worry."

No, he knew me. Knew me too well. Well enough to be concerned about how much I'd worry, but I didn't want Gwen concerned about that too, so I kept it to myself.

She tilted her head in thought. "I didn't think much about it when he said we were updating the security system here. It just happens sometimes, needing an upgrade, but this was a pretty expansive upgrade. That was more than a year ago now. Then, on Monday, we all of a sudden had a second set of security guards working the doors."

More than a year ago.

That letter had to have arrived while I'd been pregnant. All of this had to have begun around then. Had Hudson been acting *off* for that long, and I'd missed it?

"I know what you're thinking," Gwen said, assuming she could read my mind. "But you've had a lot going on. Being a mom and taking care of one kid is enough of a handful. You had a hard pregnancy and birthed *twins*. Your home life probably seems like it's turned upside down. If there's been something going on this whole time, how the hell could you be expected to spot it? Even if Hudson has acted differently, you'd probably attribute it to not enough sleep and the new chaotic life."

I guess she *could* read my mind.

"Or maybe it hasn't been that serious until recently." I still hated the idea that I could have gone so long unaware of something weighing so heavily on my husband. "You did say the extra security started this week. And that's true at home too."

"Good point. Maybe something changed. The threat got more real." She suddenly narrowed her eyes. "Should you even be here?"

"Oh my God, you sound like Hudson." I stood up and smoothed my hands down over my skirt. "He's gone out of his way to make it safe here. Obviously. And at least here I have something to do. At home, I have nothing—"

"—except being the mother of two kids under one, and a preschooler," Gwen interrupted.

"I have nothing," I repeated, louder, "that challenges my *mind*, and I'll end up obsessing over those letters until I drive myself crazy. Trust me. It's better for everyone that I'm out of the house. Besides, I didn't want to cancel on Lee Chong on such short notice. It's taken long enough already for these pieces to fall into place."

I followed Gwen's glance up to the clock on the wall. "But your appointment with Lee Chong isn't until this afternoon," she said. "Why are you here so early?"

"I wanted to drop off my materials for the presentation before I ran my other errand. Which I should be getting to now if I want to get back in plenty of time." I stood, picking up my purse from the floor beside me. I'd already unloaded my laptop with my PowerPoint presentation and the drawings I'd mocked up for the event space stored on it.

I was certain once Mr. Chong saw them, he'd see why we were the perfect buyers.

Gwen sat back in her chair, a brow raised. "Errand? You said you were safe because there was extra security here at The Sky Launch. Is it really smart for you to go anywhere else? And why do I have a feeling that whatever this errand of yours is, it isn't going to make your husband very happy?"

"Well, *he's* not making me happy right now either," I huffed.

But she was right. It *was* probably wise to make sure someone knew where I was at all times. Ideally, someone who wasn't Hudson Pierce.

"Look. He can't expect me to sit back and let him do all the work on this by himself. Some of those threat letters referenced things in his past, things that I couldn't make any sense of, but that doesn't mean there isn't somebody who can."

She sat forward, suddenly alert. "Don't tell me you're going to Celia Werner about this."

"No." Though that *was* an interesting thought. And potentially better than my own. I considered, then shook my head. Facing that dragon was one step too far. "She isn't the only woman who knew Hudson before I did."

"Okay. Good. Because for a minute there I thought you'd truly gone crazy." She smiled as though she wasn't quite sure if she'd gone too far in her terminology.

I grinned back, letting her see me accept the phrase with no harsh feelings.

"Hey, you don't think *she's* behind these threats, do you?"

I'd already considered it. How could I not? Celia in my life, weaseling in near our family was a constant concern for me. "She just had a baby," I said, sharing the conclusions I'd come to on my own. "She can't possibly be so obsessed with us that she's been hounding Hudson for the last year and a half—could she?"

Gwen's shrug said she was as undecided about that as I was. On one hand, it didn't really seem like her style. Celia usually preferred subtlety. On the other hand, if this was something she'd put someone up to, we could be certain that whatever her game was, this would only be her opening gambit.

"For the moment, I'm giving her the benefit of the doubt. Because of the motherhood and marriage thing. But she's certainly on my possibility list," I said.

"Hard to imagine that you might have enemies worse than her," my friend said sympathetically.

"I know, right?" A chill ran down my spine at the thought of someone worse than Celia. For once in my life, I was thankful for Hudson's bodyguards.

* * *

Thirty minutes later, with Brody, today's security sidekick, I rang the bell at Mirabelle's boutique in Greenwich Village. She opened the door, already babbling.

"Laynie! You don't have an appointment today. What are you doing here? Of course I'm so happy to see you. And you never have to have an appointment to come by. I will always fit you in. Do you need something to wear for an occasion? Something special that I can help you with? Is Hudson taking you somewhere special? Or is this a social visit? And who's the stocky bald guy brooding in the corner? Did you finally hire a personal assistant? Not the type I thought you'd go for, but to each her own."

My sister-in-law was in her usual perky mood. No one could simultaneously energize and soothe me quite like Mira, without me ever getting a word in edgewise. She hugged me and shoved a glass of champagne into my hand, then rushed off to attend to another client before I could answer a single one of her questions. I watched her flit around tirelessly and felt a pang of envy. The energy and speed she naturally had in her body had likely helped her regain her pre-pregnancy body with little effort.

It was a tempo I recognized, but had never achieved physically. Even before the children, when I would run regularly, I never had her energy. Only my head, my thoughts, ever traveled that fast. That unstoppably. Watching her was like seeing my mind personified.

Sometimes it was exhausting to look at, and I had to turn away.

Finally, she had a moment free, and she pulled me aside into a consultation area near the dressing rooms where we could sit and talk.

"So what is it? Need a dress or an escape? I'm happy to provide both."

I chuckled as I finished off the last of the champagne she'd given me, then set the glass down on the table between us. It was neither, but between being here and the bubbles, it *did* feel like a momentary breather from my frenetic worrying.

"Actually, I wanted to ask you something. I thought you might be able to help enlighten me about Hudson. About his past." I swallowed.

The corners of her mouth turned down slightly. "That's an odd request. I am intrigued. What exactly do you want to know?"

I hadn't yet decided which way I was approaching my conversation with Mira before I'd arrived, whether I was going to tell her about the letters Hudson had received or not, but on the spot, I decided to be transparent. I explained to her everything that I knew, what I'd seen—the extra security, Hudson's refusal to tell me any more. After telling Gwen earlier, I had the story down to a concise narrative.

Mira's face was expressive as I spoke, her mouth gaping, her eyes wide. By the time I was done she was no longer sitting in her seat, but up out of her chair and bouncing around the room.

"Oh my God, Hudson!" she exclaimed. "I can't believe he was keeping you in the dark like this. Doesn't he understand anything about his wife? Of course you're going to obsess about it. Of course you would want to investigate on your own. Does he not know you? Does he not think of you as a partner? Marriage is supposed to be a two-way street! This is absurd! I'd kill Adam."

"Exactly!" It was so relieving to know she was on my side, that she understood where I was coming from. It had been a risk coming to

Hudson's sister. She might've felt inclined to defend him, being his blood relative and all. "That brings me to why I came to you. I was hoping you would maybe be able to shed some light on the past. Maybe you could direct me to who might've sent the letters? He's not helping me, since he's not letting me know what angle he's working." I sat back, pleased that this had gone so easily.

To my shock, Mira turned her frustration back to me.

"No way. Because what are *you* even thinking, Laynie? Going off behind his back like this? It's one thing for him to keep something from you, but you're just as bad. Isn't this the kind of thing that's got you in trouble in the past? Tip-toeing around him? Two wrongs never make a right. And I am not about to get in the middle of your marriage squabble. You two need to work this out. You go back to him and you get him to open up to you. And thank you *very* much, for bringing whatever drama safety issue this is to *my* store. Did you even think about that? You're a mother now. You have kids. *Kids!* You can't go chasing down the bad guys like there are no consequences. Now promise me you aren't going to follow up on anymore of this bullcrap and you'll leave the investigating to the people who do that for a living."

"Mira! I can't promise—"

She cut me off. "Promise me, Laynie, or I'm calling Hudson and telling him what you're up to. I am a mother, too, in case you forgot, and if you won't be safe, keep *us* safe, I'll make sure it happens."

I sucked a breath in and held it, afraid if I let it out, I'd explode. Not just because I didn't want to give up my investigation, but because I had so much bursting inside of me, so much emotion and anxiety building up about these threats and nowhere to put the energy. What was I supposed to do with all of it? Let it keep hold of me and my thoughts, let the obsessions take root in my mind? I didn't want to be the insane, fixated woman that my husband seemed to think he'd married.

But I definitely didn't want to put other people in danger—not Mira. Not my kids.

Not even me.

"Okay. Fine," I promised woefully.

"Thank you," she said, sharply. Then she walked out of the consultation room shutting the door loudly behind her. All the energy I'd
felt in her presence had collapsed into sheer exhaustion. I was no closer
to uncovering the truth than I was before, and I'd upset the only sister
I had in the bargain.

A second later the door opened again. "I'm bringing something for
you to try on, by the way, so that if I bump into my brother later and it
comes up that I saw you, I won't be lying when I say you stopped by to
get a new dress." She left the room again, slamming the door as hard as
she had the first time.

I supposed I'd forgotten she'd always been on *our* side—Hudson's
and mine—as a team.

And there *was* absolutely one thing I could always count on Mira
for without question—picking out the right outfit.

She sent her assistant back to the dressing room with a stunning
Diane Von Furstenberg wrap, color-blocked in luxurious shades of dark
blue. It fit perfectly when I put it on, accentuating the hips I'd developed
over the last few years, hiding the belly that had been a souvenir from
childbirth.

It made me feel sexy and alluring.

Womanly.

Like the Alayna I'd been when Hudson had fucked me in front of
the mirror in this very dressing room all those years ago. The one whose
very worst flaw had piqued the interest of the very best man she'd ever
met. Not like the Alayna of today, the one who'd almost forgotten to
brush her hair before leaving the apartment and had to change her outfit
once already this morning after the baby spit up on it.

I smiled at my reflection. At least the trip downtown hadn't been
a waste. The dress was going home with me. Hudson had, of course,
been right—I wasn't spending enough time on *me*. On *us*.

Something told me that the look in his eyes when he saw me in
this would be every bit as hungry as it ever was in those first heady days.

"It's exquisite," Stacy, Mirabelle's longtime assistant said, peering
over my shoulder.

"You think so? I like it, too." I appreciated Stacy's opinion, and I trusted her. We had a rocky start when we'd first met, and though we weren't exactly friends now, we were friendly. She'd once had a crush on Hudson—but, seriously, who hadn't? Unfortunately for her, she'd ended up the victim of one of Celia Werner's games and had believed that Hudson liked her back.

Yet another victim I'd forgotten to list.

I'd been swept into the game too. Been tricked into believing there'd been more going on than there had been—not between Stacy and Hudson, but between Celia and Hudson. My investigations back in the day had led me to cornering Stacy, thinking she had the proof I needed to determine the nature of Hudson and Celia's true relationship.

She hadn't, in the end. But seeing her now, remembering that she was a part of Hudson's past, had the gears in my overactive mind whirring in a new direction.

"Stacy, I'd like to ask you something," I said, spinning toward her. I paused, remembering my promise only moments ago to Mira, then immediately disregarding it. This wasn't a fresh investigation, after all, merely exhausting my options in the place I'd already started one.

"I know I said I would never involve you in any drama again, but I wouldn't ask you if it wasn't important. Do you know of anyone who might be . . . jealous . . . or maybe angry at Hudson? Angry enough to . . . threaten him in any way?"

Stacy laughed incredulously. "Are you kidding? That's about everybody in the New York City phone book. He's richer than fuck. Of course people are jealous of him. And he's a businessman. Of course people are mad at him, too." She stepped forward to untie the bow of the wrap at my waist. "You want me to bring this up front for you?"

I put my hand on hers, halting her. "I'm serious." Then my thoughts went another direction. What if . . .

I dropped my hand, and took a step away. "Stacy, are you still hung up on my husband?"

I had it in my head that it was a man sending the letters, but it could as easily have been a woman. Stacy would've known about his past, and she'd known about my bedrest. What if she still resented everything that happened before?

She straightened, her height going up by another full inch, it seemed. "Are you for real?"

The anger rolling off her was thick, blanket thick. I began to think I'd made a serious mistake in my accusation. "I'm sorry, that was probably a stupid—"

"You have some nerve, Alayna Withers *Pierce*. After everything you put me through before. Putting me in the middle of your soap opera drama. Dragging me into your personal shit, and what did I ever get out of it? More accusations? I've never been anything but loyal to Mirabelle. Never done anything but admire the Pierces. You have *some nerve*. You can get someone else to ring up your dress."

She stomped off toward the door then stopped suddenly. "Oh, and tell your guy to stop hanging out around here. Three times this week I've seen him. He's making our clients nervous."

She left, slamming the door almost as loudly as Mira had, before I could ask what guy she was talking about. Before I could apologize. For the second time in a quarter of an hour, I'd alienated someone I liked.

And for what?

I sighed as I finished undressing myself. If there was a strange guy hanging around Mirabelle's boutique, it could mean that Hudson had sent extra security here as well, which meant the danger extended further than he led me to believe.

Or the guy *was* the danger.

The one thing I knew for sure was that this investigation would be a whole lot easier if I had Hudson working with me.

CHAPTER TEN

HUDSON

I pushed *stop* on the video screen, shutting off the current remote interview, as soon as I heard the elevators doors open into the loft. When I'd left Alayna that morning, telling her to stay put, I knew she had no intention of doing that. Typical Alayna. But I hadn't expected her to show up here.

To my surprise, it wasn't Alayna who walked out in a fit of energy, but my younger brother.

I exchanged an annoyed glance with Jordan.

"Satcher Rutherford, man . . ." Chandler began. "You sure how to pick them, Hudson."

It was enough of an intro to keep me listening.

"I mean, he knows his shit, for sure. The Rutherfords own over sixty successful nightclubs around the world—New York, Atlanta, Las Vegas, Brazil, London, Tokyo—and Satcher is himself responsible for at least half of those clubs."

He took off his jacket and threw it over the armchair, then began loosening his tie while he talked. I tried to bite down the gravel of irritation that he was making himself comfortable. I didn't want this to be a long visit. I hadn't wanted this to be a visit at all.

His DNA must have contained none of the people-reading genes I'd gotten, because he droned on. "Thank God I did my research first, because the way you sent me out of that meeting a couple of weeks ago, I thought I was looking for a consultant to help us out with our reopening. Obviously Rutherford is way above consultation pay himself, and from what I've discovered in my digging, he's not into sharing information. I realized this needed to be an investment opportunity for him. So that was the proposal I put together—I didn't ask you about it because Trish says you've been on *do not disturb* for the entire week and also? Because fuck you, I'm part of Pierce Industries, and I can make decisions myself. I don't need you to sign off on all my shit."

I, in fact, *owned* Pierce Industries, and Chandler *did* work for me. But I had learned he worked better when he believed we were on equal footing, so again, I bit my tongue.

"The problem is that getting a meeting with the guy is harder than getting a meeting with the Queen of England." He turned toward the fridge and snagged a water bottle from inside, then leaned against the kitchen counter facing us, looking as self-assured as a guy who'd gotten a meeting with the Queen.

He hadn't.

"Chandler, don't exaggerate. Facts only, please."

"That's not an exaggeration. I probably *could* get a meeting with the Queen of England. Genevieve has a friend of a friend who knows a guy. Remember, she's from Britain." As if all British people had an in at Buckingham Palace.

That was Chandler for you.

"If you're just here to tell us your hardships, with no question or real information, could you please do it at a later time? We actually are in the middle of something here." I didn't bother wrapping my sentiments in niceties. It would only provoke him to stay longer.

"There is a point. I have a question." He said, pointing his water bottle in my direction.

"Then do get on to it."

"I'm getting there. I'm providing the background information first. Otherwise you won't understand the question." He took a swig of water, and I could feel my eye twitch in impatience.

"So. Apparently, if you want to talk to Satcher there's a process." He put the word *process* in air quotes, as best as he could with one hand holding a water bottle. "No matter who you are. Even the grand and mighty Pierce name couldn't get around that. So I first had to talk to his guy, *again*. He's younger than me, and get this—his name is Dudley. Dudley! Can you imagine naming a child Dudley? A baby Dudley! I can't even imagine calling a baby a grown-up name like that. What do you nickname him? Dud? It was seriously the only thing that went through my mind the whole time I was talking to him on the phone. It's ridiculous. Having a guy named Dudley is ridiculous. Never name a baby Dudley."

"You seem to be thinking about babies a lot here. Are you and your fiancée expecting?" Jordan asked.

Whether he was sincere or that was his version of dry humor, I liked it. Like I said, there were many reasons I kept him on the payroll.

"No, once again, for everyone in the room—Genevieve is not pregnant. And we're not having any babies any time soon. We only think about them all the time because everyone around us has them as often as most people change their bedsheets."

That seemed to say a lot about how often—or not—Chandler changed his bedsheets. But I wanted him out of there, so I didn't interject with that particular comment.

"Anyway, Dudley, was very critical of our proposition. Did you know that Atlantic City is a dead zone right now? Why do we even have a nightclub there? Apparently nobody goes there for nightlife anymore. The whole city is, like, over."

I centered a hard gaze in his direction. "Exactly why we need to have the very best behind our nightclub opening. To bring the population back."

"Right. Exactly. I know that." He took another swig from his water bottle. "That's totally what I was going to say to Satcher. When I saw him. Because even though I didn't convince Dudley Do-Right that our nightclub was a good idea, he did think that Satcher would want to hear about it, to—and I quote—'have a good laugh.' So he advanced me to the next step, which was giving me a direct line to Satcher."

"Good job. Sounds very productive and somewhat amusing." I stood up, ready to usher my brother out.

"Wait. I am nowhere near done."

I took a deep breath in. I'd been afraid of this. I stuck a hand in my pocket and urged him to continue with a nod of my head.

"So I call Rutherford. I was expecting to talk to a secretary or something, but it was his actual direct line. When he answered, as soon as I introduced myself as a Pierce, the phone somehow goes dead. I give him the benefit of the doubt—maybe there was a lousy connection. I call him back. I go straight to voicemail. I called him back again. Straight to voicemail. I called him back four more times. Finally he answered."

At least my brother had fortitude. If that's what that was called.

"This time he let me get past my last name and propose a meeting to discuss an investment opportunity. He said he didn't want to have anything to do with Hudson Pierce or Pierce Industries. You were obviously not kidding when you said he did not like you."

I could feel Jordan's gaze on me, could feel the questions in his head that he had yet to ask.

"But I told Satcher, no worries. I really don't like you either. You're a fucking asshole. Everyone knows that."

I pinched the bridge of my nose, hoping to ward off the headache that immediately threatened to take over the space in my skull.

"Hey, it got me a meeting," he said.

"I suppose you do what you need to do." I didn't have to be happy about it.

"Or, I *thought* it got me a meeting. Because when I showed up at his New York office, his secretary seemed surprised. She said he must have made a mistake about his calendar, and he wasn't even in the office that day. 'He must've double booked.' I didn't buy it. He wanted to humiliate me and waste my time, and he succeeded. I looked like a goddamn idiot. This time, though, I was smart—I got the secretary's information. Shelley. Cute plump redhead. Little flirting with her got me her cell number as well as Satcher's cell. Called him later that night, told him there must've been a mixup, pretended to give him the benefit of the doubt. He apologized. Said he appreciated my tenacity—my tenacity! How fucking patronizing.

Like I was an intern instead of a peer in his field! He appreciated it so much he set up dinner for the next night at Gaston's."

"Good work," I began again with my exit spiel.

"He stood me up again." Chandler took another swig of water. "I'm telling you—this guy is Douche Juice with a capital D. It's a wonder the two of you aren't friends."

I narrowed my eyes. "In other words, you've taken the very long route of telling me that you've been unsuccessful in this endeavor."

I headed to the wet bar and poured a glass of Macallan. Two fingers.

"Au contraire! I made another phone call. This time to Shelley. Used all my charm and discovered that Mister Douche Juice isn't even in the country right now. But! He's opening up a new club in Austin and will be there in person tomorrow. I fly out first thing in the morning."

I picked up the glass and turned toward him, my brows raised in surprise. "Good work! Sounds like you really didn't need me at all." It felt surprisingly nice.

"Here's where I need you," he said, stepping over my congratulatory toast. "I need to know what the fuck you did to this guy to make him hate you so much and how the hell I'm supposed to get him to want to work with us now."

So much for that feeling of relief.

I crossed over to him, took the bottle of water out of his hand and replaced it with the glass of scotch.

"Well, thank you, bro. But it's only two-thirty. A little early for a drink, don't you think?"

"You asked me how I suggest you deal with him. This is my answer."

He scowled, but he took a sip of the scotch. "And why does he hate you?"

I didn't even think before I answered. "We had a schoolboy rivalry. Simple as that."

"No fucking way it's that simple. Not when he's going out of his way to mess with me because of my connection to you thirty years later."

"*Thirty years* . . . It was half that long ago." I paused a moment to do the math. Time flew faster than it had seemed. "Twenty years ago, anyway. How old do you think I am?"

"Don't worry about your age, Hudson. You look good for pushing forty."

"I'm not pushing . . ." I trailed off when I saw Chandler flash his cocky grin and realized he was trying to press my buttons.

I usually didn't let him rile me up. The pressure was obviously getting to me.

"Might this Rutherford be our guy?" Jordan asked, leaning forward.

"No," I dismissed quickly. Then I reconsidered. "Perhaps. If he's really still holding a grudge."

"What guy? The guy for this job, because if he's not, tell me now before I fly to Texas tomorrow." Chandler asked. "And is he really still holding a grudge?"

"Jordan's talking about something else. He's definitely still the guy for the Atlantic City job." I rubbed my hand over my face. "Unless he is *our guy*," I muttered to myself. "Which is very unlikely. I couldn't possibly have wounded his ego enough to push him to this extreme now."

I felt both men's eyes on me, but it was Chandler who spoke first.

"Want to tell us what happened between you and Satcher and let *us* decide if he deserves to hate you today? Let me rephrase—because I know you don't want to tell me anything ever, especially anything that has to do with you or your past, but maybe you could make an exception this once."

He was right—this wasn't a tale I wanted to tell. Jordan should hear it, but I could wait and tell him later, when we were alone. I'd worked very hard to protect my brother from knowing about the games of my youth, and there wasn't any reason to change that now, but perhaps he did deserve this one sliver of my history.

I glanced at my watch to confirm the time. Two twenty-four, to be precise. I didn't have to rush off just yet.

Unfortunately.

"Fine," I sighed. I needed a drink first.

I headed to the bar and poured another glass of scotch for myself while Chandler slung himself into my armchair.

"What's all this?" he asked, gesturing to the screen set-up where we'd been watching more victims from my past be interviewed for the sham tell-all. "Binging Scandal on Netflix?"

Jordan responded before I got the chance. "Something like that."

"Nothing at all like that," I corrected, not wanting Chandler to get the idea that I sat around on my ass, accomplishing very little with my days and still taking all the credit. "Remote interviews." I took a swallow of my liquor, embracing the warmth of the burn and the way it loosened the tightness of my jaw and shoulders.

"As I said," I began, returning to the couch with my drink in hand, "we were kids when this took place. I've known Satcher for as long as I can remember. Our families were very close friends. I'm several months older than Satcher, but it worked out to being the same grade level. Before high school, we'd usually only seen each other on the rare occasions where our parents would bring their children to socialize with them—birthday parties, summer events. We didn't tend to ever enjoy each other's company, but it was never an issue until we were freshman together."

"Hold up, hold up," Chandler interrupted. He sat forward, pausing dramatically before asking, "Our parents had friends?"

I wondered for a moment if he was trying to be smart, but then remembered that Chandler was eleven years younger than I, and had seen a very different side of our parents then I had. "Yes. A long time ago, they had a small group of friends. It consisted of the Werners, the Rutherfords, and two other couples. They were all very entwined in each other's lives, especially the Rutherfords and our parents. They were almost as wrapped up in each other as they were wrapped up in business and shopping."

"Why do you sound so sour about it? It's kind of sweet, thinking about Mom and Dad hanging out with friends like regular people." Chandler had that puppy-dog look in his eyes that he often got. He was the kind of guy who overly romanticized most situations.

"There was nothing sweet about their entangled lives. It was scandal and dysfunction and alcoholism, each of them enabling each other in their addictions and encouraging one another to further ignore their children."

"Oh," he said nodding his head as though he understood. "Mom gave people attention other than you and you got jealous. Got it. Your life is suddenly becoming quite clear."

I stared hard at him and scowled. "If you want me to go on, you will keep your inaccurate commentary to yourself."

He mimed zipping up his mouth, but his eyes gleamed like he'd scored some point in an imaginary game he undoubtedly thought he was playing with me.

I ignored him, and instead focused on Jordan. "As I said, Satcher and I didn't have much to do with each other in our younger days. Not much that mattered, until we were freshman, and finally in the same school together, where it became obvious that he had an agenda to earn a certain notoriety among our peers. Apparently, he felt that said notoriety would be best achieved by engaging in a feud with me. I'm still not sure why he chose me to be his rival—perhaps because I was the head of my class, an obvious choice, or because of our parents acquaintanceship—but our freshman and sophomore years were very tense, to put it lightly."

"Like what did he do? Steal your girlfriend? Instigate a fight after study hall? Did he get you sent to detention?" Obviously, Chandler had forgotten he'd zipped his mouth shut.

"I have never served a day of detention in my life," I said, making sure the air, and facts, were clear. "Our rivalry was much subtler than that. Yes, there were stolen love interests, both on my side and his, but that was nothing compared to the levels we eventually reached. Once he found out the subject of my final presentation for honors economics, he stole the idea and presented it before I did. I had to come up with a brand new idea and work frantically through the night to have mine ready the next day. Another time he convinced a student teacher that I was obsessed with her, and she ended up transferring classrooms because of it."

I didn't mention that I'd gotten him back for that one by writing a series of love letters to the men's rowing coach on Rutherford's personal stationary signed in his name. That situation had been quite sticky, leading to the coach confronting Satcher one day in the locker room. Thankfully, the kid knew judo and the teacher was fired.

In retrospect, I suppose the teacher was less thankful.

Of course, Satcher's real wrath got taken out on me. Quietly and unnoticeably to the adults around us.

The two of us had kept on our war through two grades. I'd practiced manipulation on Satcher Rutherford, matching each of his moves with one of my own. We'd been quite alike, the two of us, each smart and witty, but where I had been cold with my calculations, he'd been passionate. His moves always had flair. He'd intrigued me for that reason. I'd envied him that—his heart. His fire. His ability to both feel and plot. It wasn't a brand of power I'd encountered before, and I hadn't understood it. He'd been a good chess player, for that reason. I'd seldom been able to guess his moves. Often, he'd had me cornered.

Until he couldn't anymore.

"So then what happened?" Chandler asked, eager for more. It was strange how much I enjoyed his rapt attention.

I forced myself to quit drawing the thing out. "Long story short, the two of us didn't get along, and by the summer after tenth grade, I'd had enough of it. So when both of our families summered together at the Hamptons, I upped my game."

"You know," Chandler said turning to Jordan, "this is almost as good as Scandal. And that has a Pierce Industries in it too."

I could see the effort it took for Jordan not to roll his eyes, and made a note to give him a bonus.

"So? What did you do?" Chandler asked.

"I convinced Satcher's parents that one of them was having an affair." It had been easier than I'd expected. Their marriage had apparently already been fragile and on the brink. The simple placement of a pair of skimpy women's underwear, which I'd stolen from Chandler's nanny's quarters, tangled in bed sheets, along with a spray of my mother's perfume inside one of Satcher's father's dinner jackets was all it took. It had been so simple to sneak up to their master bedroom plant the items I needed to while everyone was distracted during a summer weekend party.

I couldn't have predicted how far the stunt would go. Not only did the scandal cause the Rutherfords to separate, they also moved away from New York. "How was I supposed to know that neither parent would feel emotionally capable of handling their son on their own?" I asked innocently.

Chandler looked from me to Jordan. "What does that mean? I'm lost."

"They got divorced and sent their kid to boarding school," Jordan guessed, with no judgment in his tone, just clarification of the facts.

I nodded. "An all-boys school in upstate Connecticut. I haven't spoken to him since."

Chandler's earlier look of awe turned to one of utter shock. "But that's . . . that's . . . that's so *mean!*"

"That type of unresolved animosity from one's formative years might show up later in life." Jordan's meaning was clear—he was adding Satcher to his suspect list. Wisely, now that I'd thought about it. "I'll follow up."

"And you should say you're sorry!" Chandler exclaimed, indignantly.

I threw back the rest of my scotch and set my glass down with a thunk before setting him straight. "I'm *not* sorry. That preppy little asshole wreaked havoc in my life. I was glad to see him out of it."

For once in his life, my brother's mouth was open, but he had nothing to say.

Now I just needed to steer Chandler in the direction I wanted him to go.

I stood up and buttoned my jacket.

"I don't expect you to grovel for me either, Chandler. If that's the route you choose to go, that's on you. Frankly, I'm not keen on going into a business venture with him, either. My original intent had been . . . more subversive. If you had asked me, I wouldn't have approved of the route you chose, clearly. But since you're already walking that path, I recommend you use our dislike for each other to your advantage. Assure him that my feelings for him are mutual and that a partnership will both keep an enemy close and allow him to make money off me at the same time. He might find that gratifying. It's the only reason I'm allowing you to keep on with this proposal.

"Or, you could take the simpler alternative," I continued. "Call the secretary back, charm *her* into giving you the number of a consultant to help revive the club, and you won't have to do any more business with Rutherford at all. It's your choice."

I was snippy, but I had enough guilt built up on my shoulders for the deeds of my past without my brother adding to the pile. And, for all the things I had to make amends for, Satcher Rutherford was not even close to being on my priority list.

In fact, I was rather proud of how that one had shaken out.

Little shithead.

"Now I'd love to stay and listen to you continue to compare my very real life to some overly-dramatic television show that has obviously used the name of our company in it's scripting—Jordan, make a note to talk to a trademark lawyer—but I have another place I need to be. Enjoy your time in Austin." I crossed to the elevator and left the loft with my head held high.

I was reasonably sure that after my speech, Chandler would stay away from Rutherford. An investor *had* been a good idea, but dealing with Satcher would come with risks. And all we'd really needed was someone to help guide a re-launch. It would be an easier task to find that person, and we wouldn't have to worry about a foe from my past. A foe who very well could be currently threatening me.

But later, in the car to my appointment, I pulled out my phone and texted Jordan, just to be sure.

Make sure Chandler has security on him at all times.

Chapter Eleven

ALAYNA

"My mission was fruitless," I said, sinking into the chair across from Gwen when I returned to The Sky Launch.

Good friend that she was, she shut her laptop and gave me her undivided attention. "Tell me about it."

"Mira didn't think I should be investigating. In case it's dangerous." I propped my chin up with my hands, my elbows anchored on the desk. I left out the part where she was furious with me. I needed someone to be my cheerleader after all of this.

"I feel like I might have said the same thing . . ."

"And then you took it back, which is what makes you a better friend," I said pointedly. She hadn't really taken it back, but at least she'd humored me with my intentions and hadn't threatened to tell on me to my husband. Good enough.

Though, if the situation really was dangerous, maybe a good friend *should* have been yelling at me.

But *was* it really dangerous? Or were the letters a scare tactic? What about the guy Stacy referred to? Who was that? Why wouldn't Hudson tell me anything?

My head was consumed with questions—none of which Gwen could answer.

"Help me take my mind off it," I groaned, wanting solidarity as much as anything. "Tell me something going on in your life. Anyone from the past haunting JC?"

Gwen chuckled. "No, but . . ." She craned her neck to look behind her, seemingly making sure that the door to the office was shut. Even though she had confirmed that it was, she still lowered her voice and leaned in to continue. "JC and I did decide that we're going to go to that party."

"The sex party? The orgy party?" I did *not* keep my voice down. I practically squealed. I was deeply, deeply excited by this distraction.

"Shh." Her face turned pink. "It's called an erotic party, and yes. We're going tomorrow night, so by the next time I see you, I should be able to tell you all about it."

"I want you to tell me all about it right now." I sat forward. "What are you going to wear? What are you going to do? Oh, shit, what if you see someone you know?" This definitely was getting my mind off people who wanted to do me and my family harm.

"It's formal attire and both JC and I have decided to wear masks. We are not *doing* anything. We are simply going as spectators. That's all." She looked at the clock. "And while I'm scolding you, it's time to get you downstairs. My impression of Lee is that he's a pretty punctual man."

I stood up, once again smoothing my outfit. "All right, all right. But I want details after, okay?"

"Same to you. Tell me everything Lee says. Good luck!"

I grabbed my laptop and walked down from the office to the hostess station. I could tell the answer to my question before I even asked it, from the expectant way that she looked at me as I approached.

"Elsa, is there someone here to see me?" I asked.

She nodded with a smile. "Yes, Mrs. Pierce. He's waiting for you in Bubble Room Four."

Gwen was right about Lee Chong and his penchant for punctuality, it seemed. Just like my husband. By my clock I still had another seven minutes. But then, Hudson always said that on time was late.

I hustled across the floor and up the stairs to the bubble rooms, only stopping to catch my breath when I was outside Number Four. And then

I paused, wondering if I should knock on the closed door, or walk right on in. It was always these details that fussed me.

I decided walking in was the strongest—and the bravest—so I threw my shoulders back, took another deep breath, put on a bright smile, and walked in the door. "Mr. Ch—Hudson." I froze, halfway to the table, my eyes locked on the man sitting there, who was definitely not Lee Chong, but was still familiar.

"What are you doing here?" I quickly replayed the conversation I'd had with Elsa. Neither of us had specifically mentioned Mr.Chong's name. There'd obviously been a miscommunication.

"I could ask you the same thing, Precious," he said, that sly grin of his turning up the corner of his mouth. "You said you weren't going anywhere today. When I told you to stay put. Remember?" His gaze pierced into me. Challenging me.

I scowled. "Not a princess in a tower. Remember?" I retorted.

"Which is why I thought you might care to have lunch, away from the penthouse. Join me, will you?"

Automatically, I started toward the bench opposite him, then stopped myself, remembering that Lee Chong was waiting for me, either in another bubble room, or was about to arrive. "No. I can't."

His brow lifted questioningly. "You can't?"

"I mean, I'm not happy with you. Why would I want to have lunch?" I hugged my laptop to my chest.

"For exactly that reason. To make up." His voice rumbled, sending goosebumps skittering down my arms.

Damn, he made making up sound so . . . tempting.

But right now I couldn't make up even if I wanted to. I chewed on my lip. "That's really sweet of you, Hudson, but I'm going to have to decline. Enjoy your lunch." I swiveled on my heel and headed toward the door.

"Lee Chong isn't meeting with you," Hudson called after me, freezing me in my tracks.

My hand was hovering above the knob, and now I wanted to punch it through the wall.

I spun around, my pulse racing. "How did you know about—"

"He called me last night before I left work. Wanted to know if it was okay to discuss major purchases and renovations with my wife. He seems to be a bit of a traditionalist—used to only dealing with men."

I threw my head back and cursed under my breath. "Traditionalist, you say? Wonder how he's going to take it when he finds out his daughter's a lesbian."

"What was that?"

"Nevermind." Lee Chong's daughter's affair with Liesl was the least of my concerns right now. "And so what—you told him no? Is that why he's not here today?"

Hudson leaned back, looking surprised. "Of course not. I told him The Sky Launch belongs to you. What you do with it and how you choose to run this business has nothing to do with me. It bothers me that you would think that I would say anything different."

I sighed and took a couple steps forward. "I'm sorry, H. It's just, you're here, and he's . . . not."

"He said it was due to an unrelated matter that he needed to reschedule. I assumed that he'd called you directly as well."

I practically laughed. "Bullshit. You knew he wouldn't call me and reschedule—the traditionalist who doesn't want to deal with women—and that's why you were here. To catch me in the act of doing something sneaky behind your back."

He smirked. "Me? Do that?"

How could there be seven years between now and when we'd first met and still be so much electricity between the two of us? It sizzled, crackled in the air. Made my skin tingle. Made my pussy ache and throb.

"Come sit down. Join me for lunch, Alayna."

He knew he had me. I didn't have to vocally admit it. I walked over and sat down on the bench across from him, setting my laptop next to me and putting the napkin across my lap.

He turned and pressed the button next to him to call the waitress, who showed up immediately and took our orders. When she was gone, Hudson steepled his hands together and placed his elbows on the table. "Do you want to tell me about this grand plan of yours? How it involves

Lee Chong and his event space?"

As hesitant as I had been to tell him for all these months, I suddenly did want to tell him, kind of badly.

There were a lot of things I wanted, actually.

I wanted this to just be a casual lunch date. I wanted there to just be sexy electric heat between us. I didn't want there to be dark and heavy terrors hiding in the tension that surrounded us.

But that was our reality. I was willing to face it, if Hudson would only let me.

"Are you ready to tell me everything about your investigation on this threat against our family?" I asked, killing the light mood between us.

He didn't answer, but his expression said it all—that he wasn't talking about it.

"Yeah. That's what I thought." I put my arms around myself, and suddenly I felt very old and very tired. Like I'd been awake for days, like I'd been running from something. In a way I had been running—running from the full force of this shadow. I hadn't let it sink in. Hadn't actually held the idea there was somebody on this earth who maybe wanted to do real harm to me. To my children. To the tiny precious angels that gave my life meaning and joy.

My throat began to tighten. I bit my lip to distract myself, but it didn't work.

Across from me, Hudson seemed to be in a very different mood. His gaze tripped around the bubble room. "We used to do very fun things in these," he said wistfully, seductively.

"I had babies, Hudson. No one has fun in bubble rooms after babies," I snapped.

"The babies don't mean—"

I cut him off. "The babies mean everything! Someone's threatening them, H!" I meant to say more. Meant to tell him this should be something that we dealt with together and that it wasn't fair he had forced me into the dark to deal with it alone.

But I couldn't say anything, because I immediately burst into tears. Not little trickle-down-your-face tears, but full out sobs that shook my body as they wracked through me.

I didn't remember moving or Hudson reaching for me, but next thing I knew, I was in his lap, and he was kissing my head, holding me, and rocking me in his arms, murmuring words of comfort. "I got you. I won't let anything hurt you. I won't let anything hurt our babies. I swear to you, my love. My precious. Nothing will happen to any of you. Ever."

And as I cried into his suit jacket, I wondered if it was possible to trust someone so much, and still not be sure you entirely believed him.

CHAPTER TWELVE

HUDSON

We didn't eat lunch at The Sky Launch.

I asked the waitress to box up our orders to go, and on a whim, I brought Alayna back to the loft above my office. Then, after she silently picked through her salad, I tucked her puffy-eyed self into the bed where she fell fast asleep.

I sat in the armchair next to her and watched her while she dozed, long limbs curled into herself, her facial features relaxed and at ease. In this state, she seemed as carefree and burdenless as Brett. Oh, that I could keep her like this forever.

That I could keep them all like this.

The first time I had made love to Alayna, had been inside her and felt the tremendous impact of our worlds colliding, it had been in this very room. And then, as now, I had watched her afterward, knowing I could never let her go, that I had to have more of her, even as I prepared to push her away. She had never been just a game to me, but I had thought that I could hold her at a distance. What a fool I had been.

How long had it been before I learned that I couldn't ever shut her out for good?

Not long, truly. Our courtship had been a whirlwind, mere weeks passing.

What the fuck was I thinking, believing I could shut her out now, after years of building a life together?

She stirred in the bed beside me. A slight *mmm* escaped her throat, her head tossed from one side to the other. Then her eyes popped open. Her expression was unsettled until her gaze found mine, then a warm smile played on her lips.

"Did I sleep through the entire afternoon, or did you abandon your work obligations just for me?" she asked stretching, her breasts jutting deliciously forward, pressing against her dress as she did.

I let my eyes wander down to her cleavage. "I've rearranged the entire week's schedule for this project. Which has been very much for you."

Her smile faded. "This project being the one where you are investigating those threatening letters. Right?"

"Right," I admitted. It felt like relief and terror at once to tell her so.

She sat up, and with a sigh tilted her head against the headboard, the wheels in her brain obviously spinning a mile a minute.

I moved to sit beside her on the bed and held my arm open, inviting her in. She came without hesitation, her heat soaking into me, confusing my cock about the mood of the situation.

Subtly, I readjusted myself and pulled her in tighter against me.

"I'm scared, Hudson," she said, her voice vibrating against my chest.

It was the last thing I wanted to hear. "I know, and I don't want you to be scared. I want you to let me worry about it so you don't have to be scared."

"I know that's what you want, but that's not how things work. Especially not for me. It's one thing to have this menace looming over us, and to not know anything about it. It makes my mind go crazy. Makes me imagine the worst things, no matter how safe you tell me I am. How protected you try to make me feel. It's a whole other issue, a whole other hurt, to realize you've been shutting me out."

My lids closed momentarily with the squeeze of my heart. "I know, precious. I am—"

"Let me finish. Please," she stopped me.

I held my next words, though I knew they would likely end the need for anything else to be said. She deserved space to be heard, and I needed to give her that.

"You used to have such a thick wall around you. I remember thinking if I could only get inside, if I could just break down your barrier, everything would be okay between us. That we could be perfect together." She fiddled with the button on my shirt as she talked, twisting as far as it would go one way, then twisting it back the other. "And I was right, H. When you finally let me in—we were magic. I felt whole and unstoppable with the complete Hudson Pierce at my side. That's what makes me feel safe, Hudson—you. When you give me all of you. When you stand beside me and treat me like your partner. When you hold my hand and tell me we got this."

She pulled away, sitting upright and looking down at me. "I get what you're trying to do here, keeping this away from me. I get that you don't want me to have to feel it. But you also shouldn't feel this alone. This isn't us at our best. Us at our best is a team." She put her hand over mine, gripping my index finger tightly. "We need to do this as a team. We don't work any other way."

I waited a full three seconds after she'd finished talking to make sure she was done. "I was actually thinking the same thing. While you were sleeping."

Her expression warred between doubt and victory. "Really?"

"Yes. Really. I think we need to lay all our cards on the table. No more walls. I need you with me on this."

Her eyes began to glisten. Cautiously, she asked, "Are you just saying that because you know you've lost?"

I shoved back the growl I felt coming on. "I did not lose."

"It sure sounded like you lost to me. Because I got what I wanted, and you're giving me what I . . ."

"That's not a loss," I corrected. "It's a concession of both parties."

"Actually, I really don't feel like I had to concede much of anything at all." She flashed a mischievous grin, the kind that sent shocks straight to both my heart and my cock.

God, this woman.

I surrendered. A hundred times. A thousand times.

Which meant she was about to push me out of bed and plead with me to walk her through everything. I knew how her brain worked, how eager she got. She didn't like to wait on an idea once she had it.

I, on the other hand, would be happy sitting here admiring her for a little while longer, if she'd let me.

But as she climbed over me, instead of continuing out of the bed, she stopped, and sat straddling my waist. Her fingers went back to playing with my buttons, but this time she undid them, one by one.

Her grin turned naughty.

"I didn't bring you back here to seduce you," I said, my cock growing thicker underneath her.

"Maybe it's what I need." Her voice came out breathy. "Besides, it looks like I'm the one doing the seducing." She threw my shirt open and ran her palms over my bare chest, igniting sparks of fire in my veins. I liked her like this—hot, feisty, empowered.

But I liked the reins in *my* hands even better.

I slipped my hand under her skirt and traced the silky skin of her thigh until I reached the crotch panel of her panties, which were already wet. Hooking my thumb underneath the flimsy material, I found her tight bud and began massaging it, exactly the way I knew she liked.

She let out a sweet whimper that made me instantly turn to steel.

"Take off your dress," I ordered, barely restraining myself from tearing it off for her. She reached behind herself to undo the zipper, and though she struggled with it, I let her do it alone, not wanting to move my hand from her pussy. Wanting to watch her strip just for me.

We'd always been explosive together. I had no complaints about our sex life, but it was rare these days that we had the opportunity to take our time. I didn't always get to fully enjoy these interludes, didn't always get to relish in the way she gave herself to me, every time, so freely, so completely.

The way I always gave her all of me.

Did she even realize it in our fast and frenzied stolen moments? That she still owned every single molecule of my composition? That she still resided in every hidden corner of my being?

She pulled her dress over her head, and as she did I sat up and unfastened my cuffs, quickly yanking my unbuttoned shirt from my arms and discarding it on the floor. By that time, she'd lost her bra as well, and I gazed happily at her tight nipples standing at attention. I cupped one breast in my hand, the familiar shape and weight of it sending relief through my body.

Fuck, I loved her body. Every inch.

I would've delivered a prayer of gratitude, of adoration as I worshiped, but my mouth was already suckling on her other breast, my tongue licking reverently along her nipple before my teeth grazed along the sensitive skin.

That earned me another one of her precious whimpers, this time she added a sweep of her hips along my aching groin. My cock was still imprisoned beneath my suit pants and my boxer briefs, but even with so much between us, the movement was ecstasy and elicited a growl of my own.

"You're killing me," I said, planting kisses in the space between her breasts as I traveled to her other nipple.

"Then I guess I should do it again." She slid her pussy over the ridge of my cock again and again, torture that deserved to be paid back with another nip of my teeth on her tit and a light pinch of her clit through her panties.

She squealed, a delicious sound that I needed to taste. I swallowed the tail of it, pulling her toward me and covering her mouth with mine. I kissed her long and deep, kissed her as though I had forgotten her flavor. Exploring her as though I'd never taken the time to discover every part of her mouth before.

She took it all. Kissed me back with equal fervor, wrapping her arms around my neck and pressing her breasts against my chest where I could feel the tips of her nipples, still wet from my affection, pressing against my skin.

When I pulled away, it was only because I had to be inside her, because I couldn't wait another second to be connected to her. Breathlessly, she wriggled out of her panties, a move she made hot as fuck even when she was in a hurry. Especially when she was in a hurry and needy.

I was just as needy for her. While she undressed, my eyes never left her. I stripped out of my clothes at the same time and laid down again on the bed. Then I pulled her back to sit across my upper thighs.

I fisted myself, pumping up and down even though I was ready for her.

She watched me, as hypnotized as the first time she'd watched me handle my own cock. It turned her on. I could feel how much it turned her on by the way her pussy leaked on my leg. She bit her lip and eagerly began to line herself up, which did things to me. Her eagerness. Her anticipation. It somehow gave me patience for days. I could drag things out a long time—and I often did—just so I could enjoy her excitement.

Today was not one of those days.

Today I was eager too, eager to show her that she was still as close to me as she'd ever been. That there weren't walls between us. That any barrier I had put up had been a mistake, that I had never wanted there to be anything between the two of us.

I pressed my crown to her entrance, and she sat down on me, taking me in fully, with a sigh that I echoed.

Jesus, how could she still feel so good? Every time. Tight and warm and familiar and home. I could sit there, unmoving, and still feel like I'd found heaven.

And I knew from experience it only got better from here.

I thrust into her, a couple of short stabs to warm her up, and then let go full-force, clutching onto her thighs, hips bucking up and up and up. It was never enough—never hard enough or fast enough or deep enough, no matter how we were positioned. I always wanted more of her. Always wanted all of her.

Good girl that she was, she reached down to play with her own clit, and instantly she grew tighter and hotter. My eyes became glued to her fingers as they stroked along the bundle of nerves, making it turn hard and plump and slippery. Then when she stiffened with her orgasm, my gaze ran to her face so I could watch the pleasure as it made its way across her features with vivid expression.

I sat up to hold her, knowing she'd be worn out and weak, wanting her close to me.

She felt even tighter wrapped around me at this new angle. I let out a satisfying grunt and cupped her face in my hands.

"I need you safe, precious," I told her kissing along her jaw. "In every way. If everything I have done to make you feel safe has made you feel like we're growing apart, then there's no point. I need you to feel as safe as you are. I need you with me." I drove into her with my cock, a slower pace, but still deep, reminding her we were connected. Reminding myself that I'd merely forgotten for a moment that we were tethered to each other in everything—the good *and* the bad.

She looked into my eyes. "Together," she said. "We're doing this together. You'll keep me safe. We'll keep the kids safe. Together."

"Together," I repeated before taking her mouth in a searing kiss as my thumb returned to her clit to rouse another orgasm from her beautiful body. Carefully monitoring her signals—watching her breathing, listening to her sounds, feeling the way she clamped down around my cock—I could time her impending climax. A few more quick pumps of my hips, and we found our release together.

Together.

I was still inside her when we collapsed together on the bed, our limbs tangled around each other. She'd said she'd needed this. The truth was, so did I. Needed to feel this much a part of her.

I needed to let her into the investigation too, even more than I'd needed to make love to her. I needed her with me, despite preferring that she be kept safe and sheltered from it. I needed her, even though I hated more than anything that she had to know she had a reason to be scared.

Honestly, I needed her because I was scared too.

CHAPTER THIRTEEN
ALAYNA

Hudson was on the phone when I got out of the shower and wandered into the front room looking for him. He had cleaned up first, and was wearing some khakis he must have stowed somewhere in the loft. Khakis and nothing else.

My stomach performed somersaults as my eyes traced along his broad shoulders and down the sinewy strands of his biceps. He was so strong. So capable. So worthy of being my protector. I trusted him with every part of me.

He turned in my direction as he heard me enter the room, his eyes dilating at the sight of me wrapped only in a towel, but he kept focused on his conversation.

"Thank you," he was saying. "We both appreciate it." He paused to listen. After a second, his eyelids shut briefly before he opened them again—his version of an eye roll. "Yes, Mirabelle, I should have talked to Alayna earlier, but we are working it all out now. I promise. We will see you Sunday and you can interrogate me about it then."

I bit back a smile. So Mirabelle had been on my side too.

I was less irritated with the way things at the boutique had turned out, knowing she'd chewed out Hudson as well.

"She's watching the kids?" I asked as I patted the ends of my hair dry with a towel.

"Yes. Jordan's team is taking them over to her house. She'll keep them for the weekend."

We'd decided this before I'd showered, but I needed reassuring of the plan.

"And it won't be too much of a handful for her? Having all those kids plus hers?"

"I sent Payton to help, and Mirabelle has a nanny of her own. She also said something about Sophia coming by—you know how she likes to hover over the grandkids." He picked up a button-down that he must've pulled from the closet and began putting it on.

"And it will be safe enough at her house?" I hated asking, because it felt like the other Alayna—the one who worried too much. The one who fretted over nonsensical, ridiculous things.

But I reminded myself that this time the question was warranted.

"Mirabelle's house has state-of-the-art security," he said reassuringly. "And on top of that, we have some of Jordan's guys watching. Mirabelle already knows, so she won't kick them off the property."

I nodded, taking a deep breath in and then letting it go. Letting go of the worry. Or at least letting it loosen a bit.

Maybe all it did was redirect my worry. His comment about men at Mirabelle's reminded me of what Stacy had said when I'd been at the boutique, and then I had a new concern. "H, does Jordan have men watching Mirabelle's store too?"

He looked at me carefully. "Would you prefer the answer was yes or no?"

"I would prefer the answer is *true*," I said back with a huff, although I did hope it was a yes. If whoever was hanging around my sister-in-law wasn't one of ours, the implications were concerning.

He chuckled. "There are men watching her store while she's open. But don't take that to mean that the threat has extended further than those letters you read. I've just been taking extra precautions."

I loved that about him—that he was always extra cautious. That he never missed any details. I relied on that trait now. "I'm glad you did. Though Stacy's noticed them, and I think it might've been a good idea to give her and your sister a heads-up, because both of them can be pretty dramatic when they want to be about anything out of the ordinary. But I'm glad you are looking out for them."

He shrugged, as if to say he thought his methods were completely fine. I hadn't really expected otherwise. His confidence, that unshakeable force, was something that I found very attractive.

I shook my head again, tossing the towel I'd been using on my hair onto the floor.

"By the way, Jordan stopped by with some clothes for you while you were in the shower. He picked them up from the penthouse. I laid them on the bed for you." The heat of his gaze trapped me, pinning me in place. "Or. You could wait to get dressed. And I could get undressed again."

Warmth spread over the entirety of my skin, but I pulled away from his stare and marched toward the bedroom. "Stay dressed. That wasn't the reason we asked Mirabelle to take the kids."

His sultry tone followed after me. "You mean it wasn't the *only* reason."

"I don't seem to remember it being on the list at all." I found a pair of panties and stepped into them, long past the embarrassment of Hudson's assistants seeing my personal items. "We're supposed to be working as a team to figure out who's harassing our family."

I began to put on my bra, reaching behind me to do the hook-and-eye.

"I think we work best as a team when I'm inside you."

His voice was closer this time. I turned and found him in the door-frame, watching me.

Honestly, if he kept looking at me like that, he was going to win this dispute.

I hurried to pull a T-shirt over me, hoping he'd be more focused if I were more covered. "Can we at least eat dinner first?" I asked. "I'm starving."

"Dinner first," he nodded, but he didn't move. And didn't stop staring.

"Dinner where we lay everything out on the table? Clear things up?

Get on the same page?"

He nodded again. "Everything on the table."

"Not me on the table," I added quickly, in case he was taking this another direction. "The things you've been keeping from me."

"All of that is a part of everything," he smirked.

I could agree to that.

But I made a mental note that before there was any more sexing, I also wanted to talk about to the New Park School incident as well. With all that had been going on and not speaking to him, I hadn't told him yet. And I was really desperate to find out about Judith Cleary's threat.

"Good. Thank you." I walked to him, draping my arms around his neck. He responded by wrapping his arms around my waist and pulling me closer. I gave him a quick kiss that I could tell he would easily make longer if I let him.

I didn't let him.

But I liked the mood he was setting. I wanted to follow it through. "Can dinner be out somewhere?" A couple's getaway *hadn't* been the purpose of this weekend, but maybe Hudson had the right idea. We hadn't had much time together lately. I couldn't even remember the last time we'd been on a date.

He looked down at me regretfully. "That sounds wonderful, precious. However, since we sent extra men to be at Mirabelle's, the team is a little stretched. I'd prefer we stay in. This building has an armed guard twenty-four seven."

I frowned. The bubble of my date night was burst as fast as the idea had come.

His statement also reminded me that he seemed to think we were in real danger. Not Alayna's overactive imagination version of danger, but the kind of danger that made him feel like he wasn't enough to keep me safe on his own.

Seeming to sense my distress, he quickly worked to soothe me. "Compromise? We order in, but eat on the rooftop. How does that sound?"

"Romantic. Thank you, H." I suddenly remembered I had my dress from Mirabelle's with me. Maybe this could be a sort of date night after all. Threats and tension and secrets revealed notwithstanding.

I moved my hands to his chest and began to push away so I could finish changing, but he pulled me closer, and spun me so my back was against the bedroom wall.

"Why didn't you tell me about Lee Chong and your plans for The Sky Launch?" he asked, his expression serious.

My stomach dropped a little to hear him. His tone wasn't angry or judgmental. Rather, he sounded hurt. As hurt as I had been when he hadn't included *me* in *his* life.

We *did* say all secrets on the table, and I *did* want to tell him about this, but it felt so insignificant next to everything else going on. How could I possibly spend tonight's valuable time together blathering on about vinyl records when our family was at risk?

So I downplayed. "It really isn't anything I spent much time on. Just a passing—"

"I saw your plans. You've obviously spent *extensive* time on it." Again, there was no accusation.

"You saw my plans?" I hadn't shown anyone but Gwen.

"I found the folder on the desktop of your laptop. Your PowerPoint was very thorough."

A burst of indignation shot through me. "You went through my laptop!"

He went on as though there were nothing upsetting about that at all. "While you were sleeping. The plans were brilliant. I loved every detail. The coffee shop and merchandising area was one of the highlights."

I was only somewhat mollified by his compliments, and attempted to cross my arms over my chest, but he still had me trapped against the wall, and he grabbed my arms instead and pinned them over my head. "Why are you fussing?"

"You looked at my laptop behind my back," I grumbled.

"And you went through those letters that I had laid out while I was sleeping," he said, with a smirk.

He didn't quite have the point he thought he did—those letters were out in the open, versus my closed and stored laptop. Not that I was going to argue it with him, so we just held each other's gaze for several seconds.

Finally, I asked, "You really thought it was good?"

"Brilliant," he repeated, sincerely. "Why wouldn't you tell me about that? Did you think I wouldn't support you? Did you think that I would object to you expanding the nightclub?"

I suddenly felt vulnerable, my arms in the air, his eyes piercing into me. Seeing into me. Poking around in the deepest parts of me. Just like he'd always done so well.

I lowered my head. "I thought you'd say it wasn't the right time." My voice sounded smaller than I meant it to.

"Why? Because the twins are still so young? It was you who said you wanted to be home with them. I can't believe that I ever gave you the impression that I wouldn't want you working if that was what you wanted. I have always supported you in—"

I cut him off. "Because I didn't think you thought I could handle it. Not so soon. Not so soon after . . ."

His brow furrowed for a second before he understood my meaning. "That's your fear talking, Alayna. It's not fair to use me to personify your doubts. If you say you need to work, then you need to work. If you say you need to be on a beach in the Virgin Islands, then that's where we'll go. If you say you need another baby—"

I stopped him right there. "I don't need another baby."

He smiled. "You know what you need. And I'll support whatever that is."

I felt my eyes getting wet. "But you don't really think my head's a crazy mess?" My voice cracked. "The other day, it seemed like you were afraid of my state of mind."

He dropped my wrists so that he could cup my face with one hand. "Your mind is the reason I fell in love with you, precious. Your sexy, brilliant, incredible, crazy, mess of a mind. Maybe it feels like it's chaos in there sometimes, but I promise I wouldn't want you any other way."

That right there was why I didn't want him any other way, either.

* * *

"Damn," Hudson said when I walked out onto the roof forty-five minutes later.

While he'd ordered tapas and set up a table and chairs, I'd put on the wrap dress I'd purchased earlier in the day. I'd done what I could with what makeup I had in my purse, styled my hair, and by the time I was done, I thought I looked pretty dang good for a mother of three.

I looked pretty dang good, period.

"Turn around," Hudson said, practically growling out the command.

I complied, spinning slowly. Seductively.

"Are you sure we have to eat dinner first?" he teased. "Because I'm suddenly hungry for something other than food."

Actually, he was probably dead serious, from the way his eyes had turned dark and liquid. It was amazing to me, seeing this now, that I had ever worried we had lost our spark. What we'd lost was the kind of raw honesty, the uninhibited lust you could only get when you're completely focused on the other person.

But it seemed that, along with my own confidence, our communication was back.

"I'll feed you," I promised. "Whatever you want to eat. But first you assured me we'd talk."

"I did say we'd do that, didn't I?" The sensual darkness in his eyes stayed, but his smile turned from predatory to warm, and I wondered to myself for the thousandth time—how did I get so lucky?

He took my hand and walked me to the round table set up in a small corner of the roof. Somehow he'd managed to scrape up a tablecloth and a pair of candlesticks as well. It was exactly the romantic scene I'd imagined.

"This is perfect, H," I said, as he pulled out my chair for me to sit in.

"*You're* perfect. Stunning, really." He seemed to remember something and added, "Also, you're smart, funny, brave, and enough. According to Mina, it's not appropriate to only compliment a woman on her looks."

I laughed. "She's amazing."

"She's you."

"She's you, too." I sat down, and he pushed my chair into the table.

"She is," he agreed, then went to sit at his own seat.

The food was already set out on the table, the wine already poured. My stomach grumbled. I hadn't eaten much of my lunch, and I was hungry, but food still didn't interest me as much as details. Not with so many questions left unanswered.

"What was the first letter you received?" I asked, watching as Hudson began loading items onto his plate.

He looked at me sternly. "You need to eat, Alayna."

"I'm not going—"

"I will talk, as long as you are eating."

I quickly grabbed a roll and stuffed a piece of it in my mouth, smiling smugly in his direction. "I'm eating," I said when I'd swallowed. "Now go."

He laughed to himself, as though he shouldn't have been surprised that I would have behaved any other way. Then he sighed, seriousness settling back over him like a suit. "The first letter arrived when you were five months pregnant with the twins."

I rewarded him for beginning the story by scooping some goat cheese and mandarin salad onto my plate.

He went on. "You had just been put on bedrest. The letter had shown up mixed in with some files from Human Resources, folded in a plain white envelope, no address. It was a mystery how it got to me without being screened, which made it unusual right off the bat. The language as well was deeply personal. Not many people were aware of your bedrest situation. That was still new—and it's not like I spend much time discussing our personal lives with other people regardless. Normally a vague letter such as that wouldn't cause alarm, except for those details. I handed it off to Jordan, who assured me it was nothing. A prankster. Someone with a chip on his shoulder. Possibly someone even in the building—which would explain how they'd known about you, perhaps a stray word from Patricia overheard. Jordan said he'd get to the bottom of the matter. He didn't recommend further action at that time."

"But you increased security at home and at The Sky Launch." If it hadn't been that big of a deal, why had he made that move?

Hudson looked only mildly surprised that I had learned this

information. "You've been doing your own investigating, I see. Yes, I did increase security. The letter made me realize we hadn't had an update in a while, and the personalization had jarred me—I won't lie. I was more anxious than usual, with your difficult pregnancy, and I recognized that I might be overreacting, but it was better to be safe than sorry."

"And you didn't tell me because . . ."

"Because I knew I was being ridiculous. Paranoid. I wasn't about to concern you with something that should have been a dead issue. Especially when Dr. Addison had warned that you needed to stay away from stress." He lifted his glass of wine and took a swallow. "Certainly, you can understand that."

I paused. Studied his face. Searched for any of his tells to see if he was manipulating the story. Not that I didn't trust my husband, just . . . sometimes he liked to think he was saying and doing things for my benefit, and occasionally that involved a little futzing of the truth.

Everything about his expression and his posture though, said he was sincere.

"Yes. I can understand why you didn't tell me then. Go on." I placed another forkful of food in my mouth to demonstrate I was keeping up with my part of the bargain. Hudson swallowed back a broiled shrimp himself before continuing.

"I'd almost stopped having nightmares about the first letter when the second letter came. It showed up in the mailroom, addressed to me personally, so it was screened for toxic substances, but not read. It was delivered to me in a stack with a bunch of other items at the penthouse, because you had just given birth."

My mind played quickly through the lines I remembered from the letters I had read. "That must be the one that had a line like, '*Congratulations, you must think you're the man of the year twice over.*'"

"That one," he confirmed. "This was letter two, so it was obviously more alarming. Jordan ran all the tests, traced the return address to a post office downtown. Every lead led to a dead end. Again, Jordan believed it was just someone jealous of my life. Someone particularly triggered by my happy family. He didn't believe there was any real threat involved, and indeed, since the language in that letter was much more benign, it was easier to put out of my mind."

"And you didn't tell me about it because I just had twins and it wasn't a big deal and even your head of security wasn't worried. Blah blah blah. Right?" I was giving him a hard time, but that was our thing.

"Would you have said something, were you in my place?" he challenged as he popped a cherry tomato in his mouth.

"Probably not," I conceded. "But definitely the third letter—"

"Came six months later." That's all he said.

That was all he had to say.

Six months later, after the birth of my twins, I was in the height of my postpartum OCD. Whatever threats he'd gotten then, of course he wouldn't have shared them with me. It would've been against the advice of everyone around him, against the advice of my therapists, against his own better thinking.

God. Poor Hudson. Having to deal with this and me, all at the same time. He must have felt so alone. Some partner I'd been.

"Alayna, don't you dare blame yourself for anything," he said sharply from across the table, reading my mind.

I pulled my eyes up quickly to meet his gaze. "How do you even know what I'm thinking?"

"Because I know you. And it's not your fault. Whatever you're blaming yourself for. I didn't want you to be concerned with it. That's why I didn't tell you. Not because I didn't think you couldn't handle it. Or because you weren't strong enough."

I appreciated his kind, comforting words. I even thought he partially believed them. Believed that the reason he hadn't told me was because he wanted to do this on his own, and not because he worried about breaking me.

But we both knew who I'd been back then.

"Thank you, H," I said, reaching my hand across the table to wrap it around his. "Thank you for bearing all of this alone. I wish that I had been there with you, because I hate for you *ever* to have to bear things alone. But I'm so very grateful that you are the kind of man who does.

Who looks out for me and his children like that."

He squeezed my hand back, and began to rub his thumb along the back of my palm, caressing it. "The last two letters have come much more quickly. None of them have had fingerprints, none of them have led to any substantial location. All of them from random post offices in New York City. The last one was delivered to the penthouse—"

I inhaled sharply. I hadn't known that.

"It's when the picture of you arrived. That was last Friday. The bodyguards came after that."

Last Friday. The night of Nash King's birthday party. No wonder Hudson had acted so distant and preoccupied. And without something concrete to assign it to, I'd immediately blamed myself for not interesting him.

You really can't take the crazy out of the girl.

"Do you have any leads? Any suspects?" I asked him.

"I don't know if you caught them, but there are specific references to a scheming manipulative Hudson. While those could be coincidence, Jordan and I are assuming that they indicate whoever is sending the letters is someone from my past, someone who was part of one of my games."

"I thought as much." I hadn't realized the references were vague to him as well. I had hoped they would have led to something more concrete.

Hudson went on to tell me more about the tactics he and Jordan had used to go through potential suspects, the lists Hudson had drawn up of people he could remember in the past that he had wronged, people whom he believed might still be out to get him.

"There are so many, it's like looking for a needle in a haystack. I kept a digital journal in the early days of my experiments, but once I began working with Celia, she took over the journal writing. There have been too many years, too many casualties . . . Honestly, until that photograph of you, I'd begun to believe it was someone who just wanted to vent. But if he—or she—is upset enough to go to the trouble of following you, of taking your picture and sending it to me . . . Well."

"I know," I said so he wouldn't have to say whatever he was imagining. The idea of someone following me and my children, being so close, it turned my insides to ice. That had to be exactly how Hudson was feeling. How scared. How beside himself.

Thoughts of the children and Hudson's past suddenly reminded me of something I hadn't told him. "Does Judith Cleary have something against you? Could it possibly be her sending the letters?"

Hudson's brow rose. "Judith Cleary? However did you hear that name?"

I told him about Mina not getting into New Park School, about the reason why, and about my confrontation with Judith Cleary and the message she had for my husband. "She's on the Board of Directors. She obviously has it out for you. Why is she so against you?"

He frowned. "I did not manipulate or scheme Judith Cleary." He hesitated. "Much."

I sat back in my chair. "Obviously, she has some kind of grudge against you."

"And I have one against her. That woman is petty, narcissistic, and self-involved." His jaw was tensing with irritation. "She had Mirabelle kicked out of their girls' club after Sophia showed up to one of the parent meetings drunk. While I don't condone my mother's behavior, she most definitely shouldn't have taken it out on her child."

Awesome. . Judith Cleary was *actually* a bitch, and not just because I wanted her to be one in my head in order to justify my behavior that day. I did like it when things worked out.

"So what did you do? Because you must've done something for her to be mad at you." I'd already decided that whatever it was, I was in full support of it.

Hudson smiled slyly. "I had her kicked out of the country club. For unfit citizenship."

I laughed. "You would think she would've learned her lesson. Here she is trying to take it out on another kid. What a bitch."

His face grew serious. "I'm sorry I ruined Mina's chances for going to our legacy school. I will call Judith and grovel. See what I can do."

"Please don't bother. We don't want that kind of school, our daughter playing with those kinds of people. We can find something better.

Besides, there's no way you'd apologize convincingly."

He didn't disagree as he took the napkin from my lap, dabbed at my lips and set it down on the table.

Together we looked out over the city, lit up with lights. It was beautiful, being on top of the world. Breathtaking, thrilling, a little overwhelming, but worth it.

I tilted my head and peered over at my husband. "I know we've had many rooftop dinners in our marriage, but this was nice. I mean, the conversation sucks, but the rest of it I'll keep."

"I know something we've never done on a rooftop."

"We've had sex on a rooftop before, H. You're losing your memory." That wasn't a night I'd ever forget. It had been his mother's birthday, but I'd been the one getting the gifts. Hudson always had been good with his mouth.

"Sex was not what I was referring to. And don't you dare think I don't remember that night." His reprimand was low and serious. It made my spine feel tingly at the base.

Still. After all this time.

I grinned. "Then what are you referring to?"

Instead of answering, Hudson pulled out his phone and flipped through a few pages on his screen before setting it down between the two of us. His Spotify app was open to one of my playlists.

"You follow me on Spotify? I thought you just used that app to play lullabies for the babies." All these years, and the man could still surprise me.

"I saw you added this one a few weeks ago," he said, standing from his chair and walking over to mine. He reached over to his phone and pushed play, then held his hand out to me. The familiar strains of our anthem came out of the tiny speakers. "The babies love this particular song," he said, pulling me from my chair and into his arms.

"What are we doing?" I asked, though it was obvious.

"We're dancing. We've never danced on a rooftop." He turned me gently to the beat, and I relaxed into his arms. "This is good, right?"

"Super good. And it's our song." It was strange how I felt like I could melt and come together all the same time. How he could undo me and fix me simultaneously. I pressed my face against his, listening carefully to the words of *All of Me* as they played. It was a new version, not the John Legend original that Hudson had first played for me all those years ago. This one was a duet between a man and a woman.

"I like this arrangement," I told him. "Before it was always as if you were singing it to me. John Legend's voice—I always imagined it was you telling me that you were giving me all of you. But in this version, there's a woman singing too. And I like that because I feel like I'm saying it back to you. Telling you that you get all of *me* too."

His grip on me tightened suddenly, and he pressed his lips to my temple. "This isn't how I dreamed our life would be," he said, his voice thin and stretched. "This isn't the future I dreamed I would give you."

I leaned back so I could look him in the eye. "What do you mean? Our life is fantastic. I couldn't want for anything. You gave me three children. You've given me a home. Given me my nightclub. My books. My friends. My sanity. Everything I have that is good and wonderful is because of you, Hudson."

He shook his head. "I also gave you my past. I gave you security guards. I gave you a reason to go to bed at night scared."

"And I gave you OCD and obsessions and difficult pregnancies."

"Those weren't your fault," he protested.

"And neither is any of this yours now." I stopped moving, but held onto him at the shoulders.

He attempted to move me again, to start the dancing, but I didn't budge. He gave a frustrated sigh. "The things that are happening now— these threats—Alayna, you have to face that they've come about because of somebody I once was. That they are happening because of things I once did. I caused this. I'm the one to blame."

God, he could be so stubborn. Stubborn in his martyrdom.

Well, I could be stubborn too.

"You were the man you were because of terrible circumstances. Because no one showed you that you could be somebody else. Because your mother and father convinced you that you were unfeeling and uncaring, and you believed them." He started to try to speak, but I continued over him. "And it doesn't matter if everything you did was with your free will, because whomever you were before is what made you into the man that I fell in love with. The only reason there is any *now* with us is because there was once a *then*."

I brought my hands up to his face, rubbing my thumbs along the rough five-o'clock shadow on his jaw. "We were both broken, Hudson. And we fixed each other. When you first played me this song, the perfect future that I dreamed of with you? Was any future with you at all. And you've given me that and so much more. I'm sorry if you find our life together disappointing, because it's been more wonderful than I could ever imagine."

"No, precious, I didn't mean that. I haven't been disappointed for a single second. I'm only disappointed right now, through this. That I can't keep you safe and—"

I cut him off. "I *am* safe. I'm with you. We are together, and that's all I need to be safe, remember?"

He gave a curt nod.

"We're going to figure this out," I reassured him. It wasn't often that I was in this position, where I was the one bolstering my husband. He was usually the foundation, the anchor, the levity.

Surprisingly, it comforted me to be able to be that for him now.

He kissed me suddenly, locking his lips to mine and holding them in place for several long seconds. When he broke away, he said, "I'm still going to give you that future I dreamed of. We'll get rid of this baggage from the past, and then we will be safe for good."

He was so solemn, it was as though he was making a promise. As though he were adding to our wedding vows, and I took them in, placed the words inside me along with the other things he'd said, sworn to me on the day we pledged our lives to each other.

"I believe you," I told him. "I'll be here when it happens. I'm here until then too."

The song finished, but we held each other longer. Clutched each other tight.

Then, when we finally broke away, I threw my shoulders back and said the words that I knew we were both thinking. "We both know what we have to do to make progress on this. And I'm ready. Are you?"

"If you're with me, I am," he said earnestly.

"Okay then." I took a deep breath, and tried to ignore the anxiety creeping along my skin. "It's time to call Celia."

Chapter Fourteen

HUDSON

There were a myriad of reasons I hadn't wanted to go to Celia Werner Fasbender.

I didn't trust her.

Any information she shared would come at a great cost.

Seeing her would likely cause my wife stress. Seeing her would likely cause *me* stress, for that matter.

I didn't necessarily want her to know there was someone threatening me and my family, didn't want her to know the predicament that I was in, for fear she'd take advantage of it.

Because, as I'd mentioned before, I did not trust her.

But, if I were being honest, Jordan and I were essentially stalled on the investigation. It took Alayna's insight for me to finally face that matter, to finally accept that this was not something I could handle on my own. While Jordan had continually pushed to take the issue to the FBI, it was only my wife who was brave enough to say that we needed to step into the dragon's lair.

Wasn't that where all journeys ended up eventually?

It had to be handled delicately. I thought about it in great detail, how it would go, what she would say. Even after feasting on Alayna, loving her and pleasuring her to the point of exhaustion, the dilemma of adding Celia to our hunt kept me up all night.

As soon as it was late enough in the morning for human interaction to be appropriate, I crawled out of bed and texted my old friend. I had considered calling, but I was sure I knew how that would go. With enough time to talk to her and enough information from me, she would have no reason to meet us in person, and I felt strongly that this was a matter that needed to be addressed face-to-face.

Celia was a woman who was always playing some game. Every word that came out of her mouth, every side glance, every gesture was the move of a pawn. The slide of a rook. Even the text I sent had to be carefully crafted.

I need to see you.

She was already awake, or my text had woken her. She responded quickly. She was smart enough not to ask why or try to gather more from me here. It had to be that, because I certainly didn't believe she was still loyal, not even somewhere deep inside her, underneath all the hard, cold, thick layers that I had helped her build. Her only questions were *where* and *when*.

With that settled, I left a note for Alayna, then went down to the office gym for a run. When I returned, she was awake. Coffee was brewing and she'd found the eggs in the refrigerator and was making omelettes.

"Tomorrow. 6 PM. Celia will meet us at Randall's for drinks."

Alayna—my precious, my world, my light, my life—she turned and smiled at me as though I had given her the key to a brighter future instead of announcing we were walking into the gloom of the past.

Hopefully, her optimism was warranted.

* * *

As Alayna had requested, we spent the next day and a half going over the video files of the interviews conducted with possible suspects. While I paced the room and tried not to succumb to drinking all the scotch in the loft, Alayna sat stoically, taking feverish notes about the men and women describing the heinous crimes of my past. This was the vulnerability that I hated most—feeling out of control, like a spiraling fall into black nothing. She'd known vaguely about my games, but never in this precise detail. She'd certainly never experienced the horror of listening to it from the victim's side.

Somewhere in the midst of the terrible confessions, I had an epiphany—it hadn't just been Alayna I'd been protecting by keeping all of this from her. The letters, the danger from my past—I'd also been protecting myself.

"That wasn't the man I married," she'd say occasionally as the worst stories were told, seeming to know that I needed comfort, and it helped, but still—by the time we were ready to meet with Celia on Sunday evening, I was tense and on edge.

Other than the occasional reassurance, Alayna had been oddly quiet for the most part, whether processing all she'd seen or letting me have my space, I wasn't sure. But on the ride to Randall's bar, she became herself again, anxious and fretting and full of questions.

"Why did we choose Randall's? We don't usually go there." She twisted her fingers together nervously, the very definition of wringing her hands.

"It was a random point between our location and hers," I answered, not mentioning that Celia and I had gone back and forth on this matter. She had wanted to meet on her turf, I had, obviously, wanted to meet on mine. The office, her hotel, The Sky Launch—all locations were suggested and dismissed, finally settling on using an app that found meet up spots at an equal distance between two points on a map. Randall's it was.

"She knows why we want to see her?" she continued to fidget.

"No." I was terse.

"Then why did she agree to meet us? That doesn't seem like her. To walk into a situation without knowing what she was dealing with? That seems highly suspicious. Doesn't it?" She was working herself up.

I stilled her hand, wrapping it in mine and caressing it with my own, an attempt to calm her. "I suspect that she thinks that I'm going to discuss business with her," I said. "She wants me to let her and her husband purchase equal shares in Werner Media so that our three-point alliance no longer favors us."

"Of course she does," Alayna huffed indignantly. "Did she really ask you that directly? Or are you just guessing?"

"She asked directly. She said that if I don't let her buy shares, they will find them somewhere else. That was a few weeks ago." It seemed so much longer in the past. I had barely thought about it with everything else going on.

Alayna pulled her hand away from mine brusquely. "You spoke to her recently?" Her eyes burned into me, not quite accusing, but warily.

I should have realized she'd have that reaction.

I reclaimed her hand in mine, placing my fingers through hers so that it wasn't as easy for her to pull away. "I spoke to her, but just once. We have a business relationship. There will be times that we have to speak." I didn't mention that *I* had been the one to call Celia, that I'd been concerned about the engagement party details for Chandler and Genevieve. It wasn't a good time for Alayna to believe that I was so worried about her mental health that I would resort to calling her foe.

Perhaps that was manipulative on my part.

Add it to the list of things I was guilty for.

"You're right," she said. "I overreacted." She was silent a moment, and then asked the most brutal question of all, the one I'd really hoped to avoid. "Are you sure Celia isn't the one sending the letters?"

We'd promised to be honest. "No."

* * *

"She's late," Alayna said, when we'd been sitting at Randall's for nearly seventeen minutes.

Of course she was. Celia would want to make an entrance.

"Maybe she hit traffic coming from downtown." I took a swallow of my scotch. "Or she had a hard time getting away. You remember how it is when your baby's that young."

Alayna glowered at me. "Are you defending her?"

I sighed heavily. "No. Just, she's not even here yet. I thought we could save the judgment and the daggers until she's earned it." Because if she was still the Celia that I knew, she was going to earn it.

"How very fair and noble of you." She brought her glass of Sancerre to her lips. And with her sour expression and red wine lips, for a split second I imagined her the Lady to my Macbeth, the one who could truly undo her husband's enemies.

Then the image was gone, and I had to laugh at myself. Alayna as Lady M. Preposterous. It had always been Celia who was calculating and vengeful and steely. Bitter and focused to the core.

And I was not someone who wanted his enemies undone. I had made them. I was resolved to make amends, and leave vengeance for another man. Another man's wife.

I flipped my eyes to the door as the aluminum frame caught in the light, indicating it had opened. Then—cool, crisp, dressed in red, her blonde hair pulled up—there she was.

"Speak of the devil," I muttered to myself.

Alayna turned her head toward the entrance, but the door wasn't in her sightline. Which meant she wasn't in Celia's sightline either.

Celia, on the other hand, saw *me* right away.

She smiled, not too brightly—with the smile of an old acquaintance, which was what I supposed we were now, on our best days.

After checking in with the hostess, she started toward our table, and, though her stride never changed, I could tell the moment that she saw Alayna. Her posture changed. Her chin lifted. Her shoulders rounded backward. Whatever promise she had of being helpful when she walked in, there was less of a chance now, and her body showed it.

I didn't regret bringing Alayna, though. I wouldn't. I wouldn't have even come if not for her.

It was also obvious the moment that Alayna saw Celia.

My wife was the most beautiful woman in the universe. Nothing compared to her soft brown eyes, her perfectly curved figure, her dark tresses that bent and kinked whichever way they wanted and yet some-how created the most beautiful mane of hair. Her face was interesting. Her flaws made her intriguing. And most importantly, who she was, the person underneath, shone through her physical form. She was passionate, and fiery, and wore her emotions for all to see. It was these things that truly made her spectacular to look at.

But she could never see herself the way that I could. Secretly I suspected she wished she were more refrained and controlled.

Which is why when they met Celia's, I saw her eyes flash with envy.

Unwarranted envy, in my opinion. Celia was an attractive woman, but she was cold. There was no fire. There was no passion. She might as well have been made of marble and placed on a shelf of one of the fancy homes she decorated for all the life she brought to a room.

Except, maybe she'd changed.

I was still holding out hope that she had.

"Hudson, Laynie," she said in greeting when she arrived at our table.

If I were a gentleman, I would've stood. I didn't.

She sat down at the far end of the booth. Alayna sidled closer to me, likely by instinct.

"I didn't know we were bringing our significant others," Celia said to me, as though we were the only two at the table. "Should I call Edward? He doesn't have any plans."

"That won't be necessary," I said quickly. I was determined to get straight to the point. Determined to let her know right away that this was not going to be a conversation about our businesses. "This conversation doesn't involve him. It does, however, involve Alayna."

Celia's eyes narrowed into tiny little slits as she moved her focus to the woman next to me. "I'm intrigued." She studied my wife much more closely than I liked. "How are you, Laynie? It's been so long since we've seen each other face-to-face. You look . . . *tired.*"

I felt Alayna tense next to me, and I put my hand on her thigh to steady her. This was a cat and mouse game, nothing more. Celia loved taunting. It was best to ignore her.

"What can we get you to drink, Celia?" I raised my hand to flag the bartender.

"Nothing. Water, I suppose." She angled herself in her seat, crossing one leg over the other.

"Really?" I dropped my hand to the table before the bartender noticed me. "You were the one who suggested we meet at a bar, and you're not even having a drink?" Now *I* was letting her get to me.

I knew better than this.

"I'm nursing. I can't drink, unless I'm going to dump it all after, and I'm not." She reached over to my scotch glass and pushed it closer toward me. "But we all know you're in a much more agreeable mood when you've had one of these. Hence, the bar."

It was meant exactly as it sounded—to plant a seed. Does Hudson Pierce have a drinking problem? Like his alcoholic mother? Like his wife's dead father?

I didn't want to do this.

"I changed my mind. We don't need to meet with you. This isn't going to get us anywhere. Alayna, grab your purse. We are leaving." I pulled out my wallet, digging for a fifty to leave on the table. Celia was trying to push my buttons, trying to prove she still *could*, but I didn't need this. Alayna didn't need this.

Apparently, my wife felt differently.

"Hudson," Alayna said, putting her hand firmly on my bicep. "We should stay." Her eyes were pleading, her voice measured, and I knew—I *knew* how hard it was for her to sit in the same room with Celia, let alone at the same table—and if she was telling me that we should stay, then we needed to stay.

I put my wallet back in my pocket, but left my money on the table, so we could leave when we needed to.

And Celia gloated, as though she'd won the first point. "Thank you. I would hate to have wasted this trip. Now, since Edward is not involved in this matter and Alayna is, I am assuming that we are not here to speak about the three-point alliance?"

It seemed Celia was as interested in getting to the point as I was.

"That is—" I was interrupted from concurring by my wife.

"Like Pierce Industries is going to sell you shares. Did you forget that we have the majority for a reason? Hudson needed to have something to hold—ow!"

The majority had been acquired to keep Celia in line. I wasn't sure this was the best time to remind her of that, when we were about to ask her a favor, so I silenced Alayna with a gentle pinch of her thigh.

"That is correct," I finished. "We are here to ask you for . . ." I couldn't bring myself to say *favor* and chose a different word instead. "*Assistance*."

Celia tilted her head. "This is interesting. You must be mighty desperate if you're asking me for help. You have to know that's going to indenture you to me."

I could feel Alayna's claws come out. Probably because she was digging them deeply into my upper thigh.

"Why don't you hear the situation out before you start bartering about payment?" I suggested, trying to ignore the fact that I was being treated like a pin cushion. "At one time, you and I helped each other with no strings attached. Especially when we found the outcome benefitted both of us. You might find this is one of those times."

Celia opened her hand in a gesture of ambivalence. "Go on then. I'm listening."

I already regretted this. But we were here. And Alayna believed this was our best shot. "We have received a series of threats recently. Letters, addressed to me, containing menacing language toward my family."

Celia eyes went wide. "And you think I did it?"

"No, we didn't—" I began.

"Well . . ." Alayna said softly.

I threw her a glare that clammed her up then returned my focus to Celia. "We didn't come here to accuse you. But the threats reference the past. The time when you and I were . . ." I glanced at Alayna. It was much harder to have this discussion in front of her than I'd imagined.

"Playing together," Celia finished for me. The expression on my face must have told her what she needed to know. "I see. Do you have these letters with you? May I read them?"

I reached into my jacket pocket and pulled out the photocopies I'd made. I paused, taking one last moment to doubt, then slid the papers across the table toward her. I finished off my drink in one swallow, ignoring the knowing look Celia shot me when I did.

She read through them quickly, her brows creased as her eyes skimmed the lines. I remembered suddenly that she'd always been a lover of words, always excelling in literary arts. Like my wife. In another lifetime, would they have been friends?

That was another future I'd once dreamed.

"This reference about the mask you wear," Celia said, now on the third letter, "could be referring to that masquerade party we went to." She went on reading and soon shook her head. "But none of the rest fits."

That was the problem—none of it fit one exact scenario, one precise dictum. Not that I could see, anyway.

She continued on through the letters when she got to the fifth one, I said, "That one contained a picture of Alayna in the park with the twins. She hadn't known she'd been photographed."

Any decent human being would have found that fact chilling. Celia merely looked up at me and said, "Hm."

Then she gathered all the letters together and handed them back over to me. "I do think you're right, that it's someone from the past. But it's like a scavenger hunt. You have to do a lot of digging before you can figure out what these vague clues mean."

I didn't take the letters. "We were hoping that you would help us put those clues together."

She considered for possibly half a second, her hand moving in toward her body as though to keep the letters, but then suddenly she pushed them back in my direction. "I can't do that. I can't take these." When I didn't take them, she set them in front of me on the table. "I'm sorry that I can't be more helpful, I just can't."

Alayna, who'd behaved very well in my opinion, practically bolted up from her seat to lean across the table toward her photo. "You can't? Or you won't?"

I put a soothing arm at the center of her back, ready to pull her down if need be. "We don't have to take up much of your time, Celie," I used her childhood nickname. Every manipulation tactic I had in my book was fair game at this moment. "If you even just allowed us access to the journals so we could piece together—"

"The journals?" This mention startled her. "I don't have them here. They're in London. I'm sorry. It's not going to work. I can't help you." She pulled her shoulder bag over her arm. "Now, if you'll excuse me, I really must be going."

She slid out of the booth and walked in a clipped pace toward the door.

"Dammit," I muttered, hurrying after her before I could change my mind.

"Celia, wait." I managed to close in on her before she left the building. "This person could come after you, too. I might only be victim number one. You aren't innocent here. Your past is as tainted as mine."

"And I understand I'll be on my own if and when that happens. I can't help you, Hudson." She was stubborn. She was iron. I knew this about her. I'd made her like this.

But she had a *kid*.

I thought she'd found true love. I'd thought she'd changed. "I really thought you'd softened," I said, disappointed more in myself, in my erroneous optimism, than her.

Her expression twisted into something I couldn't read. "You know nothing about me, Hudson. Not anymore."

I felt Alayna walk up behind me, just as Celia turned again and walked out the door.

She was right. I didn't know her anymore.

And that made us more lost in this investigation than ever.

∗ ∗ ∗

"She's playing us," Alayna said the minute we were alone in the penthouse. "She's the one behind all of this. She expected us to come straight to her and we played straight into her hands. We're so stupid!"

We. Never mind that it had been Alayna who had wanted to meet with her. Alayna who had wanted to stay.

I followed my wife into the living room where she was already pacing back and forth. "Don't you think I've already considered this possibility?"

My eyes wandered over to the wet bar, but after Celia's comment and my earlier glass of scotch, I decided to hold off.

"I know you considered it as a possibility. But now I'm saying that's what it is." She flipped to face me. "Do you realize that's what it is too? Because what else is it? It's either that or she's just plain mean."

I sat down on the arm of the sofa and rubbed my hand over my chin. I'd thought about it during the silent ride home, thought about each of Celia's expressions and gestures and tried to analyze every single little detail. Perhaps I didn't know her anymore, but I knew *people*. I could *read* people. And if I had to try to read her . . .

"She seemed spooked," I said, remembering her reaction to the mention of the journals.

Alayna stopped suddenly, midstep. "Spooked? What do you think *we* are?"

I started to answer, but the elevator dinged.

"The kids are home." I stood up to meet Payton and the security guards who had brought them back from my sister's.

Payton was already walking toward the nursery when I stepped into the hall, a baby carrier in each hand. She turned toward me. "They're all asleep," she said quietly. "You can take Mina from the bodyguard."

I nodded and went to the foyer to retrieve my daughter from the man who was protecting her.

Alayna appeared as I was tucking Mina into her bed. She leaned over our little girl and kissed her on the forehead. Then she threw herself in my arms.

"If it's Celia," she whispered, "that means we aren't really in danger, right? She just wants to scare us. She wouldn't ever really *hurt* anybody. Right?"

I didn't answer.

I ushered her out of the room, and when the door clicked shut behind us, I told Alayna what I didn't think she wanted to hear at the moment. "I really don't think it's Celia."

Her face fell, but she was distracted from her disappointment by Payton as she returned from the twins nursery.

"We had a great weekend. Mina really enjoyed the time with Aryn. I think Holden is getting a new tooth—he's been extra fussy and a little feverish. I gave him Tylenol two hours ago and he didn't eat much tonight. I'll check on him again before I leave." She checked our expressions to see if we needed anything else. "I'm going to go get their things from the car."

"Thank you, Payton," Alayna said, walking her toward the door.

"Oh, I almost forgot." I hadn't followed them so I didn't see what was being handed over, but I could hear rustling. "There was that birthday party on Friday afternoon. Mina got this from one of the parents. Probably an invitation to another one. You know how it's always the same kids invited to them."

The hair stood up on the back of my neck, and I started at a brisk pace to the foyer.

"Hudson . . . ?" Alayna called, her voice lilting with concern.

"I'm here," I said, arriving next to her. She was holding a small red envelope. The kind used for thank-you cards and party invitations.

I took it from her hands. It was sealed, unopened. "Where did Mina get this?" I asked again.

"She said a parent gave it to her," Payton answered slowly, as though she were afraid she were in trouble. "One of the dads at the party."

I exchanged glances with my wife. *A man.*

"Where was this party?" I tried not to sound as concerned as I felt.

"At Central Park."

Outside. Accessible. Anyone could've been there.

"Thank you, Payton. Make sure one of the guards walks with you down to the garage." I waited until she was in the elevator and the doors were closed before I carefully opened the envelope. I wanted to preserve the flap, in case it had been licked instead of sealed with a envelope sealer. I pulled out the card inside. It had a monkey on the cover holding a single balloon.

Was I being paranoid? Was this really just a children's invitation to another birthday party?

But when I opened it, the words I found written in the familiar blocky handwriting chilled me to the bone. *There is an enjoyment of correctly predicting how people will react.*

Alayna looked up at me, puzzled. "But what does that mean?"

"It's something that I used to say," I said.

"Who would know that?"

Only one person. "Celia."

CHAPTER FIFTEEN

ALAYNA

"She can't get away with this," I said grabbing my purse from where I'd dropped it in the foyer. I opened it to make sure that my phone was inside. "What hotel is she staying at?"

Hudson was still holding the card, still ruminating on the words. He looked up at me, his eyes glazed, and blinked. "Alayna, you're not—"

I cut him off sharply. "Not going to talk to her? Oh yes I fucking am. What hotel is she staying at? I know you know, and if you don't tell me, I'm going to text Genevieve and ask her."

Hudson tucked the card inside his suit jacket, next to the letters he'd photocopied for Celia that she hadn't taken.

"Confronting her is only going to play right into her hands. Just like you said earlier." Somehow my husband could remain cool and calm. I didn't know if I envied that, or wanted to smack him for it. "We'll take it to the police tomorrow and handle this the correct way. File a restraining order."

Like a restraining order was going to do anything. She hired people to deliver her messages.

I dug my phone out, and started to text Genevieve, my hands trembling. I was determined to get the answers I needed one way or another, but my fingers couldn't seem to work properly.

After I made three errors in a row, I turned my frustration on

Hudson. "She got my child involved. Our four-year-old little girl. Give me the fucking hotel name, Hudson, because I am going to go there and give her a fucking piece of my mind, and so help me, if you don't let me do it right now, you know that I will do it later. So you might as well just tell me."

He ran three fingers across his forehead, a sign that he was in a more agitated state than I'd given him credit for.

The elevator dinged, and Payton walked in, a diaper bag over one shoulder, Mina's backpack in her arms, as well as one of her favorite stuffed animals. She startled at the sight of us still in the foyer.

"Payton," Hudson said, turning to her. "Would you be able to stay a couple of extra hours? Alayna suddenly remembered an errand we needed to run."

An errand. At eight-thirty on a Sunday. That better be code for beating the crap out of an arch nemesis.

But I was grateful he was making the decision to do this with me rather than putting it off until Jordon could be involved.

"Sure. Mind if I borrow something from your library to read, since the kids are all sleeping?" she asked.

"Yeah, that's fine. Take your pick of whatever," I answered automatically, already pushing the button for the elevator to re-open so we could hurry. The thought of waiting even a second longer suddenly felt like a risk that grew with every moment we weren't running toward the only real clue we had.

And if we were playing into her hands, well—at least I felt like I was *doing* something.

"Aren't you coming?" I asked Hudson impatiently. No danger could truly exist with him by my side.

"Thank you, Payton. Make sure you set the alarm." He followed me into the elevator then hit the button for the doors to close as I fidgeted.

"You better not think you're going to come up with some classic Hudson Pierce way to distract me from this. I *am* talking to her." That woman didn't frighten me. I'd given her a black eye once. I could take her down this time. There was no incentive on earth like protecting your children.

Hudson pulled his phone from his pocket and started typing. "Nope, I'm not trying to stop you. I'm texting the driver now. You reminded me that when you get your mind set on something, you don't let it go. But if you think I'm going to let you do this on your own, then *you* don't know *me*. Besides, I have a feeling this will be entertaining. I wouldn't miss it for the world."

Awesome. I was preparing to go into the ring, and he'd decided to just take a seat in the stands. I'd been hoping he'd be the guy who wiped the sweat off me and made me chug water in between rounds, but maybe that was pushing it.

Hudson spent the ride toward Celia's hotel on the phone with Jordan, catching him up on the latest. I listened, halfheartedly, but everything he said only worked me up more. Either his words reminded me of what happened, pissing me off all over again, pissing me off at *her* all over again, or they made me pissed at him.

I didn't like to feel that way, so it was easier to try and fix my anger on Celia.

"Yes, I'm certain that Celia is the only one that I shared that quote with," Hudson said halfway through his phone call, "but something doesn't line up. This doesn't feel like her M.O. I can't put my finger on it, but I still don't think she's behind this."

"Oh, she's definitely behind this," I said, even though he wasn't speaking to me. "And I don't know what you mean by this isn't her M.O. Riling us up? Trying to scare me? That's totally her."

I knew she was behind it the minute she refused to help us find who was behind the letters. No one could read them—no *mother* could see a threat to another woman's children, and not want to help. Besides—the "coincidence" of her wanting to reclaim shares from our alliance just as this was happening was too much.

It was obvious to me now. She planned to use our family to benefit herself.

Over my dead body.

"She's usually trying to terrify *you*," Hudson said, moving his mouth away from the phone to placate me, to try and refute my certainty. To defend her. "She isn't usually trying to terrify *me*."

Whatever. Wasn't that the same now that we were married? She'd just gotten more creative with her tactics. That's what people did over time—they changed up the game. They didn't stop playing.

Which is how I knew my husband was a good man.

And the light I saw in him only served to highlight the darkness in her.

But Hudson had gone back to his call, so I kept my comments to myself, letting the fury build inside me until my leg was trembling and the sound of my blood rushing could be heard in my ears.

"Shall I come in with you?" our driver asked when we arrived at the hotel. He was doing double duty as security, and if I were alone, Hudson would kill me if the answer wasn't in the affirmative. Even together, it made sense to me.

So I said, "Yes."

At the same time, Hudson answered, "That will not be necessary."

I glared at my husband. "You don't even want to try to intimidate her? We'll look a whole lot stronger if we go up there with a bodyguard on our side."

Hudson made an impatient sound. "I'm trying to prevent a scene. I'm sure she will be more than intimidated at the sight of you as worked up as you are and me behind you. You can circle around, Andrews. We won't be too long. I'll text when we're done."

Even through my irritation, I was impressed that he knew the name of this particular driver. There were so many new members to the security team, I hadn't yet gotten a chance to learn everyone. I was lucky some random guy hadn't come up and said that he worked for Jordan. At this point, I might've believed them, gotten in the car, and let him take me wherever he wanted.

It was nerve-wracking to realize that my fervor to solve the case could well have blinded me to other details.

I really needed to do a better job of noticing my surroundings.

My surroundings at the moment were quite posh. Celia—or her husband—had nice taste. The hotel was definitely five stars. The kind of place that took the security and privacy of its guests seriously.

The kind of place I'd dealt with in my *own* past, too.

"Do you know her room number?" I asked, surveying the lobby. The bar was right next to the front desk. An older couple was getting up from their seats.

"I do," Hudson said smugly. "But how do you expect to get up to her floor? The elevator requires a key card to work."

I rolled my eyes. "Oh, God. It's as if you've never stalked anyone." I continued to watch the older couple as they exited the bar and headed toward the elevators. Timing my steps, I managed to make it there right before them, then stopped, searching through my bag as if I was looking for my key. When the couple pressed the elevator button, and stepped inside, I stepped on after them, still digging through my purse. Hudson hurried and followed in, too.

"What floor?" the lady asked after she pressed her own button, using her key card to make it light up.

When Hudson didn't answer right away, I poked him with my elbow.

"Oh. Twenty-seven," he said.

"I haven't found the key yet. Just a minute. I know it's in here," I continued my pretend purse exploration, letting out an anguished sigh.

"We can get you up," the lady said, using her key to push the twenty-seventh floor button. "You're on your own after that."

"Thank you. My mother's in the room so if I can't find the key, she can at least let us in. That's so helpful. Thanks again." I dropped the search, and settled in at the back of the car next to Hudson.

"You probably didn't even grab it," he said quietly, but loud enough for them to overhear. "You're always leaving the room without the key. My forgetful girl." With a light press of his lips to my temple, the couple smiled at us and looked away.

Maybe he'd never stalked anyone, but of course he was good at these games, too.

In another life, it might have been fun to play them together.

But in this one, we weren't those people anymore. And we were *better*. Our life together was precious, and it was worth protecting.

I tapped my hand along my thigh anxiously as we rode up. The elderly couple got off. We climbed higher. Top floor. And then it was our turn.

I pulled out of the car then remembered I didn't know the room number. I turned back and looked expectantly at Hudson.

"2705," he said, answering the unasked question.

A quick glance at the signage on the wall said to go left. I made the turn, my confidence rising with each step that I took. I counted the doors as I passed each one. *The Presidential Suite*, read the sign outside 2705.

"Of course," I muttered, raising my hand to knock. My heart was pounding, and all my outrage was reaching a boiling point.

My children.

My *children*.

Hudson halted me before I could pound my raised fist. "We should be adult about this," he said. "Handle this civilly. In an appropriate manner."

"Mm hm." I was noncommittal as I spotted a doorbell. A fucking doorbell in a hotel room. I reached for it.

"Alayna, you hear me? You're going to behave, right?"

"Totally." I pushed the bell.

It was quiet for a moment, no sound came from inside. Then there were voices, first too muffled to make out followed by Celia's voice increasing in volume as she presumably walked toward the door. " . . . probably turndown service."

Turndown service. That's where I should be—in bed, relaxing, waiting for turndown service with no cares in the world. Instead of scared out of my freaking mind, worrying about my children and their safety and whether or not someone was actually after them.

The door opened, and as soon as I saw Celia standing there in a white silk robe, her face and hair fresh and clean from a shower, I lurched.

"How dare you? How *dare* you?" I screamed in her face.

Celia took a step back, caught off-guard, allowing me entrance and

Hudson came in behind me, immediately grabbing my arms, probably afraid that I'd end up swinging.

He wasn't wrong.

Well, he could hold my fists, but he couldn't hold my tongue. "It's one thing to mess with me, but you crossed a line when you involved my child. You are unbelievable, you know that? It's unfathomable that anyone, let alone another *mother*, could do this to someone else, just for kicks. *How dare you?*"

"Civil, Alayna, remember?" Hudson said at my ear as I struggled against him.

"Jesus, what the fuck?" Celia flashed her blue eyes wide, her expression alarmed and innocent.

"Exactly, what the fuck, Celia?" I yelled.

"Hold on, hold on," Hudson wrangled my wrists behind my back, so that he was holding them with one large hand. The other pulled out the card that we'd received and handed it over to Celia.

Like that was a smart move.

Celia opened the card and read it, her face going pale. She looked genuinely concerned. She was a better actress than I'd given her credit for.

"Where did you get this?" she asked.

"Someone gave it to Mina at the park," Hudson answered.

"Oh my God," she exclaimed.

I was done with the charade. "It was you! You're so fucking sick. Hudson said you'd changed, but you will never change. You have no heart. Manipulating and conniving. Does your husband know what . . . what a . . . *dragon* he married?"

I bucked against Hudson's hold on me, seriously wanting to tear out her throat. His grip remained firm as he shouted out commands—"stay", "calm"—and Celia rattled on indignant protestations of *it wasn't me*.

Suddenly a booming voice cut through the noise. "What the hell is going on here?"

The room suddenly grew silent, all attention focused on the man who'd entered the room. Hudson was even startled enough to loosen his grip, and I pulled away from him, quickly taking two large steps to the side and out of his reach. He didn't try to come after me. He was too busy watching Celia, noticing the way she had turned every bit of her focus to the stranger.

Not really a stranger, I supposed. I'd never met him, but I knew who he was. Edward Fasbender, Celia's husband. Genevieve's father. The owner of Accelecom, the company that had recently joined forces with Pierce Industries and Werner Media to create a three-point alliance, determined to corner the media technology market.

My first impression, even with his shirt unbuttoned at the collar and his cuffs loosened, was that he was a very intimidating man. There was a palpable change in the air when he walked in. He was at least a decade older than us. Powerful, formidable. Much like Celia.

Though her stance had weakened since he'd entered the room. Had she finally met her match?

"Edward," she said, taking a step toward him. "It's nothing. Hudson and Alayna are . . . old friends."

"Old friends, my ass," I blurted out.

Hudson threw me a sharp glare, as though warning me silent. It felt patronizing as hell, and I made a note to tell him later.

"Is there a problem?" Edward asked, coming further into the space. "I didn't realize that you and Hudson Pierce had been friends, darling."

Celia, who always had something to say, who always had her best face on—lowered her eyes demurely, saying nothing.

It was startling to watch. Made no sense.

And then it hit me—her husband really *didn't* know about Celia's past.

Which meant I had leverage.

I stepped around Celia so I could speak directly to Edward. "Actually, there *is* a problem."

"Alayna," Hudson hissed. Then, addressing his peer, "Edward, you haven't met my wife."

"No, I haven't. And I hear we are about to be family." He stepped closer, and I found there was something oddly charismatic about him, and also oddly frightening. He didn't offer his hand, simply studied me as though inspecting a new suit he wanted to purchase. "It's a pleasure to meet you, Alayna."

"It's really just a misunderstanding," Celia said, her voice shaking almost imperceptibly.

"I'd like to hear what Alayna has to say, if you don't mind?" His stare pierced into his wife like a knife at her throat, until she lowered her eyes again. "Alayna?"

Feeling bolstered, I lifted my chin up. "Hudson and I are being terrorized. We have reason to suspect the threats may be coming from your wife."

"That's not necessarily true," Hudson said behind me, and I swear to God I wanted to punch him in the nuts. How much more fucking evidence did he need? For someone who claimed to be here to back me up and maybe enjoy the show while he was at it, he was awfully quick to abandon me.

At the same time he corrected me, Celia protested again. "I haven't done anything to you. I didn't send a single one of those threats."

Edward put his hand up, silencing his wife again with the mere gesture.

"If she didn't do it," I continued, "She could prove it, and help us find out who is threatening us, at the same time. It would be easy, if she'd let us see the journals that she kept from the time that she and Hudson . . ." I paused.

Here it got tricky. Exposing the exact nature of Hudson and Celia's relationship to her husband would remove the leverage that I had. I just had to dangle the possibility in front of her.

"Hudson and Celia had a working relationship in the past," I finally said. "I don't mean to butt into your marriage. It would be truly cruel and devious to interfere with your relationship." I glared at Celia. "And so I apologize if this is the first you are hearing about their former partnership. But my family's safety is on the line, and this is truly important."

Edward nodded, his face stony and stoic. If I'd ever thought that Hudson was unreadable, he was Dr. Seuss compared to the dense text of Edward Fasbender.

I watched, and waited.

"I see," he said after a moment, and then it was his turn to surprise me. "I *do* know about Hudson and Celia's working relationship, of course."

"You do?" I felt gutted, losing my one ace as quickly as I gained it.

"I do. Celia tells me everything. Don't you, darling?" He moved to put his arm around her, and she fit perfectly into the crook of his. As though she'd always belonged beside him. "Well, almost everything."

Celia bent her head at his last remark, a clear sign that she felt guilty over something. It was an exchange that Hudson and I were not meant to understand. Frankly, I was more concerned about where we stood now as far as the journals.

But Edward cleared that up too. "I can guarantee you that Celia is not behind this. And to prove it, we will have the journals flown here from London. They can arrive here by Tuesday. You may come back then. Now, if you don't mind, Celia needs to get some sleep. Our baby will be waking up in about five hours for her feeding, and you are correct, Celia really is a dragon when she hasn't gotten enough sleep."

* * *

"Damn," I said, when we were in the hall and the door was shut behind us. Despite the tension that had played between us all evening, despite my irritation at his behavior inside, I was desperate to discuss what had just happened. "I've never seen Celia kowtow to anyone before. Did you see the way he just *looked* at her and she bent to his will?"

"I told you she fell in love," Hudson said grabbing me by the forearm and directing me down the hall, past the elevators.

"What the fuck are you talking about? *Fell in love?* That was not love. That was some kind of mind control trick or maybe he has, like, a voodoo spell on her, or maybe he's blackmailing her or something. It's not love. And where are you taking me, anyway?"

He pushed through a door and pulled us into the stairwell. "Love doesn't always look like love to someone on the outside." He pushed me roughly against the wall, and caged me in. "This probably isn't going to look a lot like love right now, either. Turn around."

I was so used to doing anything he said, I began to turn in the tight space. "What isn't going to look like love? Why?"

I heard the sound of his buckle, followed by his zipper. "The way I'm going to fuck you. Because I'm mad at you."

Sudden warmth spread over my skin, and a fire began low in my belly. God, I loved it when he was like this—dominating, demanding, desperate.

Except . . ."Wait. I'm mad at you too." I started to turn back to face him, but he put a firm hand on my back, keeping me in place.

"Good. You can tell me all about it while my cock's inside you." He kicked my legs apart.

I spread them even further. I didn't want to fight him. Not really. Not at all, actually.

"Well. If you can't figure it out on your own, you were a total asshole to me in there. You should've stood up for me. Instead, you practically defended her." I felt my skirt being lifted, felt his fingers on my crotch panel as he pulled it to the side, clearing a path for him. My heart sped up even as my stomach sank a little, remembering what had just occurred. "You tried to hold me down. Which was demeaning and patronizing and . . . oh."

He thrust into me with one bold stroke, completely distracting me from my chain of thought.

"Are you done?" he asked, sliding out of me, only to return again full force.

If I had an answer, it was lost to the moan that came out of my lips. Fuck, he felt good and thick and furious.

"Good. Then I'll tell you why I'm mad at *you*." He snaked his arm around my waist and dipped it down to my pussy to rub my clit. As soon as his fingers touched the surface of my sensitive bud, my knees buckled and I had to press my forearms against the wall to steady myself.

"You said you were going to be civil," he said, as he continued to hammer into me, his fingers driving me mad at the same time. "You didn't trust me when I said I didn't think she was the one. You could have lost us the chance at getting access to those journals altogether."

I could feel an orgasm spiraling through me, whirling like the cyclone in our lives, taking over, forcing me to hold on tighter.

Somehow I still managed to gather my thoughts enough to say one last thing. "I did get us the journals. *Me.*"

"And Jesus Christ, I've never thought you were sexier." He brushed his nose against my ear then nibbled, hard. "Put your legs together. Make it tight."

I brought my thighs together, tightening the space between my legs, my pussy naturally gripping him harder. With his praise and admission of how hard my strength turned him on, along with his expert caresses of my clit and his quick staccato jabs, it was only another minute before I was crying out his name.

Over and over, my favorite mantra.

My favorite prayer.

"Hudson, Hudson, Hudson," as my limbs shook with pleasure and my vision went dark and spotted with lights.

He grunted out something incoherent and finished while I was still trembling with the aftershocks.

I was limp and boneless when he turned me around to claim my mouth, the only reason I was still able to stand because he was holding me so tight. *This.* This was why he was so perfect. We could fight, and bicker. We could pull and yank at the tension surrounding us, and still he would fight to come back to me.

And when we came together again, we were always explosive.

My lips were bruised when he pulled away, or they felt bruised. Swollen, at least. Well kissed. To me, it looked like love.

I leaned against the wall of the stairwell, and watched him as he pulled himself together, trying to empty my mind, trying to hold onto the post orgasmic haze he'd given me.

But thoughts will enter as they will, and the realization that hit me suddenly took my breath away.

"Hudson," I said reaching for him, clutching to him when my hands made contact with his chest. "If it's not Celia, if Celia didn't do this . . . if she didn't send the letters . . . if she didn't send the card—it means there is somebody out there who wants to hurt us.

"And he touched our little girl."

Chapter Sixteen

HUDSON

It was another sleepless night. I'd tossed and turned, unable to get comfortable. Unable to rid my mind of the image of a man, some stranger approaching my child. My precious little girl.

Alayna and I argued over how to handle Mina's involvement. We both flipped sides so many times, it was impossible to say which of us thought we should talk to her about the man who'd given her the card and which of us wanted to keep her sheltered and not alert her to any fear.

At one point, Alayna said, "It was probably someone the asshole hired. Not him personally. Probably some nobody who was given the task of passing a birthday invitation out to a particular little girl."

"And if that's true," I came back, "then that hired delivery man might lead us to our real guy."

"She's four years old, Hudson. She can't possibly relay any information that's useful. We might as well not involve her at all." She stormed out of the room, slamming the door behind her, only to return a minute later. "Unless there was something really remarkable about the man. She *is* a smart kid. If the guy had a limp or an accent . . ."

By that time, she'd convinced me not to pursue that avenue of investigation. "I'll send Jordan to talk to the mother that handled the birthday party. We'll start there first. Mina will be a last resort."

When I left for the office on Monday, we still didn't have a firm certainty of what tactic to take with our daughter. We'd agreed to put it off one more day, both of us knowing that every minute that went by increased the risk of Mina forgetting anything she might recall about the encounter.

Christ, she was just a little girl! She shouldn't have to be a part of this at all.

On the drive to work, I dealt with another issue. Or tried to. Celia.

I had things to say to her. She had acted oddly from the moment we had spoken to her about our threats, and while her husband was acting reasonably and responsibly by having the journals brought to the States immediately, something had still been off.

It should have been *her* who had offered to help, not a man who was, in many ways, a rival as much as a peer. It would be better, I believed, to confront her alone, without her spouse present. Without *my* spouse present, for that matter.

I called her cell phone. I let it ring until it crossed over to voicemail before I hung up. I tried again with the same result, then decided I would try to speak with her later.

Later happened as soon as I arrived on my floor and found her waiting in my lobby, our eyes met.

Without saying a word, I unlocked the door to my office, then stood aside gesturing her in. I followed her, shutting the door behind me.

But before I could address her at all, I discovered she had something to say as well.

"You really fucked up, Hudson," she tore into me before I could even get behind my desk. "And you can't blame that on me. This was your doing. *You're* the one who brought this to my house."

She was tense and cryptic, pacing back and forth in front of my desk like a smoker jonesing for her next cigarette break.

There were ways to handle this woman. I knew them, every one. I had long ago become a pro at managing Celia Werner when we'd run our experiments and games together. I could turn the situation around.

But I was tired. Worn out. Exhausted from arguing and digging and wading through the emotions and remnants of the crimes of my past. I had precious little energy left, and she didn't deserve to have it wasted on her.

I slammed my fist down hard on the desk, making her jump and cutting her off. "Did you do it? Are you behind this? Yes or no? Once and for all."

Her face wrinkled in anguish, as though I'd slapped her. "No! I told you, I didn't—"

"Then I *didn't* fuck up. We need those journals. We need them to solve this. Whatever it took to get them, I don't regret it." I was dismissive and final.

She ignored my cues, insisting on her innocence once again. "I have *always* been real with you. No matter what I've done, what schemes I've pulled. I have still always been honest with you, when we were face to face. So when I say I didn't do this, you should know I'm telling the truth."

I sat down in my chair and looked up at her as though I were surprised to still find her standing in front of me. "How could I know anything?" I asked innocently. "I don't know you anymore. Remember?"

She nodded, her lips tight. She kept nodding and she stared at me for several hard seconds.

Then without another sound, she turned around and left my office.

I should have felt good about it. She'd walked out like a wounded animal. It should have been a victory.

But I wasn't convinced I was in a war with Celia Werner Fasbender. There was no victory to be won here. Not really.

And if I was wrong, then I knew she'd find a way to have the last word.

* * *

It was an entirely different Celia who answered the door when Alayna and I arrived at her hotel room the following morning.

"Come on in," she said, as invitingly as though we were the first guests to arrive for bridge night. "I've already ordered tea and coffee—I didn't know which you preferred in the morning," she said looking directly at my wife. "I also have an assortment of fruits and breakfast pastries, in case you haven't eaten yet. I know sometimes it's hard to remember to take care of yourself in times of stress."

Alayna and I exchanged a glance.

"I've already eaten," Alayna said blankly. At the last minute she added, "Thank you."

Celia's smile didn't falter at all. "They're here if you change your mind."

"How about we just get started?" I said, determined to move this along as quickly and as efficiently as possible. It was one thing when I'd followed Alayna over so that she could speak her mind. That had been on Alayna's terms. Today felt entirely different. Today was out of my control. And where my wife was involved, I resented not having that control.

I was the one who felt responsible for her being here. I hated that she had to do this, had to sort through my worst stories and spend the day with a woman who had worked so hard to bring her pain—especially when it was debatable whether or not she was done.

"Where are the journals?" I asked, keeping the ball rolling.

"Since you're obviously not hungry either, Hudson, they're in here. Follow me." Celia made a left down the hall, and walked deeper into the hotel suite. Alayna started after her, but I grabbed her hand first, lacing it through mine. I wasn't sure if it was to bring her comfort or for my benefit, but it felt better going into this with our hands joined.

"Is Edward working with us as well?" I asked as we walked after Celia.

"No. He went into work. It's just us and the nanny," she said leading us into the dining room.

Then there they were, the journals from our past, spread out on the dining room table. Eleven in total, I counted. Black and slender and harmless, except for the words that they contained.

My stomach rolled, and I was suddenly grateful that I hadn't accepted any of the food Celia had offered.

I was also glad it was only the three of us. I wasn't sure exactly how much Celia had told her husband about the contents of the books before us, and while a part of me hoped—for her sake—that he was aware and accepting of her former sins, there was absolutely no reason he needed to participate in the airing of mine.

"I don't know if you had a plan about how to attack this," Celia said, tucking a stray hair behind her ear that had fallen from the loose bun gathered at the back of her head. "But I was thinking that you and I, Hudson, could each grab a journal and start reading through it. When we come to a name of someone involved in an experiment, we could record the name as well as any other details that may be important regarding the subject. Such as whether or not we believe they might still have hostile feelings toward you or me. Most of those references in the letters seemed vague, but if we come across anything that seems to possibly be referenced, then we can note that as well."

The three of us stood around the table, none of us moving. It was precisely the manner that I had planned to sort through the books, but having Celia take charge threw me off-kilter. Made me doubt the method.

"If you have another plan . . ." she offered, seeming to sense the source of my hesitation.

But I didn't. "No. This is good." I dropped Alayna's hand so I could remove my jacket. I hooked it on the back of one of the dining room chairs, and then sat down, ready to get to work.

Celia took the cue and sat down across from me.

"What should I do?" Alayna still stood next to me.

Celia looked to me to answer. It was my turn to read her mind. Not only could Alayna miss relevant information as she read through the journals, it also somehow felt strange to ask her to try. The walls were down between us, she knew my secrets, and I was sure many things I was ashamed of would be revealed during the course of the day. But I didn't have to force her to read through the shock and horror of my former days.

I could protect her from nothing else, it seemed, but the details.

"You can do the recording, Alayna. As Celia and I read, we will call out information. If you could track it and sort it, I think that would be the best use of your time."

She brightened slightly. "I have my laptop. I could build a spreadsheet."

I smiled reassuringly in her direction. "That would be very helpful."

Which was the truth, but I also knew how much my wife loved making spreadsheets. Hopefully it would keep her mood up as well.

"Let's get to it, then." I reached for the nearest journal and opened it up.

Celia took the one in front of her, and began reading as well.

The journals were small, each five by eight with one hundred lined sheets inside. Celia's print handwriting was feminine and clearly legible. She wrote in expressive prose, hinting at her love of literature in the eloquent passages. It was much different from the way that I had recorded our experiments before she'd come along. Mine had been like science reports—all data and analysis. Concise. Clinical. I had never thought to include nuances such as the emotional state of either of us throughout the schemes, or the addition of references to outside material to back up our hypotheses and conclusions.

A few pages in, I realized she hadn't only recorded our history together, but had also revealed deep pieces of herself. These truly functioned as diaries as well as journals. Was this why she hadn't wanted to share them with us? Because the sharing made her vulnerable?

She couldn't possibly be as vulnerable as Alayna and I were at the moment. Or as vulnerable as my children. Could she?

I brushed aside sentimentality and forced myself to concentrate on the goal.

"Monica," I said, reading the first name that came up. I remembered this one—Monica wouldn't be a threat. She hadn't even realized she'd been played. It had been a simple jealousy ruse. A quest to see how long a new woman I was dating would tolerate an overly close relationship with the former flame, played by Celia.

Monica had dropped me the first time she'd found Celia fresh from a shower, wearing only a robe in my apartment. *Good for you, Monica.*

"Graham," I added when I came across her last name. "Monica Graham. No threat level. Nothing that connects to anything in the letters."

"Timothy Kerrigan," Celia called out a minute later. "And Caroline Kerrigan."

I looked up at her.

"Book one," she said, holding it up, as though she thought that was why I'd given her my attention. "I picked it on purpose. I like chronological order."

"Mm," I replied, not sure what other response to give. Tim and Caroline had been our first real game together—an attempt to break up a pair of newlyweds in her building. As we had worked tirelessly to try to bring their marriage to an end, I distinctly remember the thrill of feeling like Celia and I had found a new beginning. I had decided I would never be the type of man who could share myself with anyone, but in that single scheme, I had found one part of my life that no longer had to be lived alone.

Now, at the memory, I felt guilt and shame.

And regret?

No, not that. Opening that door to Celia had been the first step in a long journey to finding Alayna. I would never regret that, no matter how dark and twisted the path got before Alayna's sunlight found my world.

Next to me, Alayna had pulled her laptop from her purse and had already begun developing the spreadsheet. She speedily recorded the information, then asked some follow-up questions—the date, any known phone number or address or email, whether either of us had seen the subjects since the scheme had taken place.

It was a good system, and the work moved steadily like this through the morning. We decided to wait until all the data was gathered before making any conclusions about any particular subject, but a couple of times I picked up my phone and called Jordan, requesting that he look further into this person or that. It was exhausting and tedious, but it was the most productive I had felt on the investigation since the whole thing had begun.

We'd been working for almost three hours when a small cry from the other room reminded us that we weren't alone. A moment later, a robust German woman appeared from somewhere in the suite, carrying the baby, still fussing.

"Excuse me, Mrs. Fasbender. I think she's hungry. She won't take the binky," the woman said, speaking softly as she hovered over Celia.

"It's about time for her to eat," Celia said glancing at the clock. "I'll take her. Thank you, Elsa."

I tried to concentrate on the words I was reading instead of watching while Celia took the baby in her arms, and walking with a little bounce in her step, as she crossed over to the living room and sat in the armchair.

But I couldn't look away.

She expertly adjusted her blouse and positioned the blanket around her infant daughter so she could nurse while remaining modest. Then she slumped into the chair, her feet propped up on the Ottoman in front of her, and cooed at her baby.

It was fascinating. And breathtaking. The kind of scene that would make a well-treasured photograph, if someone were to capture the image. It was natural and sweet, and I was reminded of a Celia Werner that I once knew. A young, vibrant woman who only wanted to be loved. To *feel* love.

"*I remember what it's like to be in love,*" she'd whispered to me once in the dark. "*I'd like to feel that again . . . someday.*"

She had been vulnerable then, and in response I'd been angry and offended. I hadn't believed in the emotion. I had thought her a fool, had believed she'd been ignorant and brainwashed. I'd been the atheist, laughing while she prayed to her God of romance.

I had been so afraid she would leave me, that I would be alone again in the world of coldhearted manipulation. Then, in the end, I had been a convert. I'd been the one to leave *her*.

I *wanted* her to be changed, I realized.

I wanted to believe that this Celia that I watched, while she cuddled and caressed her infant, was as geunine and real as she seemed.

I wanted her to be changed because we'd once been friends, and I wanted her to feel love, the kind of love that can't break through without morphing you into the best kind of person. The kind of love that I had with Alayna.

I wanted her to be changed because it let me off the hook.

Because if she wasn't changed, then she was just another victim to count among the others. Another person I had schemed and played with and betrayed.

Was I seeing, then, only what I wanted to see?

"Even grizzly bears care for their baby cubs," Alayna whispered next to me. And if I wanted to be judgmental about her spite, I couldn't for even a moment. My wife deserved to hold her grudge against Celia as long as she felt she needed to. I owed it to her not to try to persuade her otherwise.

When I turned to her, I expected to find her scowling at me, silently reprimanding me for whatever kind thoughts she assumed were playing in my mind.

But I found that despite what she'd said, she was also watching Celia, and though I couldn't quite read what she was thinking; her expression was soft and her eyes compassionate.

"What's her name?" she called across the room, a question I hadn't been bold enough to ask.

I traced her gaze back to Celia who was now holding her baby across her shoulder, rubbing her tiny back.

"Cleo," Celia answered, smiling as she said it, as though it were a word that couldn't be said without a happy countenance.

"Is she a good baby?"

My gaze returned to my wife. Trying to read her. Trying to determine if she meant the question to discover something she could lord over her later, or if she was genuinely interested.

Her expression said the latter.

Celia hesitated a moment before answering, perhaps trying to determine the same motive. "She is, for the most part. I have a terrible time getting her to burp though." Her voice grew higher as she addressed the baby. "Too much of a little lady, aren't you?"

Alayna pushed her chair from the table and stood up. "Can I try?" She started working towards Celia before she got an answer. "Brett's the same way. I swear it's because she's trying to get extra cuddle time. But I learned a few tricks." She held her hands out towards Celia.

"It's worth a shot. She gets terrible tummyaches when she doesn't. Thank you."

Gently, she handed off her daughter to Alayna, who lit up at the presence of a baby in her arms.

I stared at them as they chatted easily about burping techniques, and wondered with a sudden tightness in my chest if this was the thing that the two of them might finally bond over. Not any of the other things I'd assumed they'd be likely to share an interest in—books, business, *me*—but something as simple and universal as motherhood. I couldn't tell if it was a one-off moment, or the beginning of something that could change all of us forever, but it felt precarious, like balancing a tray full of expensive china while walking along a tightrope. The slightest breeze in the wrong direction would send everything crashing to the ground.

I desperately didn't want to be that wind.

I shifted my eyes back to the text in front of me, finding the spot on the page where I had left off, but stared at the words for several moments before actually resuming reading.

A few minutes later, Celia returned to the table, leaving Alayna to rock back and forth on her heels, doting on Cleo. A pleasant, thick sort of hush fell over the room, and I tried not to breathe for fear of disturbing it.

We were beginning to settle into this quiet, when Celia started to giggle.

I peered sharply across the table at her.

"Remember the Pascal sisters? You tried to convince them you were twins." She giggled again as though remembering something particularly funny about the scheme.

I rolled my eyes. "There hadn't been any point to that game."

"Yes there had been—it was for fun." She brought up one foot underneath her on the chair. "I could never figure out whether you were that good at fooling them or whether they were just that clueless."

I frowned dismissively. Then I remembered how I'd acted that one, using a slightly different voice for one of the "brothers."

"I think they were relatively easy to fool." I began chuckling now. "Why would two brothers have two different accents?"

"Right? I don't think I've ever laughed harder."

"That *was* fun, wasn't it?" I'd never really labeled it as such. Or, I hadn't in a long time, too absorbed in the guilt and shame to remember that I had enjoyed myself. Had enjoyed the plotting and the playing and the companionship of that time, when I'd felt little else. I'd forgotten that even then, when I'd thought myself lost in the darkness, I was still capable of silliness, the kinds of pranks anyone might play.

It felt good to remember that, to recognize that I hadn't been completely hollow, that those years together hadn't been all wasted.

"And did the Pascals think it was fun?" Alayna's question cut through the moment, reminding me that my thrills had a cost.

I sobered quickly. "No, I'm sure they did not."

"She's burped," Alayna announced flatly, delivering Cleo to her mother. Celia took the baby then left the room to return her to the nanny.

Alayna took her place next to me once again, saying nothing as she resumed work on her spreadsheet.

I considered her carefully, irritation pinching just under my skin. She deserved her spite—I did understand that. But this was jealousy, and that I begrudged her. What right did she have to be jealous? Didn't she understand that any joy I had found in that time of cold, dark nothingness was shallow compared to the depth of happiness I'd found with her? Didn't she realize that I had barely been alive back then? Didn't she understand that my life *began* with her?

She had nothing to envy. She was my everything. Every moment I had lived without her was cold and empty in comparison.

"Hudson, I forgot to show you that I had this ready," Celia said returning to the table with a paper in hand. She slid it across the table so Alayna and I could both see it. It was a diagram of a room, a proposed seating arrangement. With tiny circles around larger circles to indicate designated seats, names labeled next to each one.

"I hope you find that suitable for Chandler and Genevieve's engagement party. I tried to be thoughtful about where I placed you. As you can see, I didn't put you in the back, though I did appreciate the suggestion."

I could feel my balance start to shift, feel the tray of china in my arms begin to slip from my grasp.

"Hudson suggested a seating arrangement for the party?" Alayna asked, her tone slightly confused, but underneath, a realization.

She wasn't dumb. She'd never been dumb. She was the smartest woman I knew.

"Yes," Celia answered before I could gather myself enough to intervene. "He called me right after they got engaged, concerned about any unnecessary tension between, well, *us*. He requested that he be allowed to approve the seating arrangement."

Alayna turned her attention slowly toward me, her eyes brimming, her expression full of pain and betrayal. "You thought I couldn't handle it." It wasn't a question. It wasn't even quite an accusation. It was a bitter acceptance of the painful truth.

"Alayna . . . precious . . ." I was wordless, stammering. I couldn't deny it—I had done it. For her good—to protect her. Always, to protect her.

She didn't understand.

She snatched her purse from the floor and stuffed her laptop inside then pushed away from the table with a mumbled, "Excuse me. I have to go."

"Give us a minute," I muttered to Celia as I jumped up to follow my wife. I threw a glare over my shoulder though, making sure Celia felt it, because there was every chance that she'd meant to stir up this drama, that it hadn't been an ignorant misstep. Finding out which wasn't the most immediate priority on my agenda.

Alayna was outside in the hall when I caught up to her. "This isn't what it looks like. You can't let this get to you."

"Can't I?" she lashed back. "Isn't that exactly what you expected I would do in Celia's presence?"

Annoyance coursed through my body. "Oh, for Pete's sake. That isn't fair. You were obsessing. I was trying to make it better for you."

"Awesome. Seems to be working really well, doesn't it?" Her anger radiated off her in spikes like barbed wire.

I tried a different tactic. "Look," I said gently. "I understand. It's tense in there. It's difficult to trust Celia—"

She cut me off. "This has nothing to do with Celia right now, Hudson. Don't you get it? This is so classic. You don't even see how you manipulate people. You're the one making me crazy! Look at yourself in the mirror."

I was acting on little sleep. My emotions were tangled and stretched, my bandwidth thin. "You've overdramatizing this. As usual. This is why I didn't want you working on this with me."

"That's bullshit. That's an excuse so that you don't have to face the fact that you broke my trust—not in the past, Hudson, but now." An angry tear escaped, and she wiped it away quickly with the back of her hand.

It made my stomach twist, the guilt roiling around, and instead of taking the time to step back and acknowledge that, I lashed out. "I am not going to take responsibility for your overactive mind."

Shit. It was a low blow. Something I didn't even mean. I took responsibility for all of her—she belonged to me. That was my job. A job at which I was failing miserably.

She looked as though I'd knocked the wind out of her. It took a couple of breaths before she could spit out her next words. "Typical. Not taking responsibility. Have you stopped to think for a second that might be exactly why we're in the predicament we're in at the moment?"

She'd cut deep with that one, stabbing me exactly where she knew it would hurt. It was the one problem with letting someone see every part of you—they knew how to best wound you with your own worst truths.

But I knew her too. "That's enough. Go home. Better yet, go to work. You need something to keep your mind busy while I try to save our family. Why don't you go fixate on The Sky Launch?"

I turned back toward Celia's hotel room door and hit the buzzer, refusing to let myself look back at Alayna. Refusing to let myself believe that I'd acted in any way except in her best interest.

Refusing to admit that I'd done anything wrong at all.

CHAPTER SEVENTEEN
ALAYNA

" . . . and the woman raised her arms above her head, her wrists bound together, remember. Then she dropped them really fast and, like, sort of shot her elbows to the side, and broke through the binding." Gwen used her arms to demonstrate as she spoke. "There was, probably three layers of duct tape around her wrists too. It was freaking amazing."

Her rapt audience of one, Liesl, leaned against the bar and stared at Gwen with wide eyes. "No way. Nothing breaks through that stuff."

"Way," Gwen insisted. "It didn't even look like it took any effort. That's how easy it was."

"This changes my vision on everything. I really thought that standard duct tape was the impenetrable fix-all. Maybe I *do* need to call a handyman about that pipe in my kitchen."

I chewed on my lip, my mind wandering from the discussion of Gwen and JC's night at the Open Door, the sex party they had attended the previous Saturday. I meant to listen, but I had other things distracting me. I'd come straight to The Sky Launch after having left Celia's hotel more than an hour before, and I was still fuming.

Stupid Hudson.

And stupid Celia.

Or maybe it was stupid me.

Maybe I *was* blowing everything out of proportion. It was so hard to tell. We'd been tense around each other, Hudson and I, both of us so worked up and anxious about this stranger out in the world, threatening to hurt us, engaging with our child. It was only natural for us to be jumping down each other's throats. It would be easier to dismiss his shitty comments and his shitty behavior if Celia hadn't been involved.

Especially when Hudson started acting like she was human.

But then, I supposed, why wouldn't he? She'd even seemed human to *me* at times this morning. She'd been cordial and helpful and, with her baby, she'd been just a regular mother.

But she was a woman who had done terrible things to people. Not just me, but the people whose names I'd entered into my spreadsheet. She'd scammed them and hurt them and thought it was all just for fun. Who could do things like that and not be a terrible person?

The answer, of course, was Hudson.

Hudson had done those things with her and I knew he wasn't terrible. But he'd changed.

Why was it so impossible to believe that Celia could change too? If there could be two versions of him, why not two versions of her?

There were certainly two versions of me.

And, worst of all, Hudson couldn't tell when I was one Alayna versus the other. That was the piece that had truly gutted me. He was so willing to give Celia the benefit of the doubt, and yet I didn't deserve it? Would he always treat me like I was that crazy, fragile woman, even when I was strong?

Would I always be paying for my past?

I guessed Hudson was paying for his past, too. We all were, and it sucked.

"Wait," Liesl said sharply, grabbing my attention. "You said she broke through the binding—was that before or after the guy fucked her?"

"Oh, definitely after. They were playing out some sort of attack fantasy. He had tape over her mouth too—you know, so she couldn't scream."

"Damn. That's so hot." Liesl threw her blue streaked hair over one shoulder and fanned herself. "It was hot, right? Or was it too rapey to be hot?"

"It was definitely hot. And rapey. Which sounds really bad, when I say it that way. But she asked for it." Gwen thought another moment. "That sounds just as bad. It was consensual."

"Consensual rape," Liesl nodded. "I get it."

I rolled my eyes. "There is no such thing as consensual rape. It's called rape play."

"Someone's sure in a testy mood. Gwen's talking about the best night of her life over here. Lighten up."

I glared at Liesl. "And it seems she thought the highlight of the night was when a woman burst through duct tape." I moved my focus to Gwen. "If that's really the best thing you got out of the sex party, it was either the lamest sex party on earth or you already know everything."

Gwen raised her chin proudly. "I do know a lot, thank you. And it wasn't the highlight. It's just the only thing that's suitable for discussion at work in front of everyone. And it was supercool." She scowled. "Liesl's right—you do need to lighten up."

I took a deep breath in and let it out audibly. "I'm sorry. I'm in a bad mood. I didn't mean to take it out on you two."

Gwen crossed to me and knocked my shoulder with hers. "Understandable. And you are forgiven." I'd told her all about my morning when I'd first arrived. "Honestly, I don't know how we're all not in a bad mood. This job fair is insane."

I looked out at the dance floor where the fair she was speaking of was taking place. Several of the larger nightclubs in the city had gathered together to jointly host the third annual search for nightclub employees. It was our turn to provide the space, so the main floor had been transformed into a sea of unemployed. Gwen had assigned another manager to collect resumes and make contacts on our behalf down on the floor. Even watching the whole affair was exhausting. A record number of people had shown up, and the room buzzed with chaos.

"Hey," Liesl said, leaning across the bar to get a better look. "Is that David?"

I followed her gaze. "David who? David *Lindt*? Who used to work here?" I perked up at the thought of seeing an old friend, even one I had parted with on awkward terms.

"It is!" Liesl exclaimed. "David," she yelled through the noise. "Hey, David!"

At the sound of his name, David turned toward the bar, straightening his tie as he did. He saw Liesl first, then scanned his eyes across Gwen and landed on me, looking surprised when he did.

He headed toward us, and we rounded the bar to greet him. Well, Gwen and I rounded the bar—Liesl just climbed over. Which was why she was the first one to him. She jumped on him, wrapping her legs around his waist, giving him a big embrace.

I hung back while he finished saying hello to the other two. I felt a strange, nervous giddiness at seeing him. The last time we'd really spoken to each other had been at my wedding. That had been awkward too, as I recalled. Wasn't it always that way with people you'd once been intimate with? We had never slept together, and we'd never actually been in a relationship, but I *had* had his dick in my mouth on a couple of occasions. That definitely made things weird forever after.

Plus, before he'd left The Sky Launch, he pronounced that he had feelings for me. By then I was in so far over my head with Hudson I could barely breathe.

Poor David hadn't stood a chance.

We had parted as friends, the kind that politely say they'll always be there for each other, but only see one another once in six years. So I felt out of my groove, wondering if we'd pick up where we left off, two people who'd worked well together and gotten along great, or if too much time had passed for that.

"Laynie," was all he said when he stepped away from Gwen and addressed me.

"Hi," I said brushing a piece of hair behind my ear that didn't need smoothing.

We both moved then to give each other a hug, clumsily leaning the same direction, then ungracefully going the other direction at the same time. Finally we worked it out, and I found myself in David's big bear hug of an embrace.

He'd always been a good hugger—I remembered that now. And it always felt good to get a hug from someone you thought fondly of.

I especially found enjoyment knowing that Hudson would be pissed off. He'd always been jealous of David—ridiculously so—and after the shitty way he'd treated me that morning, he deserved this embrace.

Though, I did feel differently when I imagined Hudson hugging Celia. Enough differently that I was the one to end the embrace with David.

"What are you—?" I started to say, but he spoke at the same time. "I thought you were on maternity leave."

"I am." I corrected myself. "I was." Wasn't I? Because there I was at The Sky Launch, none of my plans to expand a secret. "I don't know anymore."

I felt mildly ashamed that he'd kept up on my life better than I'd kept up on his. But I'd had three kids, and he was still single and carefree. Probably.

David grimaced at my confusing response. "Hudson doesn't want you working, or what?"

Something else I had forgotten, how suspicious David had always been of the way Hudson treated me. It was unfair, but it also wasn't anything I felt this was the time to get into. I ran my hand through my hair, trying to think of the best way to respond.

"He . . . actually . . ." I'd only come into The Sky Launch today *because* of Hudson. But even though I was pouting and hiding out here for the day, I did want to get back onto the investigation, wanted to see the threats end before I truly came back to work. I wouldn't be able to focus on my job otherwise. "It's complicated," I finally said. "But what about you? Are you here for the job fair?"

He smoothed his jacket. "Can you think of any other reason I would be in a suit?"

"What about Adora?" If he was leaving Hudson's Atlantic City nightclub, I wondered if he'd told Hudson yet.

David gave me a funny look. "You don't know about the closing?"

I thought back to any conversations I'd had recently with my husband about his satellite businesses. There weren't many. It wasn't a piece of his company that he dealt with frequently enough to ask my advice over the dinner table. Although perhaps there had been a passing mention.

"I think I heard something about remodeling. Are you saying the club closed for good?" Maybe they were doing a more drastic overhaul than I'd originally been aware of.

"All I know is I no longer have a job," David said with a shrug.

A new wave of frustration rolled through me. "Oh my god, Hudson. Did he even consider that people would be out of a job when he decided to remodel?" The question was more to myself than for anyone else. He should have known better. "You want me to talk to him?"

"No, please don't." David stuck his hands in his pockets and rolled back on the heels of his feet. "Nightlife there isn't like it is here anyway. It's a dead zone. Atlantic City is not the place it used to be. I want to get back to the *real* city. I want my old life back."

An idea struck, and I reached out to grab Gwen's hand and tug her closer to us, pulling her into the conversation.

"I know! You should come back here! Don't you think, Gwen? It would be perfect to have another experienced manager like David when we get the expansion going." I turned to David. "Would that be weird? Being back here. Working under me."

David smirked. "I think I quite enjoy working under you, Laynie."

I rolled my eyes, but chuckled. I'd forgotten he was a guy with a twelve-year-old's sense of humor.

Gwen, however, frowned at the joke. She was such a prude—not like Leisl, who had returned to polishing glassware before the evening's service began. No wonder the most exciting part of Gwen's sex party was the cleanup.

"I'll put in my resume," he said. "But tell me about this expansion. Is The Sky Launch opening another location?"

I opened my mouth to start telling him about my idea when I remembered that I had my laptop up in the office. "Let me show you! I have a PowerPoint presentation upstairs. Do you have the time?"

He laughed, shaking his head. "A PowerPoint presentation. Course you do. And, yeah. I have a little time."

"I'm coming with," Gwen announced then stared at Leisl until she looked up.

It took Liesl a few minutes to realize that there had to be a manager still on the floor. And that she was bottom of the totem pole when it came to seniority. "Oh. I'll stay and keep doing my job. Enjoy your PowerPoint."

"Thank you, Liesl," Gwen said, leading the way to the office.

I turned to follow, but first lifted my head up to the bubble room where my bodyguard of the day was camped out. I gave him a wave and pointed up with my thumb so he knew where I was headed. He nodded in return.

"Hudson still has bodyguards on you, does he?" David asked as we headed up the stairs to the manager's office.

Still had bodyguards. The last time I'd had them had been because of Celia. Then I'd gone years without them. Now I had them again, so to David it looked like I'd had them forever.

It was easier not to get into it. It was easier just to say, "He's very protective."

Because that was true too.

* * *

Forty-five minutes later, I'd dazzled David with my presentation. And completely bored Gwen, who had now seen it for the seventh time and likely knew it as well as I did.

I selfishly ignored her yawns and doleful stares in my direction. After my morning, after the reminder from my husband that he always knew best, I needed a little pick-me-up. David's praise hit the spot. I'd forgotten how supportive he'd always been of me and my ideas. In many ways, David had been a better cheerleader for me in business than Hudson. David was good at what he did, knew how to run a good nightclub and all, but he didn't think outside the box very often, and so any time that I did, he was immediately struck with how brilliant and amazing and innovative the idea was.

Hudson, while always supportive of me, was also smart as hell. Sometimes it felt hard to impress a man who'd already been there and done that. Not that I needed to impress him *all* the time, but occasionally was nice. But even when I did get his praise, it was hard not to worry that he was also judging my ideas, critiquing them, coming up with a better plan that he was kind enough not to lord over me.

My plans for the expansion definitely excited David.

"This is going to knock every other nightclub off the rails," he said. "Eighty-eighth Floor is going to immediately try to copy you. You know that, right? And I predict at least three other clubs go out of business within six months. No, not three. Five."

I blushed. "Stop it. You are being way too nice." But I said *stop it* in that tone that said *go on*.

Gwen rolled her eyes, and I continued to ignore her.

He did go on. "I'm not kidding. I know you already increased business tenfold when you went to seven days a week. Adding the restaurant and the advance rentals for private, high-end events, was a game changer. There aren't any other clubs in town that even have the equity to do what you're thinking of doing, and by the time they catch up, you're already on to the next thing. Thumbs up, Laynie. You done good. Proud of you."

If it were possible to go redder, I would have. But I was also proud of me, too. This was exactly what I had hoped I could bring to The Sky Launch all those years ago when I was young and naïve and nervous as hell before my first presentation in this office. And now I'd done it. So I smiled and said, "Thank you."

"Oh, speaking of the expansion," Gwen said suddenly perking up as though she'd been half-asleep. She opened the drawer to her desk and pulled out a single key. "Lee Chong dropped this off so you can go over there any time and do measurements and whatnot for whatever you need to do architecturally. It opens the door in the stairwell that connects to ours. So you don't even have to go outside and around to get in."

I stood up from the sofa where I was sitting with David and crossed over to her to grab it.

"I know what I'm doing this afternoon," I said, slipping it onto my keyring. "After I finish helping you clean up from the job fair, that is." It was the least I could do after all that Gwen had sat through. Seven takes of my presentation was proof she was a great friend, eye-rolls or not.

"Is it really that late? I need to get going." David stood up from the couch and we said our goodbyes. Gwen had worked with him for a just couple of weeks, so it made sense that she only gave him a nod.

Me on the other hand, I let him give me another big, warm embrace. It was selfish of me, and I knew that. But it felt safe there, in his arms, at that moment. It didn't mean that I was attracted to him or that I wanted him in any way—quite the contrary. The interest I had in him even back then had been because he felt *safe*.

The truth was, I didn't really want *safe*. Not that kind of safe. I wanted Hudson and everything that went with him.

But for just a moment, it was nice to have a break from it all.

To pretend for just one long moment that there was no one in the world who had ever looked at my daughter with malice, to pretend the expansion was the most important thing in my life.

One calming breath, and it was over.

"Laynie, you can't hire him, you know," Gwen said, the minute David walked out of the room. She said it so quickly, so immediately after he was gone, that I had the sense she'd been waiting to say it the entire time he'd been there.

"Why not? I know Hudson transferred him in the first place because he was jealous, but that was before we were married. Surely he understands he's got the girl now."

Gwen gaped. "You seriously don't know? David was fired from Adora because of the sexual harassment scandal. The whole remodel thing is a total cover-up."

Now I was the one gaping. "How do you know that?" It was the first I was hearing of it, which meant it had to be a mistake.

Except, Gwen had a reliable source. "Chandler told me."

"Oh my god." Every bit of relaxation and ease from the last hour evaporated in the blink of an eye. So much for finding safe harbor in a hug.

"Oh my god," I said again. My blood was boiling. "And Hudson didn't tell me?" I was so mad I could punch something. Punch someone. A particular someone. "Jesus Christ, I can't even believe him. Was he afraid that was going to break me too?"

Add this to the list of reasons my husband was not sleeping with me tonight.

"That really sucks he didn't tell you . . ." Gwen said carefully. "You don't have any reaction to the harassment accusation, though?"

Oh. That.

My initial fury at being left out, again, whooshed out of me in a rush. I sank back down on the couch and pressed my head into the back cushion.

"You know what I kept thinking while David was here?" I asked after a moment of considering. "Why can't Hudson's people from the past be as easy to deal with as the people from mine? That was a real naïve thing to be thinking, I guess." I sighed, trying to decide if I wanted details.

I didn't. It was one too many scandals for me to think about.

"I assume that if Pierce Industries went to this much trouble to fire David and come up with a remodeling cover-up, then they have received verifiable complaints from employees, and that it's not just some rumors." I glanced at Gwen for confirmation.

She leaned across the desk and propped her chin up in her hands, her elbows resting on the surface of the desk. "I don't know all the specifics, but I know it was *several* women that filed the complaints. It wasn't against just David—there were several managers involved in the accusations. Now, I don't know how credible they are . . ."

I looked her in the eye. "If a woman feels harassed, she's been harassed." I sighed again. "Poor Hudson. What a mess."

I tried to think about the David I had worked with, the David I'd had a personal relationship with, tried to imagine him in light of these new allegations. The guy who'd given me my first managerial position, along with a shot of tequila. If I imagined Mina in my own place, how did I want her to be treated in her place of employment?

And then I had to admit that I knew things were off.

"David was often inappropriate. He was my boss, and he and I engaged in the exchange of sexual favors on the premises. During business hours. And I encouraged it."

She scowled at me. "That sounds like you making excuses for him."

"I'm not. I'm not defending him at all. I'm just owning *my* part of what happened between us. He would make jokes in poor taste. I laughed at them because I thought they were his way of flirting, and I wanted him to be flirting with me."

It was so strange how I could remember so vividly wanting that, but couldn't summon up a single ounce of the feeling of wanting *him* anymore.

"I don't know what he would have done if I hadn't returned his advances like I did." Although I could guess, based on how he'd reacted when I chose Hudson. He would have been upset, pouted. He would have made work uncomfortable and tedious until I eventually either gave in or quit.

That wasn't right. That wasn't fair. That was harassment.

"Did you like him, then?" Gwen asked, puzzled. "When I met you, you definitely didn't."

"I thought I *should* like him. If that makes sense. I was looking for a guy that I wasn't really into. I was too afraid if I was into someone, I'd get crazy over him."

She grinned. "How did that work out for you?"

I couldn't help but return the smile. "Hudson definitely makes me crazy."

And I didn't want it any other way.

We went downstairs then and helped get the club turned over from the job fair back to a dance floor. It was after five by that time. I knew Hudson would be back at the penthouse soon. I knew I should be going home too. We were going to need to have a very long talk about today, about the state of *us*. I was as confident as ever in our love. My faith in our communication, though, had been shaken one too many times lately.

But I really did want to check out the space next door for a while first, so the next time we went up the back stairs, I split off down the hallway to the private door that entered into Lee Chong's space.

It was quiet inside, and dark. I'd left my phone in the office so it took a bit of fumbling around before I found a switch to turn on some lights. A few bulbs immediately blew, the place having sat unused for so long. As soon as the room was dimly lit, I heard a noise behind me, a quick shuffling that made me nervous about mice. Or rats. The scourge of New York.

But then the shuffling sounded more like footsteps, and I walked back toward the door I'd come in, wondering if I was hearing someone in the hall outside.

Before I got to the door, another clip of footsteps made me realize I truly wasn't alone.

My heart sped up to twice its normal rate, and I began sweating profusely. I was sure I was being paranoid, but I was also creeped the fuck out. I took another cautious step toward the door, away from the sounds in the shadows, whispering curse words to myself the entire time, and wishing I had my phone.

Suddenly, a form stepped out in front of me, making me jump at least two feet in the air.

I let out a huge sigh of relief. "Oh, it's you."

That was the last thought I remembered having before the world went black.

Chapter Eighteen

HUDSON

She was punishing me.

I deserved it, I knew I did, but this—not responding to my texts, not coming home at a decent hour—this was especially egregious. It was past eight. I'd already tucked the kids into bed; the nanny was waiting for my cue to send her home.

And I would, as soon as I felt less anxious about where the hell my wife was.

The day at Celia's hotel room had been fairly productive in the end. We'd gone through almost all of the journals and made significant notes. Luckily, before Alayna had left, she shared the spreadsheet she'd made with me so that I could still continue entering the information as we gathered it even after she left. Celia and I could've probably made it through the rest of the work left to be done in another couple of hours, but I hadn't wanted to stay any longer than I already had.

Like the slow descent of a fever, my guilt and shame at the way I'd treated my wife—whether in the hopes of protecting her or not—became too distracting for me to continue staring into the abyss of my past without letting the present bleed into it.

I needed to be home to work things out with Alayna.

As important as nailing down the source of this threat was, it was equally important that she and I remain a team. I wasn't sure one could happen without the other. So I'd left Celia's a little before five, intending to spend the evening making things right with my wife.

And now she was the one who wasn't home.

She was definitely punishing me.

But I couldn't ignore the gripping panic that maybe it was something more. Surely it was paranoia, anxiety created from this looming danger. But it was cold and real and it wouldn't let go. This sickening, vivid fear that she wasn't home because she couldn't be.

I texted her again. In all caps so she knew I was serious.

ALAYNA. CALL ME NOW.

I stared at the screen of my phone, waiting for the bubbles to indicate she was responding, not even with a *fuck off*. I would take a *fuck off* right now just fine.

Three minutes passed. Five.

Nothing.

I was hovering. I didn't want to hover. She hated it when I hovered. Wasn't that half the reason she was mad right now? Because I tried to ease situations for her that I knew she was strong enough to handle, but why should she when she didn't have to? If I'd stayed out of it, never contacted Celia about the engagement party, Alayna would have been uncomfortable when we went, but she would've survived. She would've survived beautifully, with her head held high.

And if she'd needed a day or two in bed, upset and processing and obsessively looking through pictures of the event on social media, what would that have mattered?

I trusted her to come back to me when she was through her anxiety.

Maybe that was the key. Maybe she wasn't punishing me—but rather, was testing me. Seeing if I was capable of actually letting her go to work and not interfering. Not showing up, cold and demanding, when she lost track of time.

Because in truth, I was the one who wasn't strong enough.

For all that I blamed her for giving in to her overactive mind, I was the one who worried too much. Who was overprotective. Who couldn't handle the thought of her suffering, even only slightly. She was the one who alerted me to possibilities, her mind skittering from one thing to the next even as she stayed my rock.

The truth was, without me, Alayna was still brilliant and clever and lovely and big-hearted and *enough*. But without her, I was nothing.

"Mr. Pierce," Payton disrupted my musings, standing in the doorway of my office.

She had caught me standing, staring at my phone, likely looking like the idiot that I was. I shook it off and rubbed my fingers across my forehead.

"Yes, Payton. You want to go home." I needed to send her away. Send her and prove that I was not the one prone to overreacting.

But what if . . .

"I'm sorry. Do you mind staying for another couple of hours or so? I may need to run out, and I haven't managed to get a hold of Alayna to see when she'll be home. I'll pay you time and a half for the inconvenience."

She smiled. "No problem. Can I grab something off of Mrs. Pierce's shelves to read again? I finished Madame Bovary and I'm having a total book hangover."

"Certainly," I answered, half listening to the nonsense words she was stringing together. "Oh, and of course I don't mind if you turn on Netflix in the guest room either."

I was pretty sure that's really what she did when she said she was reading anyway. Might as well give her permission.

"Thanks, Mr. Pierce," she said, her cheeks pinking. A sure giveaway that I'd been right. But she swiped another book off the shelf before hurrying out of the room and down to the nanny's quarters. Perhaps two things could be right at the same time.

Alayna still hadn't answered my text. I considered putting my phone down and walking away from it, but I'd already kept the nanny. I'd already failed the test, if there was one.

But if indeed, it was a test, it existed for her too. If I trusted her to stay late at work, I also didn't trust whatever forces were working against us. And she knew that. She knew I would keep trying if she didn't respond to me. She knew I would go around her. She hated it when I did that.

On one occasion, she'd said, *"My employees need to see me as a boss, not as someone's little lady."*

I'd told her that she *was* someone's little lady, and that it would do her employees well to remember that everyone was responsible to someone else.

She'd smacked me, before laughing hard and kissing me.

The memory absolved my guilt for what I was about to do.

I hit the button that speed-dialed The Sky Launch. The number I used went straight to the office. Penny answered, one of the newer managers who had come on board since Alayna's bedrest. I didn't know her very well except for what had shown up on her background report. I'd run one after Gwen had hired her, wanting to double check that she wasn't some petty crook or a con artist. The report had come back clean.

I really *did* have have a problem with overstepping.

"Hello, this is Hudson Pierce. I'm looking for my wife. She's not answering her phone, and I wanted to check in on her."

"Oh, how sweet."

It wasn't sweet, it was pathetic. And maddening. It was too soon to understand how the father of a teenager must feel. The fearful protection, the loving panic.

"But she isn't here," Penny said next.

Finally. She was on her way home. "Can you tell me what time she left? So I can know when to expect her."

"I haven't seen her all night. And my shift started at six. Perhaps you're incorrect?"

Ice cold fear ran down my spine.

"No, Penny, she was there. You're sure you haven't seen her at all?" My mind was already running wild with the implications of what she'd said.

"I'm sure," Penny said, apologetically. "Would you like me to take a message in case she shows up?"

"No. Thank you." I was already onto my next move. In fact, I didn't even say goodbye before hanging up. I logged into the app where Jordan shared all the information relevant to our security, including the schedule of the bodyguards and each of their contact information. I should have done this first, perhaps, but a call from me directly seemed less intrusive than an interruption from an armed man in black.

According to today's schedule, a man named Alan Dawes had been assigned to her. I called him directly.

"Where are you?" I asked sharply when he answered.

"Same place I've been all day, Mr. Pierce. Sitting in one of those weird circle rooms at the club. Your wife, I must say, is a workaholic. She hasn't left the manager's office all afternoon."

Hadn't left the managers office? So help me, if Alayna had told Penny to say that she wasn't there to teach me some sort of lesson . . ."Do me a favor, Dawes—go up there and check, can you? I called the office directly, and was told she wasn't there."

"Sure thing, boss. But I'm telling you, I've had my eyes on that stairway door all day, and she hasn't come down. I haven't even gone to the bathroom. There's no way she snuck by me."

That made me feel better, marginally.

"Then she'll be up there," I said, more for myself than him. "And when you find her, make sure she calls me immediately." So I could wring her neck.

I wasn't even going to consider what it meant if he didn't find her.

When neither Alayna or Dawes had called within ten minutes, though, I knew there was trouble. I texted Jordan, told him to put a trace on her phone. He texted back two minutes later.

Her phone's at the club. What's up?

I was starting to type a reply when my phone rang. Dawes. Not the one of the two that I'd wanted to hear from. Not the one that would relieve me of this worry. I silently prayed that Alayna was being stubborn, sending me a message through my hired hand, and pressed *Accept*.

"I swear she didn't leave. Her things are still in the office, and even if she decided to go out of the firewell, we have a guy watching the door outside, and he hasn't seen her either. He hasn't left his station even once, he said. You can have Jordan verify, we all stay logged into this GPS app on our smart-watches . . ." He was talking a million miles a minute, so fast

I could hear him sweat through the receiver. I tuned out of his babbling. Only one piece of information was relevant—he couldn't find her.

"Obviously one of you fell asleep on the job," I roared. "Who was she working with last?"

"Gwen Bruzzo. The blonde."

At least Dawes was sharp enough to know that. "Keep looking for her. If you're so goddamned sure she didn't slip out, than she's got to be somewhere in the building." I clicked *End* and immediately called Gwen.

"Alayna hasn't come home, and I can't get ahold of her."

"And you've tried The Sky Launch?" She knew there was reason to be worried, it was in her tone.

"Of course I tried the club first. Her things are still there, but she's not. You know she goes nowhere without her phone, in case something happens with the kids. Was she there when you left? Did she say anything about going anywhere?" I tried consciously not to sound as frantic as I felt, but I was sure I failed.

I was frantic. I was finally starting to understand how Alayna felt.

"Oh!" Gwen exclaimed. "Lee Chong gave her a key to next door! She went over there to measure and visualize and scope out the space again. She was still there when I left. I'm sure that's where she is now. Probably lost track of time. You know how she gets."

Thank God.

Relief poured over me like a hot shower.

"Yes. I'm sure you're right. I do know how she gets. Thank you for telling me."

I was still shaking when I hung up the phone. I leaned across my desk, both palms flat on it to hold me up, and took a couple of deep breaths to calm my heart. Of course that's where she was. I knew I was being paranoid.

She was Alayna. Passionate, eager, focused. Obsessive. All the things I loved.

And why wouldn't she lose track of time? I myself had told her to go fixate on her new project, pushed her there. I'd been such an ass, and there she was, an angel, doing exactly what I told her to.

I had to make it up to her.

I stopped in and told Payton I was leaving, then grabbed my keys and went down to the garage, not bothering to call for a driver. I was eager to get where I was going and didn't want to wait for him to arrive. On my way to The Sky Launch, I stopped at a small grocery store that I knew usually carried Alayna's favorite flowers—alstroemerias. She always said you had to love the way they lasted so long, a full week. Sometimes two. They were the kind of flower that knew how to survive, and she found that to be one of the things that made them so beautiful.

It was how I felt about Alayna—her ability to survive was one of the things that made *her* so beautiful.

The store did have some fresh bouquets, and I grabbed the best of the bunch of the tiny flowers and continued on my way to the club. From the time I'd parked, got inside and started up the backstairs, I had planned a whole scenario in my mind. First I would surprise her. Apologize. Grovel. And since the event space was empty and there weren't cameras over there, perhaps my groveling would take a physical form.

I hated fighting with Alayna. But I did love making up.

The stairwell leading up to the manager's office was not the main stairway for the club. It was generally only used by the staff, though, when the club closed and people were trying to exit quickly, patrons would often use them to exit onto the street. Those were the only places that the stairs led—to the administrative offices, which were located on the hallway on the second floor, to the club on the first level, and to the street.

The only other place you could get from the stairs, was to one back door entrance to Lee Chong's event space. The locked door looked almost like a closet at the end of the hallway, and to the best of my knowledge, it only existed to meet fire codes, offering another way for people using that part of the building to exit, if needed.

It was convenient, actually, for Alayna and her plans, that the door existed. It was one less thing that would have to be added during renovations when she truly got her project underway. She would be able to oversee work without having to go far from the office and give workmen unobtrusive access to the alley so as not to disrupt business as usual.

The door was ajar when I got there, which was fortunate, because there was no other way I would be able to get in if it hadn't been open. Though I did swallow back the urge to be irritated at her carelessness. If I could walk in so easily, so could any other patron who decided to wander past the administrator offices.

But I hadn't come to reprimand. Quite the opposite.

I pushed the door open farther, and stepped inside. I remembered to shut it behind me before looking for her. The lights were on, if dimly so, so the rest would be easy, but the space took up three floors. She could be anywhere.

I debated between searching silently and calling out for her, finally deciding on the latter so as not to startle her.

"Alayna?" My voice echoed through the large empty room, sounding back at me with hollow vibration.

She didn't answer.

I scanned the room, my eyes settling on the upright piano near where I'd come in. There were two shot glasses on top of it. I crossed over to them, picked one up and sniffed. It smelled like tequila, Alayna's liquor of choice.

But it wasn't like her to take shots while she was working, not since the first time I'd seen her on the job so many years ago, anyway. But that had been a special occasion. The celebration of her graduation.

I called out her name again, then listened carefully. The lights that were on didn't illuminate the entire space—just the edge of the first level. It was possible that I couldn't see her in the dark shadows. But maybe I could hear her. I told myself again, not to be irritated. Maybe she wasn't ready to talk just because I was. That didn't change the fact that we needed to.

After listening for several seconds, I actually did hear something—a flapping sound, like one object tapping against another.

I followed the noise across the room to the opposite side of the space and found a service door, this one completely open, lightly banging against the side of the building from the wind.

My heart fell into my stomach as I crossed the threshold and stood outside in the night. I looked down the side of the building in both directions. Sure enough, the space was completely out of sightline from any of the cameras or guards that I had stationed on The Sky Launch. This door was completely unseen by any of my men. By anyone at all.

"Fuck!" I took the bouquet of alstroemerias and banged it against the side of the open door with all my strength. "Fuck, fuck, fuck!"

The flowers were battered and destroyed when I was done with them.

Throwing the ruined bouquet to the ground, I quickly ran back through Chong's area toward the offices. Whoever had come in, whoever had followed Alayna into the event space, had to have entered through The Sky Launch. I went straight to the security room, where the cameras fed footage to the televisions, and was surprised to find, not only Alan Dawes, but Jordan already there reviewing the tapes.

"When you didn't respond to my text," Jordan said, "I contacted Dawes to see what was going on with Alayna. He filled me in. We are currently looking at that stairwell to see if she somehow slipped out without us noticing."

I quickly updated them with what little information I had—what Gwen had told me, what I'd seen in the space next door. Jordan sent Dawes to go look through Chong's property, in case I'd missed something, in case she was somewhere on the third floor and hadn't heard me calling out for her.

I knew that she wasn't, but he wasn't doing any good standing behind Jordan looking at a TV screen.

Jordan changed his search from the back stairwell to the front doors, hoping to find someone suspicious or someone we recognize as a suspect enter.

I watched over his shoulder while I called everyone we knew—my sister, Alayna's brother Brian, Chandler, even my mother. No one had seen her. No one had heard from her. Each *no* made my stomach drop a little further, made my mouth a little drier, made the sweat on my brow increase.

One thought echoed through my head, over and over, on a loop—I didn't protect her.

I'd failed to keep her safe.

Penny, the manager on duty, came in to see if she could help and stayed to be another eye on the videotapes.

"Anything?" I asked after I ran through my entire contact list.

Jordan was stoic with his rundown. "We aren't having any real success. It's damn near impossible to collect data with this many people—looking at the cameras and matching ID records. If it were a normal business day, this would be a different story."

"What do you mean, a normal business day?" I asked Jordan.

"The job fair. The place was chaotic." he answered.

"Record attendance," Penny said cheerfully, not seeming to understand what that was the last thing I wanted to hear. "Quite a coup. All our hard work paid off."

"Who the *fuck* authorized a job fair on the premises?" I shouted, nearly ready to tear my hair out.

Penny swallowed visibly, finally starting to notice I wasn't as excited as she was about the increased presence in the club today.

"Alayna did, sir. Months ago."

"We talked about it last week, or the security team did," Jordan said. "She hadn't planned to be in attendance, so we didn't make any adjustments to how to handle the day."

My legs suddenly felt like they couldn't hold me up anymore. I backed up against the wall, hoping it would keep me from falling to the ground.

She wasn't supposed to be in attendance.

Of course she wasn't. She wasn't back at work yet, not officially. She'd only come in because I'd sent her. I'd pushed her into danger with my harsh words, and my shame over the journals. This was my fault. All of it, my fault.

Jordan spun around on the rolling office chair to face me.

"When do you want to call the police?" He was earnest, but on task. Thank God I could trust him to keep his head about him in a crisis.

I ran my hand through my hair and closed my eyes tight. I didn't want to make the wrong choice. It was almost ten-thirty. She'd been missing, by my count, for almost five hours. If the police even took me seriously at this point, with such relatively little time having passed, it would only be because I had my name and my money behind me.

It was a big *if*.

And did I want to spend the rest of the night trying to convince them to look into this when I could be scouring the city? Was sitting in a station where my time was best spent?

"Not yet," I answered, hoping it wasn't the wrong answer. "They won't let me help. This whole thing is about *me*. This is personal. Whoever did this wants to hurt me for something I did in the past. I'll figure it out faster without being babysat by some smug detective who will just want to ask questions like whether she was having an affair."

Any good detective would want to focus on the fact that we had a fight the last time we'd seen each other too.

The thought of that made me want to throw up. What if those were the last words that . . . ?

I wasn't going to think it.

But someone with a badge would think all kinds of things, the wrong things.

"I'm going to get my man on these tapes then, an expert in tech who can maybe give us a fuller picture of what's happening than we can see. We'll do fingerprints on those shot glasses and a full sweep of the event space, check out where our prime suspects were this afternoon." Jordan had a whole list of marching orders to give to his team.

"Okay. Alright. That's good. That's all good." I pushed away from the wall knowing what I needed to do, my own task separate from Jordan's. "I'm going to go work on this from my end. Text me when you find something."

I sped the entire way to my destination. I parked in a handicapped space, barely even remembering to take my keys with me when I left the car. When I got up to her floor, I didn't give a single fuck that it was nearly eleven at night, that I might wake up everybody in the building. I hit the buzzer three times, then pounded on the door.

Celia finally opened it, standing there in the same robe she'd been in days before when Alayna had come to tell her off. She was the only person who could help me, the only person who could see what I might have overlooked. And for that, she looked like a goddess waiting to deliver her benevolence.

I pushed inside, grabbing onto her so desperately I almost tipped us both over. "Find her," I begged, my voice raw. "Find my wife."

CHAPTER NINETEEN

ALAYNA

The first thing I became aware of again was the spinning of the room.

No, the room wasn't spinning—*I* was spinning. Spinning so fast that it made my insides spin too. In my belly, then up through my sternum, up, up . . .

I was going to vomit.

I sat up a little, because I'd been lying down, and with my hand covering my mouth, I looked for a place to throw up as the saliva filled my mouth and my stomach jumped.

"Here, you can puke in this," David said, and suddenly there was a small plastic trash bin under my face, just in time to catch the contents of my stomach.

My body shook violently as I retched, over and over. After I'd emptied everything in me, the waves of nausea kept me leaning over the bin. I dry-heaved until my throat was raw, my stomach cramping and clenching.

David held my hair up out of my face the whole time, sweeping away the strands that fell loose while I heaved, and even though I felt like I was on the verge of a seizure, I was conscious enough to think, *how nice of him to do this for me.* It would suck if he weren't here. Wherever here was.

Except . . .

Where *was* I?

And how did I get here?

Still bent over, I tried to figure out what the last thing I remembered was before this moment. I'd been at The Sky Launch. In the office. With Gwen and David.

No, no. There was more.

I'd gone to the space next door. Lee Chong's space. I'd heard a noise behind me, and when I turned, there was David. Which was weird because I thought I'd let the door shut behind me. It must not have clicked all the way.

"Oh, it's you," I had said then, relieved to see him instead of some creepy stranger. Hudson's threat from the past was really starting to make me paranoid. "I thought you'd left."

David had two shot glasses filled with amber liquid in his hands. "I got caught downstairs with old faces," he'd said. "I thought we should toast to all your success before I left. For old times' sake."

I'd thought that was strange. I'd been down there too, cleaning up from the job fair and hadn't seen him, but I'd been preoccupied, so I supposed it was easy to miss him. What had given me pause me for a moment, though, was what Gwen had told me about his sexual harassment accusations. Should I really be consorting with a man like that?

But people made mistakes.

I knew what David was and who he was. He wouldn't be inappropriate around me, not any more than I could handle. He was likely trying to make sure I knew he didn't have any lingering feelings. Or he wanted a chance to clear his name. Both of those were natural impulses. And after the way we'd parted, the way I'd chosen Hudson over him . . .

I'd met him as a confident man, and left him looking at me like a kicked puppy.

I'd owed him a toast.

But how had a simple round of shots gotten me this hungover, sick as a dog, lying in a strange cot in a strange room, while early morning sun streamed through the single window?

I was sure I could figure it out if my head didn't feel like someone was using it for a kickdrum.

I sat up a little more, done with the vomiting for now, and propped myself up on my side with my elbow.

Letting go of my hair, David wiped at my mouth with a damp wash-cloth. "You're coming out of it now," he said. He was sitting on the edge of the cot next to me. How long had he—had we—been there? He set the rag over his thigh, and bent to the floor to pick up a water bottle. After unscrewing the cap, he handed it to me. "Here. Drink this. It will help."

I took the bottle from him and sipped carefully, trying to process his words. All my thoughts were sluggish and incomplete. Why was it so hard to think? A single realization bubbled to the surface.

"You gave me something."

"Sorry. It was necessary. You wouldn't have come otherwise. You're too far under his spell."

I shifted my eyes to look at his quickly. Too quickly, because there were two of him for a second. When he came into focus, I saw that he was dead serious.

I blinked, forcing my head to clear and scanned the room again. It was small with wood walls, as if we were in a log cabin. My vision went in and out of focus as I observed that the one solid door was shut tight. There wasn't any furniture except a built-in desk and bookshelf, a canvas stool, and the cot I was sitting on with a single pillow and thin blanket. It was dark except for the bit of light coming in at the window. Branches with full leaves pressed against the glass.

There weren't trees like that in the city.

Instantly, I broke into a sweat as my heart began to boom against my chestplate. "What are you talking about? What did you do? Where are we?" My voice was shrill and panicked.

In contrast, David was calm. So very calm. He smiled at me warmly. "We're home, Laynie."

The hair stood up on my arms, and goosebumps raced across my skin. I wanted to move away, but I was frozen in place, listening to his confusing, strange, dreadful words.

"I bought this place for you. I know it's not as fancy as the places you're used to, but we'll make it ours. I didn't have time to prepare it properly. I wasn't expecting to bring you here so soon. But then I saw you yesterday, and when you said you were going next door, away from his prison guards, I had to take the opportunity. I didn't know if I'd get the chance again."

This was fucking crazy. I had to be dreaming. David, the guy I'd once thought perhaps I could marry, couldn't be this crazy.

But even in my worst nightmares, I didn't feel this pain in my gut, my head.

This was all a misunderstanding. It had to be. I was confused because of whatever drug he'd put in my drink. I wasn't hearing him right. But why would there be a drug in my drink if I was misunderstanding?

I pressed my free hand to my stomach as another wave of nausea took hold. "What did you give me?"

He brushed a strand of hair behind my ear, gently. Sweetly. "Rohyphnol."

I fought against the urge to gag. He'd roofied me. He'd fucking roofied me? "Did we . . . ? Did you . . . ?" I did a mental sweep of my body, trying to determine if I'd been violated. Would I know? Would I be able to tell?

"No, no!" He reassured me. "Of course not. I wouldn't do that to you, Laynie." He stroked my hair again, almost petting me. "I want you to remember it when we're finally together."

Sheer cold terror gathered at the base of my neck and spread down my spine. I couldn't fight the reflex this time. I dropped the water bottle and bent over the side of the cot and heaved again, my body spasming, trying to rid itself of the toxin by purging an empty stomach.

Again, David held my hair, speaking to me in soft, soothing tones. When I was finished, he used the washcloth to wipe my mouth, holding my head firmly at the base when I tried to pull away.

"Calm down. Don't fight me. I'm just cleaning you up right now, baby. I know you're confused and disoriented, but trust me—I'm trying to help you."

Every word out of his mouth made my skin crawl, made my stomach threaten to attempt another round of throwing up. My eyes were watering and my heart raced so fast, I worried I might go into cardiac arrest. Had the roofie been laced with something else? Cocaine? Meth? If I weren't so weak, if the room weren't spinning so fast, I'd try harder to push away. But even if I did have my strength, he was bigger than I was. Stronger than I was by a lot. There was no way to fight him and win.

I had to try another tactic.

I could reason with him. He was being nice. He didn't want to hurt me, not really. Or he would have hurt me already.

Sitting up again, I focused as well as I could on his face. "Thank you. For helping me. But we're not going to be together, David." I spoke as gently as I could, copying his hushed tones. "I'm with Hudson. I'm married to *Hudson*. Hudson is going to want me back."

"Shh," David said, undeterred in his task of washing my face, methodically wiping the cloth in long lines over the corners of my mouth.

He wasn't listening to me.

Had he ever?

Even back then, when I'd chosen Hudson, had he truly listened?

I put my hand over his, and tried not to cringe. "David, this is serious. You can't do this. You have to take me back to my family. The police will come looking for me. *Hudson* is going to come looking for me."

David took a deep breath in and blew it out slowly, as though trying to keep his temper. "Laynie, we can talk if you feel up to it, but not about Hudson. He's got you confused. He does that—he tricks people. He's tricked you into thinking you're in love with him."

"I *am* in love with him," I said forcefully, as though volume would help.

David reached for something at his back and swiftly whipped out a handgun.

I shrieked, instinctually moving away from him, but he grabbed me by the hair, pulling hard, and put the muzzle of the weapon at my throat.

"I didn't want to use this, but I knew you might not be cooperative," he said, the tenderness gone from his voice. "It's the spell he has on you. Like I said, you only *think* you're in love with him. It's going to take time to get over that, I know, and it might even hurt a little going through the process, but I'll be here to help you through it. And when we've broken his spell, we'll be able to really start our life together."

I was too terrified to talk with the gun at my throat. And even if I wasn't, I had no idea what I'd even say to that. I thought I knew crazy. I thought I *was* crazy. This was a whole different sort. I took in shallow, tiny breaths, afraid too big of a movement would set him off. Afraid I'd accidentally knock him and his finger would slip on the trigger.

He loosened his rough grip on my hair and cradled my head to his face, his mood turning again. He pressed a firm kiss against my temple.

"I hope you can forgive me for leaving you with him for so long, Laynie. He tricked me too. He made *me* believe you loved him, like he made you believe it. But then I found out about the tricks he played on people, and I finally got it. It never made sense why you chose him—you weren't into his type before. He wasn't right for you. You're too strong and beautiful to be with someone like that, someone who put you in the shadows. As soon as I realized what he'd done to you, I started working on a plan to get you out of there. It took a long time because I had to get it right. He's smart. I had to make sure I threw the blame in other places so he wouldn't know it was me who saved you. That way he can't find us because he'll be looking in the wrong place."

The entirety of the situation began to sink in, pieces clicking into place.

"You sent the letters," I said before I'd even made the conscious decision to speak. I hadn't put it together, my head too dazed to realize it was connected.

"I did!" he exclaimed proudly. "You never guessed, did you?"

I shook my head slightly, trying not to set off another round of pain.

He must not have noticed because he asked again, sharply this time. "Did you?"

"No," I whimpered. I really hadn't. He hadn't even been on our radar as a suspect. "I didn't guess it was you."

It still didn't make sense—how had he found out about Hudson's past? The details he'd used in the letters were vague, but I'd been at Celia's long enough, listening to her talk with my husband, to realize there were some firm facts wrapped up in the threats.

"I was good. I was patient. I wanted to do it right for you." He kissed my temple again, stroking my hair like a treasured possession.

I dropped my head, the adrenaline and confusion finally running out, leaving me with nothing but fear. Bone-chilling, teeth-chattering fear. What if he'd been too good? What if Hudson couldn't figure out who had me?

What if he didn't find me? What if he didn't know where to look? What if there was finally something he couldn't fix?

David lifted my chin up with the muzzle of the gun. "Say thank you, Laynie," he said sternly, the same authoritative way I reminded Mina.

"Say thank you!" he shouted when I hadn't responded fast enough.

"Thank you," I choked out.

"Good girl. Such a good girl. You were always such a good girl," he nuzzled his nose through my hair as he praised me.

I started to cry.

Honestly, I didn't know how I'd held it in that long. I'd been teary, but now I was really crying. The full force of the situation had set in, and the enormity threatened to drown me. I was shaking as violently with sobs as I had from retching earlier.

With the gun still in his hand, he twisted my face so he could look in my eyes. "What's wrong, honey? Is it your stomach still? Does your head hurt?"

"My babies," I said, not sure if he could understand me, my voice came out so strangled. "My babies, David. I have babies."

"Oh, no, no. I was never going to hurt them. I only said that to confuse Hudson. And to scare him. I'm sorry it scared you too."

I grabbed onto his shirt, tugging at it, trying to make him see. "I can't leave them. They need me. They need their mother."

His face softened, compassion etched deep in his features.

"Oh, baby," he said, stroking my hair with the gun. "I'm so sorry for that. I wish we could take them with us because I know it would make you feel better, but . . . they're *his* kids too. Even if I thought we could somehow get them away from him, which I don't believe we can—you know how tight a hold he keeps on his possessions—we can't have any part of him with us. I can't allow that. He's too toxic. Even his DNA is toxic."

My chest shook with shallow breaths. I couldn't get enough air, couldn't bring it in deep enough to reach my lungs. I was on the verge of hyperventilating. Tears streamed down my face. Every new thing he was saying, every crazy new thing made me feel more desolate. More terrified. More out of control.

Was this really happening? How could this nightmare be my life?

David brought his hand to my cheek to swipe my tears with the pad of his thumb, the gun so close to my eye as he did that I inhaled with an audible whimper.

"I know it hurts to be without your children at this moment. *But we're together now.* You'll get over them. We just have to get them out of your system. We have to get *Hudson* out of your system, like the rohyphnol. It needs time."

His compassion was waning. His tone was more stern. More rigid.

"But I'm going to help you," he promised. "Every step of the way. I'll help you forget about him." He cradled my face with both hands, as well as he could with a weapon in the grip of one of his fists. "Oh, Laynie. I've waited so long to be with you again."

I knew what he was going to do, and still I didn't want to believe it. Because if he did this, it would only be the beginning. He would want more. He would do more.

But as much as I tried to ignore it away, it was happening—he leaned down and covered my mouth with his.

I tried to pull away, but he held me more tightly in place.

I pressed my lips firmly together, but he kept roughly working at them.

When I finally let out a cry, begging him to stop, he stuck his tongue forcefully inside. The more I squirmed, the more aggressive his kiss got, the deeper he stroked his tongue, defiling every square inch of my mouth.

I was quivering when he finally broke away, on the verge of vomiting again, too scared to even do that involuntary action for fear he'd get mad with the gun still in his hand.

He held me tight against him, nestling my head under his chin.

"I've missed your mouth so much," he whispered, poisonous lust dripping in his words. "I've never forgotten what it feels like to have your mouth on me. You were so good at taking my cock all the way down your throat. It's going to feel so good when you do that again."

"I can't! I can't!" I shook my head vehemently against his chest. I'd choke if he brought his thing anywhere around me. I'd die. I couldn't do it. I *wouldn't*.

My neck suddenly jerked back as David sharply pulled a fistful of my hair, much harder than he had the first time.

"Ow! You're hurting me!" I clawed at his hand, but then the gun was back in my face, and I froze.

He raised up with one knee on the cot so he was hovering over me. "He's convinced you you're a princess now Alayna, hasn't he? That you're too good for sucking cock? Well, you're not. Do you hear me? You're still Laynie from the bar. You're not too good for having it down your throat or in any other hole I think you should take it in, you got that?"

I'd delayed answering before, and he was more mad this time than he'd been. More unpredictable. Fighting him wasn't possible, begging hadn't worked, crying had no effect on him.

I had to say what he wanted to hear. It was my only choice.

"I get it. I do. I understand." I felt the grip on my hair loosen slightly and took that as a sign to continue. "I didn't mean that I was too good for . . ." I couldn't say it. "I meant . . ." I thought quickly. "I'm too sick. The drug is still in my system, like you said. And I want to be completely well when we're . . . when we're . . . together."

He studied me as though not sure he was convinced, then suddenly he broke into a smile. "My good, good Laynie." He sighed, releasing my hair and returning to the petting from before. "I'm so happy to hear this is as important to you as it is to me. You're already getting over Hudson."

I nodded, but he was wrong.

I'd never be over Hudson.

And I was getting out of there. To be with my husband where I belonged.

At this rate, though, the way David was moving, and if the thick bulge in his pants was any indication, I was going to be forced to suck him off—or worse—before I got the chance.

Unless I made my own chance.

Cautiously, I forced myself to put my hand on his chest. I couldn't bring myself to caress him the way I knew I needed to in order to make it truly convincing, but I managed to pat him a few times. "David," I said, making my voice light and amiable. "David, it *is* important to me. Us being together. I didn't realize you'd worked so hard for me. I want to make it special. I want to . . . clean up for you. Get pretty. Um. Shave. And . . . uh . . . do my hair up." I was improving. I had only a semblance of a plan, but I didn't have time to scheme.

His lips hovered over mine. "Don't you know? You don't need to do any of that for me, Laynie." He pressed forward, about to kiss me again.

I pushed back on his chest as his mouth brushed over mine. "But I need to! I need to wash Hudson from my body. Like you said. He's toxic. I need to get him off my skin."

I hated myself. Hated every word I said. It was almost as terrible to say them as it was to imagine what could happen to me for not saying them.

Almost.

I somehow managed not to flinch as David nibbled on my bottom lip. "Okay," he said, then kissed me anyway, like he couldn't resist himself. He prodded my tongue with his until I moved it, and he could suck it in between his lips with a moan.

My ploy hadn't worked. He was getting more invasive, more predatory. Another wave of sickening panic washed over me. If I threw up now, would he back off, or shoot me?

But then he broke away. "Okay. Washing Hudson off of you. That's smart. That's just like you. Always thinking." His gaze drew down my body lasciviously. With a groan, he stood up, adjusting himself with one hand, tucking the gun under his belt with the other.

My entire body sighed with relief.

David glanced around the empty room. "I don't have much here. I didn't have time to prepare for you."

That was my opportunity. "I know! You had to take me when you could. That's fine. But maybe we could go to the store. Just to pick up a few things." I held my breath and prayed.

He moved his head back and forth, seemingly torn. "I wish we could, Laynie. You can't go anywhere though. Not in public. People are going to be looking for you. Remember?"

"I'll be careful. I could wear a disguise." He continued to shake his head. "Did you drive far enough from the city? We have to be in the middle of nowhere, right? No one is going to pay attention to the news out here. Not city news."

I was reaching. Grasping at straws.

"Laynie," the stern voice was back. "Something you need to learn now is that when I say no, you don't argue with me. That's another bad habit you've gotten into. Hudson must have let you walk all over him. With me, though, I'm the boss, and I don't want to remind you of that over and over."

"Okay," I said quietly. Deflated. "I'm sorry," I added, afraid he'd pull out the gun again.

"It's all right. *This* time. It's only your first day back with me, and you've been gone a long time. I understand you're a bit disoriented."

Disoriented, yes. Defeated, no.

I tried another angle. "Then can you go? I could give you a list." Maybe I could figure a way out while he was gone. Another idea hit me. "I could type it into your phone!"

He bent down. "You know I can't give you my phone, sweetheart. There's no signal up here, anyway. But I can get you a pen and paper. I do have that."

Then back to escaping while he was gone. I didn't know where we were, and I didn't have my cell, so it was going to be tricky. From the birds chirping outside, the trees I could see through the window, and the lack of traffic sounds, I had a feeling we were somewhere in the woods. Getting lost in the middle of the wilderness wasn't the best of options, but anything was better than staying with David.

He walked over to the built-in desk and opened a couple of drawers, until he'd found a notepad and something to write with.

I threw my feet over the side of the cot and sat up all the way, resisting the urge to run or attack him while his back was turned. He'd move faster than I could, I told myself. And he had the gun. I'd wait until he left.

"It's a bit of a trip to town," he said when he handed me the items. "Will you be okay without me? Being sick and all?"

The pen could be a weapon, I thought as I took it from him. "Yes. I'm a bit better now. Thinking about us being together has me feeling better. All I need is some food, I think. It should settle my stomach."

"That's fantastic." He rubbed my head again, like I was his dog. "I'm going to have to be with you tonight, and I want you to be able to enjoy it."

My pen froze in the middle of the word I was writing. His greed was palpable. The way he wanted me, the weight of his lust pressing against me like an avalanche.

It would be fine. I'd be gone when he got back. He wouldn't get to *have* me.

Hurriedly, I scrawled out as many items as I could think of, hoping the more that I added, the more time he'd take at the store. *Bread, steaks, potatoes, green beans, wine, shampoo, conditioner, hair dryer, bobby pins, hairspray, toothbrush, toothpaste, shaving cream.* I wasn't sure I could get away with it, but I also added a couple of items that could potentially be weapons if need be. In case. *Razor. Curling iron.*

I tore off the sheet to hand to him and suddenly thought of one more item, an item that I hoped to God wouldn't be necessary. *Condoms.*

It felt like a betrayal to write it. The opening of a door. Like, by putting the item down, it was inviting it to be used.

I'm sorry, Hudson, I thought, as I handed the list to David. But if it was going to happen, I had to make sure it happened safely.

He scanned the list, and I held my breath, hoping he didn't call me out for the razor. When he frowned at me, I was already prepared.

"Laynie," he reprimanded. "You're being naughty. I can't buy everything you've asked for."

"That's okay. I just . . ." I'd get out while he was gone. I had to.

"I can't buy the condoms," he said.

My head jerked up in surprise. "What?"

He bent down in front of me and rubbed his palms along my bare thighs. "I've waited too too long to be with you," he said, staring at my skin as his hands ran back and forth. "I need to feel you bare. There can't be anything between us anymore. And how will we start our family if I'm wearing a rubber?"

"I . . . I . . ." I stammered. I hadn't thought it could get worse, but he *wanted* to get me pregnant? God, I was on the pill now, too. I could be fertile after missing only a couple of days.

I didn't want to think that I'd be there that long.

But . . . if I was . . .

I tried another tactic. "I was thinking about protecting you. From Hudson. He's been inside me. He's left all that . . . that toxin inside me. I don't want to share that with you."

His palms stilled, his expression turning unreadable. "So smart. I'm sure it won't take very long before he's out of you. Maybe with your period. It will clean you all out. When are you due for your next one?"

"In another week."

He winked. "I'll add maxipads to the list. I know you might like tampons instead, but from now on nothing goes in your cunt unless I put it in there."

Gross.

And lewd and wrong and creepy and I was nauseated again and on the verge of a panic attack.

David, on the other hand, had a dazed look on his face, like he was imagining things I didn't want to know about. Fantasizing. Smiling like a kid on Christmas, he rubbed his finger over my mouth, roughly tracing the line of my lips. "We're going to have so much fun together, Laynie. So much fun. I can't wait to show you."

I couldn't help it—I shuddered.

His face turned hard and mean, and he rose to his full height then stared down at me.

I frantically started to make up an apology about being cold, about having the chills—I was still sick, and all that. But it wasn't my reaction that seemed to have him upset, I realized before I started speaking. It was what he was staring at.

I followed his gaze to my hands and realized I'd been playing with my wedding ring set. I did it all the time without noticing, a nervous habit.

I stilled. But it was too late.

"That needs to come off. *He* gave it to you. It needs to go." His tone said no arguing. The gun was there too, right at eye level.

"I'm so used to it, though," I said as casually as I could. "I like the feel of it. We can pretend *you* gave it to me."

"I'll get you a ring. That one needs to go, baby, so you can move on."

He'd said I needed to obey him. But I was stubborn sometimes. Too stubborn for my own good.

"No. Please." I couldn't lose my wedding ring. I couldn't. It was stupid, I knew that, to risk my life over a symbol, but it was all I had right then. All I had tying me to Hudson and I was sure that if David took it away, I'd lose all hope.

I could almost hear my husband, though, in my head, telling me to be reasonable. Telling me to do what I needed to do to survive. Telling me to come home to him in one piece. To come home to our children.

David went to reach for my hand, and I tried to let him take it, but as he started to tug on my ring set, I pulled it away from him again.

His anger was blazing hot, the heat of it burning me just in the way he stood, the way he stared. "He still has that hold on you," he said. "I knew it wouldn't be that easy."

He turned away and started toward the door, and with him, I felt my chance at freedom slipping through my fingers.

"He *doesn't* have a hold on me!" I protested, following after him. "I want to be with *you*! If you get those things for me, I'll be able to show you how much I appreciate you. And . . . and . . . want you. I'm not thinking straight right now."

He opened the door and went out, but I had to pause in the door frame, dizziness clouding over me and turning my vision black. When it cleared again, I saw that immediately outside the room were stairs going down. I was in some sort of loft.

I didn't have a chance to look around more, because then David had returned, pushing at my sternum so that I stumbled backward into the room.

He caught my wrist roughly and dragged me across the room. "I'm still going to the store. You do need to clean yourself up before we're together. I want you fresh and pure when I make love to you so I'm going to get the things you need to do that. I'll give you another chance to take off that ring when I get back. If you don't do it willingly, I'll cut it off."

He pushed me down hard to the cot. "I also think you might be trying to trick me."

I bolted back up. "No, I'm not! I swear."

He pushed me down again, this time kneeling over me so I couldn't move. "I've decided it's okay if you are. I know it's going to take some time before you realize what Hudson has done to you. I know how you can get obsessed with someone. It's what you do. He used that against you, it wasn't your fault. But you'll get over him. And, when you finally do . . ." He gathered my wrists in both of his fists. "I'll be able to leave you here without having to do this, but for now, I'm going to have to make it so you can't run away."

I had been too focused on his face and what he was doing when he came back to notice the silver roll of tape he was wearing like a bracelet. Holding my hands with one of his, he took the tape and wrapped it around my wrists several times, then cutting the tape with his teeth.

Fuck, fuck. I couldn't get away if I was bound.

"Please, no! I'll be good! I'll take off the rings! Leave me loose! Please!"

But he wasn't listening. Or at least he wasn't responding. He put my ankles together—I'd lost my shoes somewhere in the night—and taped them too.

Tugging me up to meet his lips, he kissed me once more, deep and slobbery and possessive, before dropping me on the cot.

Then he took off, shutting the door behind him. I heard a click, and I knew he'd left me bound in a locked loft somewhere that was a *bit of a trip* to any town.

I was fucked.

I was *fucked*.

I curled my knees up toward my chest, rolled to my side, and, holding thoughts of Hudson and my babies in my head—my babies!—my Brett, my Holden, my Mina—I cried harder than I had in my entire life.

CHAPTER TWENTY

HUDSON

Celia and I spent all night around her dining room table re-reading the journals. I read the ones she had gone through before; she read the ones *I* had gone through. I even used her laptop to access my old digital records from before I started working with her. There was nothing there. Nothing. Or if there was, we were missing it.

Just after six AM, Edward came out from his bedroom, already dressed in a suit and tie. "Any luck?"

He'd addressed the question to his wife, so I let her answer. "No." She looked genuinely downcast.

She stood to kiss him goodbye, and I couldn't help but eavesdrop on their intimate moment.

"Please make sure you get some rest today," he said, softly. "Let Elsa take one of the feedings for you." The concern for his wife was apparent, and I felt a stab of guilt.

"I apologize, Edward, for keeping her up all night. I know how precious sleep is with a little one." I was sincere, even though I simultaneously believed Celia and I deserved to never sleep again, if that was the required payment to get my wife back. I was well aware that every hour that passed increased her chances of suffering something irreversible.

Things I refused to give power to by naming.

Edward Fasbender looked at me with hard, unreadable eyes. "No apology needed. It's understandable. At times we have to push the limits for the ones we love."

"Yes. That." There was nothing I wouldn't do, no length I wouldn't go to in order to get Alayna back, to find who had taken her.

"I wish you the best of luck in your search," he said then went on his way.

When he was gone, Celia said cautiously, "Hudson . . . Maybe it's not here. Maybe this isn't—"

I didn't want to hear it. I needed to have control. I needed to have a path, a direction.

"Read me the letters again," I said cutting her off. Maybe if I heard them out loud, it would trigger something else in my head.

With a sigh, she picked up the first letter of the stack and started reading through them one by one. I listened carefully, with my eyes closed, as if I'd never heard them, as if I didn't have them all memorized at this point. As if I were someone different listening.

"Wait a minute," I said, stopping her midway through the third letter. "Read the line again about playing at marriage."

It took her a second the find the place, her manicured finger trailing over the paper.

"'You played at marriage and think that makes you a husband.' He sounds skeptical of your marriage, if you ask me," Celia said. "What kind of person would say that? Who would care that much about your marriage? Somebody's else's marriage that we ruined?"

"No. Someone who doesn't think I deserve *my* marriage." *Doesn't think I deserve Alayna.* Something was coming together and I couldn't quite see it, but it was almost there. "Is that a reference to the time that you and I pretended to be married?"

She scratched the back of her head while she thought about it. "I suppose it could be. Though it would be strange if someone would want to get revenge for that scheme. I don't think that other couple ever realized they were being played."

I nodded, but not just because what she was saying was accurate, but because of where the train of thought had taken me.

"Where is that account recorded? It's not in any of the journals that we've read. Did you leave one out for some reason?" And then another piece of the puzzle fit in together. "And what about the mask reference—you said it might be reffering to the masquerade party, but I don't remember reading about that in any of these journals either. Where are those stories?"

Celia's expression seemed to indicate that something had clicked. Then she suddenly went pale.

"*Is* there a journal missing? Is there one that's not here?" My voice was getting louder with each new question. If all the answers had been somewhere else all along, how much time had we wasted?

"I forgot all about it. I'm sorry! Please don't be mad at me." She looked so uncomfortable and guilty that I was certain whatever was coming *was* something I was going to be mad at.

"Years ago . . . when I was trying to . . . when I was sure that Alayna wouldn't want you if she knew about the games of your past . . ." She trailed off, her face beginning to redden.

I'd been burning with rage since the moment that I realized for sure that Alayna was gone—rage at whoever took her, rage at myself.

It was easy to turn the rage now toward her. "What did you do, Celia?"

"I took one of the journals and planted it in the bookcase in the manager's office at The Sky Launch. I thought that if Alayna found it, she would understand who you were by reading it. That she'd—"

"That she'd read the horrible and terrible things we'd done together and leave me right away. I'm getting the picture. Fuck you, Celia." I ran my hand roughly through my hair.

I didn't really mean it, didn't really mean *fuck you*. She didn't have to tell me this. She could've said the journal had gotten lost, that she didn't know where it had gone. She'd been honest and vulnerable.

And God knew that we'd both made mistakes in the past.

"Well, she never found it," I said, calming down now that I'd put things in perspective "and she loves me anyway, that crazy woman. What we're missing has to be in that volume."

I stood up from the table, eager to be on to the next clue. "I guess we're done here, then. Thank you very much for helping me with all of this."

"Oh, don't you *dare* pull me into this and then dismiss me at your will." She stood up from the table as well. "Give me five minutes to put on some clothes and tell Elsa that I'm leaving, and I'll come with you."

I didn't argue with her, because I knew I still might need her help reading through the last journal, looking for the final missing clue. And besides, I was determined to find Alayna on my own if I had to, but that didn't mean I couldn't use a friend.

* * *

It was too early for the staff to have arrived, so I used my own key to get into the club and disarmed security while Celia headed up to the manager's office. When I got in there, she was walking around the room with a puzzled look on her face.

"There used to be a bookcase in here. I stuck it in with all the other books." She looked at me quizzically. "This is all different since I was last here."

"It was fully remodeled when Alayna was on maternity leave." The same time the letters started arriving . . .

Another piece of the picture was attempting to come into focus. "You left the journal for Alayna to find, but how did you expect her to know that it was me and you it was talking about? All the references to me just say *him*." Celia had thought it best to disguise our identities that way, not use any personal references to ourselves. Just in case.

"I put a picture of us from the masquerade ball it described inside." She shrugged, as if to say she knew she was guilty, what else could she do now but own up to it?

"Then anyone, really, who had their hands on the journal would have realized who the stories involved." I pulled out my phone and started dialing Gwen's number as I talked. "The person who has Alayna wasn't a victim from our past—he *read* our past."

Gwen answered, and I nearly tripped over my words in my haste to get them out. "I'm sorry it's early, I have a question that could be important. When you remodeled, where did all the books go that were on the shelves behind the desk?"

She already knew Alayna was still missing, since I'd called her again when I couldn't find her in the event space so she didn't delay things by asking why I wanted to know.

"Um, the books were, well . . . Some of them we threw away. Some I think we probably donated." She paused for a minute thinking. "A lot of it was David's stuff. Alayna had me call him to collect, and he came and picked up the box right before we did the remodel."

My heart started racing. "That's exactly what I needed to know. Thank you."

Before I hung up, she said, "Oh, and I don't know if this is important, but David was *at* the club yesterday. He came in for the job fair."

I looked at Celia, as if she could hear the whole conversation and was having the same *aha* moment that I was. "And he was still here when you left?"

"No. He left a couple of hours before I did. He stopped and said *hi*. Alayna invited him up to the office, and we all talked for a while, old-times chat and all that."

"Did you actually see him leave?" I asked her.

I knew her answer before she gave it, and when she did, I thanked her again and hung up. Immediately, I called Jordan. "It's David Lindt."

* * *

Jordan called his team in to the security offices, located in the basement of the Pierce Industries building. I told him I'd meet him there, promising not to get into any accidents on the way.

I didn't agree not to speed.

Knowing I was antsy to get to my destination, Celia offered to take a cab to her hotel. We parted on the sidewalk outside The Sky Launch, my mind so preoccupied, I didn't even say goodbye.

"Good luck," she called after me, when I was already halfway to where I'd parked my car.

I started to wave in acknowledgment, then realized I couldn't leave on that note. I jogged back to her so that I wasn't shouting, so that she'd know I wasn't just throwing out niceties. "Thank you," I told her earnestly.

I resisted the urge to qualify my gratitude—she hadn't been willing to help in the beginning, and it hadn't been lost on me that Alayna might be safe and in my arms right now if it hadn't been for Celia and that damn book she'd planted years ago. None of that was productive. And in the end, if we were to play that game, I couldn't forget that there would never have *been* a devious and scheming Celia if there hadn't first been a Hudson.

I'd carefully groomed her to become exactly who she turned out to be.

I'd hatched the dragon egg.

She smiled, a genuine smile, rarely seen on this woman who I'd known so long. "I'm glad I could help," she said.

I nodded, ready to leave.

But she stopped me, grabbing my hand. "Hudson, I mean that. Whatever else happens, know that I mean that."

I studied her for a moment, trying to read her motivation. It dawned on me for the first time that I might trigger the same regret and shame in her that she did for me. I was as much a reminder of *her* past as she was of *mine*. Perhaps it was becoming as compulsory to her to make amends with her victims—with *me*—as it had been for me recently.

"All right." I said in response, and that was all. Because there was nothing else that needed to be said, and I had somewhere else to be.

When I arrived at the security office, I walked into a room full of buzzing activity.

"He gave up his apartment in Atlantic City," Jordan said, briefing me on the findings so far. "His forwarding address on file there led us to an extended stay here in the city. The front desk said he checked out over the phone last night. He still had items in the room that he asked to be kept and he'd return to pick them up at a later date. No forwarding information. I've sent a man to collect those items, and he should be back here shortly.

"Gwen Bruzzo's account of seeing him at The Sky Launch has been corroborated with the video footage. We were able to spot him arriving at fourteen twenty-seven hours. He can be seen on footage for the next couple hours in the club, but he disappears around seventeen hundred hours after purchasing tequila shots at the bar. He paid cash. This is the same time Alayna left the floor, presumably to look at the space next door. We believe he followed her into the stairwell, unbeknownst to her.

"We're unable to see that because the camera angled to record that area was taken offline in the previous hour. I believe he must have used the time between leaving the manager's office and following Alayna upstairs to disable that camera. It's not an easy task, but considering he's worked at two Pierce clubs, he would be familiar with the software we use."

"We should have had a completely new security system put in when he left," I blared.

"And again when any manager leaves the club?" Jordan asked pointedly. "Not realistic and not something you need to get hung up on now. Concentrate on the task at hand, not the past. We can Monday morning quarterback later on."

It wasn't every day I let my staff talk to me like that.

But this wasn't every day.

"Though he wasn't seen again inside the club," Jordan went on, "there is footage of his car driving past the club a little before eighteen hundred hours."

He led me to a computer screen where an image was pulled up of David behind the wheel of a car. The camera also caught a woman in the passenger seat, reclined so her face wasn't clear, but I knew it was Alayna. I'd recognize her anywhere.

"She looks . . . unconscious," I said, my heart racing at the sight of my wife. I was simultaneously relieved to see her, to know we were on the right track, and devastated to realize we could be too late. But if he'd been stalking her, surely he wouldn't have . . . gone too far.

"He's likely drugged her," Jordan said, confirming my thought process. "The testing we did on those shot glasses have traces of Ro-hypnol in one of them."

A fucking date rape drug. That meant she couldn't even fight. Alive, but at his mercy.

Jordan quickly moved on, not allowing me to dwell on the worst possibilities, but I silently vowed to murder that bastard Lindt when I had my hands on him. And I *would* have my hands on him.

"I have a friend at the FBI," Jordan said, and I could tell he was wrapping up his briefing. "I've called and asked him to put an APB out on Lindt. My friend's giving us five hours before he adds the case into the system as a courtesy."

He hadn't asked if I wanted him to use his contact, but I didn't reprimand him. It was time. Jordan had made the right move. That was why he worked for me—because I knew I could trust him to keep his head about him when I couldn't.

"What about credit cards? Are you tracing those?" I asked, wishing I could be helpful.

"I have something on that right now," a woman on the team called out, flagging us over to her nearby computer terminal. "I've hacked into Lindt's bank account and found an unusual transaction within the last month. Here, an amount of forty-eight thousand dollars was transferred out of his savings account."

"Where the hell did Lindt get forty-eight thousand dollars?" I asked.

"That part's easy, he rarely spends money on non-essentials. My bank statements are filled with charges to different retailers, but his are nearly all simple bills," the woman answered. "The interesting thing isn't that he had the money, it's that it's all of a sudden leaving his account in a lump sum."

"Any idea where the money was transferred to?" Jordan asked.

"It looks like it was deposited directly into another account. Right here," she said, pointing to the line on the screen.

"I'll go over to interview her personally," Jordan said. "This trans-action may give us a lead on where to look next."

"I'll go with you," I said as I stared at the familiar name in front of me, hardly believing the coincidence. "I'm going to want to hear from her own mouth how Judith Cleary is involved in all of this."

* * *

We arrived at Judith Cleary's apartment building at exactly seven forty-seven AM. My body was flooded with so much adrenaline, it hardly registered that I hadn't slept in twenty-four hours. Jordan distracted the doorman, while I slipped quietly by and took the elevator up to her unit. I pounded on the door relentlessly until she opened up.

"Hudson Pierce. I expected to see you at some point, but I must admit I didn't think it was going to be on my doorstep. If you'd like to discuss your daughter's entrance to my school, you can make an appointment through the office. Though admissions have been finalized for next school year, so—"

I cut her off, unsure why I'd let her go on so long. "I'm not here about Mina. I don't care about your little school." As if it were her school alone, and she weren't just a board member. "I'm here to discuss something far more urgent." I nodded at her door. "Well?"

She tapped her foot smugly while she considered, and it took everything I had in me not to push her against the wall and demand answers.

Finally, after what felt like forever, she stepped aside and allowed me into her apartment. "Very well. Because I'm dying to know what's so urgent that you would need to speak to me face to face. At my home. But make it quick—I have to be at a showing in an hour and it's across town."

Oh yes, I'd forgotten she was a real estate agent. The classic rich housewive's occupation. I pulled a copy of the bank records that Jordan had given me out of my pocket and showed them to her.

"I need to know about this transaction from a David Lindt in the amount of forty-eight thousand dollars that ended up in your account. Can you tell me *why* that transaction was made? What he was paying you for?"

"Oh, that's your angle. You're trying to find something to blackmail me on, bribe me?" She rocked back on the heel of one of her shoes.

"Well, I can assure you that entire transaction was above board. Trying to use that information to get your daughter into the New Park School is not going to—"

"I told you, I am not interested in your fucking school." I lost my patience. "As soon as I learned you had anything to do with that foundation, I wanted to run a thousand miles away. I'm not putting my *child* into a place run by a board of bitches who use their elected positions to settle petty grievances. Now tell me why the fuck you accepted the payment from David Lindt!"

She stood up straighter, held her chin up high. "How dare you speak to me in that way!" she exclaimed haughtily. "You can leave now, Mr. Pierce. This conversation is concluded."

"I am not leaving until—"

"I will call security!" She already had her hand on the phone next to the door, and I didn't doubt that she would follow through.

I took a deep breath and let the oxygen clear my head. I knew how to handle a woman like Judith Cleary. The old Hudson knew exactly what to do, how to manipulate her, what tactics to use. She'd immediately assumed I was trying to blackmail her, which meant there was *something* that she could be blackmailed about. I could discover it. Could play that card once I knew what it was, and with Jordan's team on the case, I imagined it could happen before security made it up to her floor.

I knew how to do that, and I'd promised myself that I could be that old Hudson again if I needed to be. To protect my family.

But I'd done that already, set fresh plans in motion to discover who was behind this, and Alayna was still gone.

I could practically hear her voice in the back of my head telling me it wasn't the direction she would choose for me. She would rather I be honest and transparent whenever possible. She would prefer I put scheming aside, leave it for a last resort. She would prefer I become vulnerable, as hard as that might be.

"I apologize," I said, forcing the words passed my lips. "I spoke rudely and inappropriately. I'm desperate, you see. My wife is missing."

Judith's hand fell from the phone and she moved it to her chest as she gasped. "Oh my God, Hudson, I am so sorry. But I don't understand what this has to do with me."

"We believe she's been taken by David Lindt. He's a former employee who has been infatuated with her in the past. He was the last one to see her, but now we can't find him."

I took a step toward her and hung my head immediately. "You have to know that you are the last person that I would ask a favor of. But right now this transaction from his account to yours is the only lead we have."

"I see. In that case, and I'm still not sure why *you're* here instead of a police officer, but okay. She's a very rude woman herself, but her blood's not going to be on my hands."

This is where I hated the vulnerable, honest approach—because transparency made it apparent how terrible other people were. But I refrained from saying anything.

"David Lindt came to me as a client. He was looking for a real estate purchase, something out of town. He was under the delusion that he could afford something much grander. Of course I couldn't find anything in his price range, but I felt sorry for him and I ended up selling him a piece of land that I've been holding on to for a while. There's nothing much on it, silly little hunting cabin up in the woods."

She considered for a moment. "He kept talking about how he wanted to make it special for his wife who was coming home soon . . . Are you sure he is the man you're looking for? He was quite sincere about the two of them having a quiet place to really focus on each other."

It felt like my chest was collapsing inward, each breath was difficult, sharp with icy pain. "David Lindt has never been married," I said gruffly. "I believe the woman he was preparing the cabin for was Alayna."

Judith's expression turned to one of shock. "Let me write down the address for you, I'll not be having a poor Yelp review for abetting a criminal," she said, as she left the room and returned a minute later with an address written legibly on stationary.

Just as I was thinking I'd been wrong about the woman, that she really wasn't as much of a bitch as I thought, she pulled the paper toward her chest and said, "Now, I do expect a good word at the country club for this."

Then she handed me the paper.

Her mistake was giving it to me before I'd agreed.

As soon as the thing was safely in my hands, I tucked it into my suit jacket and gave her my honest response. Alayna would appreciate that, too, I was certain. "Like fucking hell, Judith. You were a nasty piece of work when you kicked Mirabelle out of the girls club all those years ago, and it's clear you're still a conniving, selfish, mean girl. While I don't care who is a member of the club you're still so keen to be part of, my mother cares deeply. She's a member there herself, as you might have known had you not been so hasty to punish my sister, and there is no room for two narcissistic witches of that caliber in one place. Thank you for the information. Have a nice day."

I left before she could call security, which she was no doubt doing, and called Jordan from the elevator, even though I would see him as soon as I arrived in the lobby. "I got the location. I know where he's taken her. We're going to need the helicopter fueled."

"I'll get on it. Mind telling me where we're going?"

"Lake Placid."

* * *

It was a ninety minute flight to Lake Placid, but it felt like ninety years. The address, it turned out, wasn't in the village, but in the woods of the Adirondack Mountains nearby.

Of course. The quiet place he'd asked for.

We filled all eight seats of the helicopter with the pilot, Jordan, myself, and five men from the security team.

On the ride up, Jordan assigned me tasks to keep me busy and feeling useful. I knew what he was doing, and I was grateful.

First, he had me locate a field where we could land the copter. The nearest spot was seven miles from the log cabin, so the next assignment was arranging for a van to be delivered from Lake Placid to the field to meet us. When that was done, Jordan had me find a hospital in Manhattan that would allow us to arrive by helicopter.

"I'm not assuming that she will be injured or harmed," he said, in an attempt to reassure me. "But since she's been drugged, you're going to want to have her checked out anyway. It's good to be prepared."

Finally, after everything else had been completed, he said, "Now call your house. Check on your kids. Talk to Mina. Alayna will want to know how they're doing. And I think it would do you some good to hear your child's voice."

He was right. Listening to Mina's sweet, floating voice brought a begrudging smile to my face. It was impossible to resist being lit up by her sunshine. She might have been a product of both of us, but she was her mother's daughter in all the best ways.

As slow as the ride up had been, once we landed, it seemed like everything moved in double time. The van took us to the address Judith Cleary had given us. Jordan didn't let us use the driveway, but rather had us park in a nearby cluster of trees, hidden from the main road. His plan was that we'd approach the house through the woods, reducing any chance of being seen before we made it to the house.

"You should stay—" he began when we started to pile out of the van.

I cut him off. "Like hell I'm staying behind."

For the first time all morning, Jordan seemed to hesitate. "Fine, but you're not going in the house until we've cleared it. You'll hang back, understood?"

Again, I had to wrestle with my ego. I wasn't used to taking orders. I reminded myself what could happen if this went down wrong, what was on the line.

"I'll hang back," I agreed, reluctantly. I wanted mine to be the first face my wife saw when this nightmare was over, but that was far less important than being able to see her face at all.

It wasn't too far of a trek through the woods to get to the cabin, though it was one that would have been better made in outdoor wear. I still had on yesterday's suit and dress shoes, and after sliding on loose dirt for the third time, I began to understand why Jordan thought I might have been better off in the van.

Finally we were outside the cabin, a dilapidated dwelling that looked like it's best days had been half a century in the past. David's car was parked outside, the doors left unlocked. I opened the door and looked inside, searching for some sign that Alayna was all right.

All I found were her shoes on the floor of the passenger side, a favorite pair of Jimmy Choos that she would never part with voluntarily. It made my stomach drop to see them abandoned like this, and I had to sit down inside the car to catch my breath.

Jordan and the team went ahead of me, and when I looked up again, they'd surrounded the cabin. On his signal, three of them burst through the front door, their guns aimed and ready.

I watched them from the car, holding onto Alayna's shoes, praying like I'd never prayed in my life. *Please, let her be safe. Please, God, bring her back to me.*

The men had been inside for only a couple of minutes when movement caught my eye in the woods on the other side of the car, away from the cabin. I scanned the trees, my heart beating in my ears, looking for the source.

Then there he was—David Lindt, coming toward the car, bent over as though hoping to not be seen.

But *I'd* seen him.

And a second later, he saw me.

He took off running back to where he'd come from, but I was right behind him, sprinting at top speed. He might have had the lead and been wearing the right shoes, but I had the adrenaline and the will. I had the fury. There was nothing that was going to stop me from reaching him.

I caught up with him before he'd disappeared into the woods, tackling him to the ground with a heavy grunt. A handgun went flying across the ground, dislodged from where it had been tucked in his belt. He had a fucking *gun*? The sight of it, knowing he had likely threatened my wife with it, gave me the extra boost of energy I needed to wrestle the larger man's wrists behind his back.

"If you touched her," I threatened, crushing my knee forcefully into his tailbone and using my upper body to smash his head into the ground, "If you laid even a finger on her, I will break every bone in your body right now with my bare hands. Don't think I won't do it, you stupid motherfucker. I'll do it, and I'll do it in whatever way hurts the most, I swear on my fucking life!"

David's response was muffled, apparently he was unable to speak clearly with his face in the dirt.

"The house is empty!" Jordan announced from the front step.

Empty?

The house was empty.

A volcano of rage burst from inside me. Vile hatred and venom spewed from my pores like lava. "Where is she!?" I screamed at the man held underneath me. "Where is she? Tell me now if you want to live another second! Tell me where my wife is!"

"I don't know!" he squealed as he squirmed underneath me. "I was in the woods looking for her!"

He was fucking lying. There was no way he couldn't know, and he would tell me if I had to torture it out of him.

Jordan must have spotted me right away, because all of a sudden he was pulling me off David while a few of his men took over handling our captive. They got him up to his feet, and immediately began asking him all the questions I was planning to ask him, just not using quite the level of violence I wanted to see.

"There's a broken window and possible signs of a struggle," Jordan told me, ever composed. "Some of the pieces of glass seem to have blood on them."

David Lindt was a dead man.

I rushed at him, throwing him against a tree, my hands at his throat. While Jordan once again tried to pull me off, I squeezed until David's face went red. Kept squeezing until it started to go blue. I intended to keep on squeezing until . . .

My phone rang. An unexpected sound here; I hadn't had a signal when we landed.

I considered ignoring it. I was in the process of murdering a man with my bare hands, after all, but then, what if . . . ?

I dropped my hold on David, stepped back as he desperately gasped for air, and pulled my phone out of my pocket. It was a number I didn't recognize. I pushed *Accept*.

"Hudson, Hudson, is that you?" The call was faint and full of static, but it was Alayna's voice. My darling, my precious.

"Alayna! Where are you?" I walked around, trying to get better reception. I was missing some of her words.

"Hudson, can you hear me?" she asked, apparently having as much trouble with the call as I was.

"Don't hang up! I'm here. I'm at the cabin. Tell me where to find you!"

I didn't seem to be getting through. "Hudson, I love you," she said, as if I hadn't said anything. "I've always loved you. Kiss the babies for me. Tell them . . . tell them I loved them . . ."

"Alayna?" She didn't respond. "Alayna, precious, talk to me! Alayna!"

The call dropped. I'd lost her.

I'd lost her and, with her, my whole world was lost too.

CHAPTER TWENTY-ONE

ALAYNA

I was in pain. So much pain. Every breath I took was sharp, stabbing, blinding pain.

Dizzily, I staggered through the wilderness, looking for bars on the phone, looking for a place where my repeated call to Hudson's cell would go through.

And now I had finally gotten to him, finally heard his voice and told him the words I had to leave him with. I'd held out for this, fought against loss of consciousness so he would know before I went.

"Let them know I loved them."

* * *

For the second time, I woke up not knowing where I was.

This room was much brighter than the last one, everything white and sterile. There was a steady *bleep-bleep-bleep* sound that matched the blip on the heart monitor next to me. Oxygen flowed through a tube inserted at my nose, and another tube connected my wrists to an IV drip.

I turned my head to look at the other side of me, and there was Hudson in a chair pulled up right next to the bed that I lay in, so close he'd fallen asleep leaning over on the mattress next to me.

The *bleep-bleep* sped up, an audible pronouncement of my exhilaration at seeing him again, seeing his face, covered with scruff as though he hadn't shaved in a couple of days, his features worn and tired even as he dozed.

I reached out to touch his prickly cheek with my fingertips, a movement that hurt more than it should have, and with my touch he jolted awake.

His face broke into the most glorious smile I'd ever seen him give.

"There you are," he said.

Here I was. And I was surprised as anyone about it.

"I thought I was dying," I told him sincerely.

He chuckled. "Not dying," he assured me. "You have a concussion, a laceration on your thigh which has already been stitched up, a dislocated shoulder, which has been set back into place, cuts on both your hands and feet, and a cracked rib on your right side."

"Oh." It wasn't a short list, but definitely none of it equated to death. "A cracked rib, huh? So that's why it hurts so much to breathe."

His brow creased in concern, and he stroked my arm. "I'll have them give you more pain medicine."

A wave of panic surged through me, and even though it was agony to do so, I grabbed on to him. "Hudson, don't leave me."

He took my hand in his and held it tight. "It's okay. I'm here. It's just a button we have to push." Still holding my hand, he used his other arm to stretch up to the panel attached to the side of the bed above me, and pushed the icon that said nurse.

Yeah, I'd forgotten that's how you did things in hospitals.

It felt like I might've forgotten a lot of things, actually, and now that he'd mentioned it, I realized my head *was* throbbing, a dull pain next to the one that seized my rib cage, but significant nonetheless. It was different than the headaches I'd had in the past, a haze that somehow also put pressure on the inside of my skull.

For a few seconds, I tried to piece together the details from what I last remembered and what was happening now, but the effort was too great.

"What happened?" I asked Hudson instead.

"I was hoping you could tell me." He rubbed his thumb along my wrist soothingly. "David's been arrested. When we arrived at the log cabin, we found him, but not you. He insisted he didn't know where you were, but then you called me. Do you remember that?"

"I do." I remembered the sweet, distant sound of his voice, and David's cell phone pressed to my ear, how the connection of the call felt like a lighthouse in a bay of fog.

Then I remembered before that, too. David. The cabin.

"I'd convinced David to go to the store, thinking I could escape while he was gone," I told Hudson. "But I hadn't counted on him binding me up before he left. He used duct tape around my ankles and my wrists. I thought it was hopeless. I was sure I'd still be there when he got back and then I'd . . . then he'd . . ."

The sickening words he'd said to me crept into my consciousness, washing me with recollected terror.

I shivered and shook my head. That wasn't important now. I'd escaped.

"Then I remembered this thing that Gwen told me about yesterday," I continued. "This trick of getting out of duct tape that she'd seen at her sex club party last weekend."

Hudson, who had listened patiently, interjected for the first time. "Sex club party?"

I shot him a warning look. "Don't get any ideas."

"I have absolutely zero interest," he promised. "Our sex life is adventurous enough."

Even under the worst of circumstances, the man knew how to make me blush.

"Anyway. The struggle was getting out of the room. David locked me in this loft at the top of the cabin. The door was not budging, no matter how many times I tried to slam my bodyweight against it. And all that was in the room was a cot and built-in desk and bookshelves. There was a stool too—that's important. I rummaged through the drawers trying to find something to maybe pick the lock—not that I know how to pick a lock—and couldn't find anything, but I did find he'd left his cell phone. It was locked so he'd probably thought I couldn't get into it.

But I figured out the password easily enough. Zero one zero two—my birthday. Turned out it didn't matter if I had the password, because the phone wasn't doing anything from that room. There was absolutely no reception. I tried over and over to make a call, and it wouldn't connect."

Hudson continued to stroke my wrist, giving me all his attention, careful not to let on how upsetting my tale was to him, which was impressive. While he could be a very patient man, he wasn't always patient where I was concerned.

"That left the window. It was just glass in a frame, not the kind that opens, and it was high on the wall, but I had to figure a way to get out of it."

"So you used the stool to break it," he guessed.

"I gave it away," I feigned pouting. "Yes. I had to stand on the desk to get the right height, and throw the stool at the glass. It took a couple of tries but it finally hit in the right spot. I brushed out the glass pieces as best I could, then I hoisted myself up." I looked down at the bandages wrapping my palms. "That's what cut up my hands.

"I cut my leg then too, going through the window," I remembered suddenly. "But the biggest problem was the loft was so far off the ground that the fall was more than two stories. I hesitated. It was quite a fall, but then I went for it. I landed on my side and my whole right side blew up with pain. My shoulder, my side, my leg, all of it was throbbing agony. I swear, I almost passed out right then."

"But you didn't," Hudson said, this part of my story evident.

"No, I didn't." That was something I should be proud of, I realized. "I forced myself to get up and get away from the house. I knew we were deep enough in the woods that I wasn't going to be able to make it to town, especially in this condition, and I didn't want to be near the roads in case David was the one who drove by and found me, but I thought if I could just get up the mountain enough to get reception on the phone, then I'd be able to call you, and you could come find me."

I'd been in such a daze, stopping frequently to take breaks and try the phone. The pain coursing through my body had been blinding. My only focus had been climbing upward, guessing at the direction by the feel of the incline as I stumbled along. It had felt like a decade before I'd finally heard the phone ringing at my ear followed by Hudson's voice.

"I wasn't sure if I really spoke to you or if it was some sort of dying mirage," I admitted. "Though, seeing as how I wasn't actually dying . . ."

"You talked to me," he confirmed. "You called, and when I heard you . . ."

He choked up, a reaction I'd never seen from him before. His eyes had gotten teary on our wedding day and at the birth of each of the babies, but he'd never lost the ability to speak, and seeing him do so now made my heart squeeze and brought tears to my eyes.

He cleared his throat, which only helped mildly. "Then when you were saying your goodbyes . . . I can't tell you what that did to me, precious. I was destroyed."

"I know," I said in a strangled voice. "Me too."

We sat for a few seconds, staring at each other, saying nothing. Processing what didn't happen, but came so close to being a possibility.

I was the one who finally broke the silence. "But you *did* find me. You traced the call?"

He nodded. "Jordan called a medic up to meet us before we even knew where you were. Then the team separated to search the area the trace said you'd be in. You'd managed to get almost a mile away from the cabin, even barefoot and in misery. You were passed out and ragged, but very much alive, thank God. It was a miracle you made it as long as you did before your body succumbed to shock. The medic put your shoulder back in place right there and gave you some morphine, and then we flew you back here to the city."

"I sort of remember waking up for part of that," I said, recalling the strange man who'd massaged my biceps and deltoids, trying to get them to relax so that my shoulder would pop in. I hadn't been aware enough to realize what he'd been doing, but now that I was, it wasn't at all like I'd seen doctors fix dislocated shoulders on TV.

"You were in and out a lot until the morphine kicked in. You were out cold after that. I'm sure you needed it."

"That sounds about right."

The nurse arrived then to check my vitals and give me more meds. When he left, Hudson told me how he'd discovered it was David who had taken me, the long night he'd had with Celia, and how she'd been helpful in putting the pieces together. He also told me about Judith Cleary and her involvement.

"I wish I'd been there when you told her off," I grinned.

He returned the smile. "I thought you'd appreciate that."

The morphine was kicking in, making me feel somber and sleepy. I was happy and grateful to have my husband by my side, but there was still a cloud lingering over me. I'd thought of David as a friend. How could he have done what he'd done to me? How could I not have seen it coming sooner? How would I ever be able to trust people after this? Would I ever feel truly safe?

"You really got him, right?" I asked. "The police arrested him?"

"Well, I almost choked him to death first, but yes. It was only your phone call that saved him from me. And after your call, when I thought you were . . . let's just say Jordan managed to prevent me from being arrested as well."

That was another scene I would have liked to have witnessed.

Still, I wasn't completely reassured. "He won't make bail or anything?"

"No bail. I have friends in the court who promised to see to that."

It was what I'd needed to hear, yet the weight of everything still lingered. A tear spilled down my cheek. "I thought I'd never see you again," I sniffed, sure I could turn this into a real sobfest if I didn't contain myself.

"Hey, hey." Hudson climbed into the bed next to me and gingerly put his arm around me. "You'll always see me again. You can't get rid of me. I stick, remember?"

I chuckled and immediately regretted it. Though it halted my tears, the laughing sent my side into spasming pain.

When I'd recovered, I said, "I'm gone for one day, and you're already stealing my lines."

"It was a day too long." He kissed the top of my head. Quieter, he added, "Never leave me again. Promise."

I was getting tired. I rested my head on his chest and closed my eyes. "I'm not going anywhere," I said, and drifted off to sleep.

CHAPTER TWENTY-TWO

HUDSON

They kept Alayna at the hospital overnight for observation, and the next day when they were ready to release her, I requested they keep her for one more night—just to be sure.

They agreed. It's hard to argue with a man who offers to donate a quarter million dollars to your research foundation.

The third day, I drove her home myself, no drivers, no bodyguards. I was tempted to give the security team orders to stay on maximum alert—after having lost her for even a moment, I only wanted to hunker down at home, keep her and hold tight to my precious family, ensure their safety through force of sheer will.

But she herself had told me before she wasn't a princess in a tower.

And even though I knew she would understand keeping a few extra bodyguards until our anxiety wore off, I thought maybe their presence was preventing us from getting to that point. Dismissing them meant we were past this. And we *were* past this, thank God.

"You don't have to carry me," Alayna said, as I picked her up out of the passenger seat and brought her into my arms.

I shut the door to the car with my hip. "Oh, Mrs. Pierce, but I do." I still felt so very responsible for not protecting her the way I should have, the way I'd promised I would, and to make it up to her I was determined to let her feel as little pain as possible. I'd insisted the hospital give her a localized anesthetic for her injured ribs, on top of the oral pain meds, and it only took a little bit of prodding to get them to wrap her torso for the ride home, significantly diminishing the agony of movement. I had to promise to remove it as soon as we got home, to encourage her to breathe deeply so she wouldn't contract pneumonia. And I *would* remove it.

Just, maybe not immediately.

I wanted to spare her every second of pain I could.

I continued to carry her as we rode up the elevator and exited into our penthouse, where a room full of our loved ones was waiting to welcome her home. I sat her gently in an armchair in the living room, while Gwen and Mirabelle and Alayna's brother and all of our family and friends doted on her as she told the story of her horrific adventure. Mina gave her a hand-drawn card and a bouquet of paper flowers she'd made herself, then ran off to the playroom to run around with her cousins.

I stood back, watching, keeping the twins from crawling all over their mother, in hopes that no one noticed how many times I teared up, so overwhelmed with gratitude. *So much* gratitude.

After only a couple of hours, I shooed everyone out, declaring that Alayna needed her rest, and I carried her into our bedroom, and tucked her into bed with a pain pill.

I brought my laptop in to work at her bedside, but mostly, I watched her sleep, amazed that I *could* watch her sleep, that she was in my bed when I truly thought for a moment that she never would be again.

How my world would have ended.

She woke up later, and I served her dinner in our room. Then, after the children were bathed and in their pajamas, I let them all come in and gather around her—carefully. As a family, we watched *Beauty and the Beast*, the animated version, and it was wonderful. Even Holden watched occasionally, when he wasn't too busy walking the edge of the bed, from my side to Alayna's, over and over again.

Brett was content to lay in the crook of Alayna's arm on her un-injured side.

Yes, kid, I'm glad she's back too, I thought.

I may have watched them more than I did the show. Which frustrated Mina, who constantly asked, "Are you paying attention, Daddy?"

"Of course," I said, because I *was* paying attention to the Beauty and the Beast story, the better one. The real one. The one where Alayna was my beauty, an intelligent lover of books who somehow healed this beast.

I forced myself to take my time through tuck-in, though it was hard. I loved these moments with my children, loved being the last thing they saw at the end of the day. And I knew they needed a parent right now to reassure them and give them extra love and attention, even if they didn't understand what was going on. Children are much more aware than adults give them credit for—I'd learned in my few short years as a father.

But I did want to get back to my wife. Every minute away from her right now was agony.

"I'm surprised you're still awake," I said when I came back into the bedroom, and she was sitting there, propped up with a pillow against the headboard. Selfishly, I was glad she was. She had slept so much in the hospital, which was good because she needed the rest, but I also missed her. Missed talking to her.

Apparently she felt the same. "I was waiting for you. I wanted to be with you a little."

I crossed to her and stroked her face. "Okay. Give me a minute to get ready for bed, and I'll come join you. Help you get ready for bed, too." I kissed her on the head—I couldn't stop kissing her since I'd gotten her back, couldn't stop touching her as much she allowed. I slipped into my closet to change into a pair of boxer shorts, my preferred garment to sleep in—when I wasn't naked, of course. I also grabbed the few items I'd stashed in there earlier when Alayna wasn't looking, and brought them with me back to the bed. I dropped the small bag on the floor beside it and reclined next to her on my side, my head propped up with my elbow. Tenderly, I caressed her thigh.

"Have I told you today how much I love you?" I asked, staring into her deep brown eyes.

"Yes," she smiled. "About a million times."

"Here's a million and one. I love you, precious."

"I love *you*. More than I can ever say." She swept her fingers through my hair. "I'm sorry," she said.

"Whatever for? I'm the one who's sorry. I didn't keep you safe. I didn't figure out who was threatening us. I didn't have the security tight enough. I never told you about Adora." The words tumbled out, the apologies I'd been holding for days.

"I shouldn't have been at work, especially when there was a job fair."

"I *told* you to go to work."

"You wouldn't have told me if I hadn't been so catty and jealous."

"If I'd let you in all the way, you wouldn't have had a reason to be jealous." I pulled her hands down from my hair to my mouth and kissed the inside of her palm. Then, in unison we both said, "This isn't your fault."

I smiled and she laughed, immediately groaning afterward from the pain. "I forgot that would hurt."

I winced as if it were me who had the broken rib. I hated that she was in pain.

She kept her palm along my cheek. "H, did you hear me? This isn't your fault."

I'd heard her. "I'm going to have to work on believing that."

I reached behind me and grabbed the bag and pulled it between us. "I do know something that was my fault. And I'm going to fix it. I really didn't let you in, not all the way. Not because I didn't think you couldn't handle it, Alayna. You're so strong, so unbreakable, you've proven it surviving everything you've been through. And because of everything you've been through I always want to keep you from ever feeling anything bad again."

She started to say something, probably to explain why that was impossible, how people have to feel pain as part of the human process, something wise and meta.

But I didn't need to hear it. I'd already learned my lesson. "I understand why I can't do that," I reassured her. "And to make sure that I don't do it again, to prove to you how very much I want you in my world—and I mean every part of my world—I have something for you." I pulled the keyring out of the bag and handed it to her.

"This is for you. A key to every door, every desk drawer, every filing cabinet that I own, both here and at the office." Every paper, every file, was hers. Every secret, every memory. Everything I owned, and everything I was. All hers.

She took the bundle of keys, more than thirty in all with labels on a large ring, and stared bewildered at the gift.

"I've also had you added to my security level. Jordan has sent you an invitation to the app that will give you access to all the passwords and links he would need to access any of my accounts or information."

It was more symbolic than anything else. She wouldn't ever really need to go through my things, though she might do it out of her own curiosity—she'd always been one to snoop. But the intention was genuine, and she seemed to understand as her eyes started to brim with tears.

"Oh, Hudson," her voice was tight. "I don't know what to say."

"There's more." I pulled up the last two items, another, smaller keyring and a paper folded up in thirds. "These are all the keys for the event space next door to The Sky Launch, and the deed, in your name. Lee Chong sold it to me, and I know I should've waited and you wanted to do this yourself, and I'm trying not to hover, but I really couldn't allow you to go back over there without installing our security cameras, and he wouldn't allow that without a purchase agreement."

She bit her lip, as though trying not to laugh. "How did you get him to sell so early? He wanted to wait until the new year, I thought."

"I had to raise my offer to get them to sell earlier. And pay cash. I'm sorry, but I'm not. I do hope that you're not upset."

"I'm not upset. I would've been too scared to go back over there if you didn't put in cameras, honestly. And considering how Lee doesn't like to work with women, he probably gave you a better price than he would've given me even *with* the earlier buy." She hugged all the items to her chest. "I love them. All of them. They are so thoughtful and perfect and . . ."

She was getting emotional, but she held back her tears. "How did you even have time for all of this? You've been by my side for days."

"You don't realize how much you've slept. Besides, you'd be surprised how much you can do with a laptop and a phone when you're sitting in a hospital room next to a sleeping patient."

I leaned over to kiss her, gently. Then I kissed her again, because she tasted so good, and I loved kissing her.

I pulled away and leaned my forehead against hers, with great effort. If I didn't stop now, I'd never want to stop, and she was still recovering. "I'm glad you love the gifts," I told her.

I had not expected the response she gave.

"Alayna, what are you doing?" I asked as her hand fondled the outline of my cock.

"Can't you tell?" she teased.

"Alayna, precious, we can't. It's too much pressure on your rib."

"I'm still wearing the wrap," she said, her hand continuing its stroking. "And I had the local anesthetic, and pain pills. The doctor didn't say that we *couldn't*. He said, when I'm ready. And I need you."

As ridiculous as it was to think that she would want sex right now, it was also understandable considering our relationship. The way we communicated had always been so very wrapped in the physical. Still, I said, "I don't like this."

"Really? It seems like you like this very much."

Damn cock. Thinking for itself rather than about what was best for her. I was already hard and aching under the manipulations of her caress.

Forcing myself to not give into pleasure, I put my hand on hers, holding it back from its divine massage. "Alayna, I always want you. You know that. But this would be too much activity for you right now."

Her expression grew somber. "Please," she pled. "I need you. I need to erase him."

Every inch of my body tensed. She'd sworn to me he hadn't violated her. "Did he . . ."

"No," she answered quickly. "He didn't touch me. But he wanted to. And I need you to help me get that memory out of my head."

I wanted to know every detail of what he'd said to her, every sickening, crude comment so I could replay it in my head as many times as I knew she would. So I could replay it and feel the misery along with her.

But just because we had no more walls didn't mean we weren't respecting boundaries. I'd given her all the keys to my life, because I wanted her in all those spaces, but if right now she didn't want to share this part of her nightmare, if that was a space that she needed to keep for herself, I had to let her. And I'd be here if she ever invited me in.

So carrying that weight for her, *with* her, was not possible.

But if she needed this—if she needed *me*—I could give her that.

I let go of her hand, letting her resume her touch. She understood the cue, and moved her hand inside the fly, her skin hot against my flesh as she wrapped her fingers around my bare cock.

"Gentle," I instructed her. "We will be gentle and slow." I kissed her, deeper than before, my tongue slipping inside her mouth. "And you should be on top, so you can control the pressure and there's less strain to your rib."

"Okay," she said, her mouth turning up again toward mine, eager for another taste of my lips. "Help me get undressed."

She lifted up her hips while I pulled the jersey dress up carefully over her torso and head, tossing it to the floor next to us. The keys jingled on her lap, falling from the dress as I took it off. I took those along with the deed and put them on the nightstand, then crawled over her to help her with her panties. She was already braless, having chosen not to wear one with her injury, and her nipples stood up in front of me begging to be sucked on, licked, and loved. I give them each a swirl of my tongue before returning to the task of ridding her of her underwear.

Again she lifted her hips, and I pulled the small bikini briefs down her legs and off one ankle then the other. When she was naked, her pussy glistening in front of me with arousal, I decided perhaps *this* was what she really needed—my mouth down here, giving her pleasure, overshadowing her pain.

I nestled between her legs, spreading her thighs around my head and licked up the length of her slit.

She shivered and I went to do it again, but she put her hand on my shoulder, stopping me. "I need you inside me, Hudson. Please."

I could never deny her anything when she sounded like that, all soft and whimpering and desperate.

I stripped my boxers off, then lay down on the bed next to her. Putting my hand at the base of her spine, I helped her sit forward and steadied her as she climbed over me. I almost called the whole thing off when she let out a yowl at the pain at turning, but then she was sinking down on me, and her entire face lit up with relief.

She began to move her hips, riding me with soft undulations.

"Slow," I reminded her when she started to speed up. But, oh God, she was gorgeous, rocking her body against mine. I slipped my hand up the side of her torso and palmed her breast, rubbing my thumb over her erect nipple. With my other hand, I tenderly brushed against her plump, swollen clit, my eyes never leaving her face, watching for any sign of weakness or pain. I was never going to come this way, so concerned about her, but I didn't care about me. This was all for her.

I saw the strain start in her features before she showed signs of it anywhere else in her body. I wasn't sure if I should slow down or speed up, rush her to her orgasm and be done with it, or continue to go at a snail's pace.

I hadn't made a decision when she made it for us, sinking down across my chest with a frustrated moan. "I can't," she said. "You were right. It's too much."

I stroked her hair, and kissed the top of her head as I ran my hands along the landscape of her back, my cock still anchored inside her. "It's okay. We don't need to."

"I know." She was quiet for a minute.

"He wanted to make babies with me," she said finally. "He wanted to be . . ." Her voice cracked. "Everywhere . . . inside me. And I thought if I could just be filled up with you, it would go away, and I would remember that I don't belong to him. That I'm yours."

My chest felt like it was ripping apart, and I fought the urge to squeeze her tightly to me. To wrap her so tightly in my love that nothing bad could exist.

"Oh, precious. You *are* mine. Not just because I'm the man lucky enough to put my cock inside you, but because I'm the man who is lucky enough to be inside your heart."

She sniffled, and I felt a tear drop onto my bare chest.

"And you're mine," I went on, "because *you* fill every part of *me*. Every cell, every molecule. Every dark shadow within me, you are there, bringing light. No one can take that away from us, no matter what they want. You're mine because I don't exist without you. How much more mine can you be than that?"

She cried softly and silently against me, and I let her stay like that, against my chest, still half buried inside her while I rubbed her back until she was done. Then I rolled out of bed, pulled my boxers back on and tended to her, removing her wrap, helping her put on a fresh pair of panties. I gave her another pain pill and made her as comfortable as possible with a pillow under her head and another under her knees.

We didn't make love, but we *had* love. So much it blinded me sometimes, brilliant and white and perfect. It illuminated my once dark world and lit every room she walked into. It hummed with its brightness. It vibrated under my skin.

I curled up next to Alayna and wrapped my arm around hers, listening to the song of our love in the even rhythm of her breathing, a hypnotic, melodious sound that lulled me into a restful sleep where there were no more nightmares or terrors or dragons from the past, just us, living happy and whole, side by side, forever.

Epilogue
ALAYNA

In the middle of the night, I woke up to an empty bed. The way Hudson worked, his mind going at all hours, it wasn't unusual to find him in his office in the wee hours of the morning. Normally, I turned over and went back to sleep.

But the anxiety from everything that had happened was still fresh in my mind. I could still feel the tentacles of the nightmare, of David's grip on me, the fear that I would be taken from my family forever, and only my husband beside me could soothe those nerves.

I climbed out of bed, slowly, wincing at the injuries and the fresh stiffness, and eased on a robe before starting my search of the house. He wasn't in the library or the living room. Wasn't in the kitchen. I was about ready to go peek in on the children, when I noticed the door to the patio slightly ajar.

I slipped out onto the balcony, feeling the hot muggy air settle on me like a blanket. "Hudson?" I called to his dark figure sitting in the chair on the other side of the deck.

He turned sharply in my direction. He was immediately alert, sitting forward as though he were about to leap up from his chair and rush to me. "Alayna. Are you okay?"

"No," I said walking slowly toward him. He started to rise, but I stopped him with a gesture. It didn't stop him from examining me all over once I reached him.

"What's wrong?"

"You're not in bed," I said. "I woke up and didn't know where you were."

His features relaxed instantly, lips turning up into a smile. "But you found me."

"That I did."

He tugged me gently into his lap, arranging me so that I wasn't putting any weight on the side of me with the hurt rib, while being sure not to disturb the wound on my thigh.

He nuzzled his face into my neck, simultaneously slipping his hand inside my robe to gently cup my breast, an intimate caress more than a sexually charged one. As he kissed along my collarbone, his thumb grazed along my nipple until it stood up, pert and proud.

"What are you doing out here?" I asked, my voice vibrating on the edge of a moan.

"Dreaming," he said, continuing his kisses up my nape and to my jaw.

"This is not dreaming, Mr. Pierce. I assure you this is very real."

His mouth moved up to hover above mine, then he lifted his eyes to meet my gaze. He studied me for a moment, then chuckled to himself before leaning back into the chair.

"What?" I played my fingers through the back of his hair.

"Do you remember the other day when Mina woke up crying? And I went in to comfort her?"

I did. I'd been changing a diaper. Hudson and I hadn't even gone to bed for the night yet, and Mina had already padded out of her room with big crocodile tears running down her face. Her daddy went to her, picking her up and carrying her back to bed with soothing words.

"Did she have a nightmare? I never asked." She wasn't usually one to have bad dreams, but everyone did now and then.

"Actually, it was quite the opposite." He chuckled again, remembering. "She told me she'd been dreaming that she lived in a house made of candy—the floorboards were red licorice and she had a chocolate bar for door. There was more. She was very detailed in describing it to me. And she was devastated when she'd woken up and realized that the dream wasn't true."

"Oh my God, she's adorable." Having children with the man I loved was one of my favorite parts of spending my life with Hudson. We had this special thing that was just ours, these little humans that we created. No one on Earth would ever find stories about their antics as charming or magnificent as he and I, but it was something we would always have together that belonged to no one else.

"How did you get her to calm down? Promise to bribe her with candy the next day?"

"Yes. I did do that. I told her we'd take a trip to the candy store." He sobered. "But then I remembered something Jack used to say when I was really little. I'd forgotten all about it. Then with Mina's dream, it all of a sudden came rushing back to me, this memory of a very similar situation when I was about her age, and my dad putting me on his knee and saying that I didn't need to cry. Because dreams don't come true from dreaming them—they come true from *holding* them."

In the distance a siren sounded, the regular whoosh of traffic passed by below, but for the most part, the night was silent around us. "Holding them? What does that mean?"

"You keep it in your heart. Think about it often. Cherish it, I guess."

Yep. That did sound like the romantic kind of nonsense Jack would spout. And it was sweet.

Sweet . . .

"Wait—you told our daughter to hold her dream so it would come true?" I looked at my husband incredulously. "You're encouraging Mina to cherish the goal of a house made out of *candy*?!"

He shrugged innocently. "We don't know enough about her yet. She might grow up to be one of those eccentric types."

"She might grow up to be one of those *diabetic* types."

"Oh come on. She's four. Who knows how the dream will change? Maybe she'll end up running a chocolate factory one day. *My* dreams obviously changed. I didn't grow up to be a train."

I giggled again. "A train? That's the dream you wanted to hold onto?

Becoming a train?"

He scowled at me. "I told you—people change." He pulled me closer to him. "Anyway, that's why I was out here. I'd had a dream that woke me up. A good dream, and I wanted to hold onto it."

In all our time together, I couldn't remember a single time that Hudson had told me about his dreams—not his real literal dreams, the ones that occurred while he was sleeping.

I cocked my head and stared at him. "Tell me about it?"

He hesitated for a moment, his hand inside my robe, rubbing against the skin of my torso. "It wasn't really long. Just a brief snapshot of an afternoon. Sometime way in the future. We were at Stern and Brett was graduating with her MBA."

Brett following in my footsteps at my alma mater—it made my chest warm to imagine it.

"She looked just as beautiful as you did, the first night I saw you at that symposium. And she was just as smart and strong and fearless and enough."

God. Our future. I'd never thought that far into it, what life would look like when they grew up. I tried imagining it now, with him.

"How did you look?"

"I still had my hair."

I rolled my eyes. "Perfect, I bet. You probably aged better than me." He would always look perfect. I was sure of that.

"I still thought you were pretty goddamned sexy. I had wanted to pull you into another dark hallway so I could mess you up before the ceremony, but Bennett was with us."

I furrowed my brow. "Who's Bennett?"

"Our son. He's an oopsie."

I almost lost it at Hudson's use of the word oopsie, such an informal word from such a formal man.

And then I started to process what he'd said. Another kid. "I'm guessing this means you aren't getting that vasectomy."

"Bennett is your favorite child! I can't bear to go out of business now that I know about him."

Whether it was his way of saying he wasn't quite ready to close up shop—or that he'd prefer not to be the one to go under the knife—I wasn't sure. Either way, I could handle that revelation. That we weren't necessarily done. As long as it wasn't happening right away. "How much later does it—*he*—happen?"

Hudson squinted his eyes. "I guess he was ten years younger than the twins. Maybe more." Jesus, I'd be in my forties. He was definitely getting fixed after that one.

But maybe that would be the perfect time for an oopsie.

I nestled into him. "Who else was there? Tell me what else we're like in the future."

"Like I said, it was only a snapshot of this moment. But I did gather a lot. Holden was there—he was already married. And his wife seemed really pregnant. About to burst pregnant. Mina got there late because she was running from work—she was managing The Sky Launch now, and there'd been some sort of crisis. Jack was there. Sophia . . . wasn't."

I was quiet, not sure what to say about a future without the woman who had made my husband's life hell, but had also still been his mother.

"That's okay," he said when I didn't say anything. "I don't know how to feel about that myself."

"I'm sure it was sad."

"It *was* sad." He let another beat go by before continuing. "Mirabelle and Adam were there. Oh, and Brett's boyfriend. She was dating one of the Bruzzos. It was pretty serious. He hinted he had a ring."

I sat up excitedly, ignoring the protest of my side. If Brett really married one of Gwen's kids, it would tie our families together in even more ways than we already were. I loved the idea.

"Which one was it?"

"Is there a difference? I don't know. One of them."

I shook my head. "You are terrible."

"I *should've* known his name. He was working at Pierce Industries. He kept trying to pitch me new ideas during the boring parts of the ceremony. Some of them were actually good."

"Man, wouldn't that be amazing? Brett marrying Gwen's son, and the two of them taking over your business when you retire. All of it, really. Sounds like an amazeballs future."

"I hope it's *our* future. But whatever future I have with you will be perfect. The only required ingredient is that you're in it with me."

I tucked my head under his chin, and thought about what he'd said, holding his dream with him. His dream hadn't included anything like, "And you didn't have a breakdown after your next baby." He didn't even say, "Yeah, you went a little crazy again, but we all survived." And it struck me that those things didn't matter to him. That his vision didn't have to include "fixing" me to be perfect. He accepted the two Alaynas, accepted that they both made me *me*.

And why shouldn't he? Hudson still maneuvered and schemed and controlled. It was why he was so good at ruling his empire. Sometimes he crossed the line and tried to manipulate me and sent me into a fuss, but I didn't want him any other way.

So maybe our whole relationship, when I'd thought we worked because we fixed each other's broken parts, was wrong. Maybe we hadn't fixed each other at all—because we didn't *need* fixing. We needed healing and understanding. We needed patience and optimism. We needed dreams instead of nightmares and light instead of darkness. We needed trust.

And we'd given each other all of that.

We'd both just needed to be loved. For who we were and despite what we'd done. For our strengths and our weaknesses too. We'd needed someone to belong to, someone who filled our dark spaces, someone who moved heaven and Earth to make sure we'd always be together.

We'd needed love.

And we had enough of that to last us a lifetime and beyond.

Epilogue 2

HUDSON

I took the rest of the week off to be with my family. To be there for Alayna when she woke from the nightmares, her heart racing, sweat pouring from her body. To make sure everyone felt safe and secure and whole before returning to work.

On my first day back, Patricia greeted me with a packed schedule and a handful of mail and interoffice items that only I could attend to. Slipped between a stack of standard contracts sent over from Accelecom, I found a single sealed white business sized envelope, my name scrawled in a masculine script on the front.

Inside was a page of hotel stationery, folded in thirds with a note handwritten in the same cursive.

I'm grateful to hear your wife is back in your arms.
You and I have unfinished business.

Edward Fasbender

Meet the man who slayed the dragon.

S LAY

(Book 1 of the Slay Trilogy)

Three years after Hudson officially quit playing games with her, Celia Werner is summoned to the office of Edward Fasbender, the most wealthy media mogul on the European continent. She meets with him, assuming he wants to hire her to decorate his offices.

Instead, he has an intriguing proposition for her.

Coming June 10, 2019

Free Story from Me!

Don't miss the FREE story in my newsletter, SWEET LIAR, starting end of May 2018, one chapter a month. Available to subscribers only.

British ad exec, Dylan Locke, isn't looking for love. He isn't looking for fate. He's definitely not looking for the pretty, young, romantic Audrey Lind.

But when the girl, who's twenty years younger than him, literally lands in his lap and asks for his expertise, he'd be lying if he said he wasn't interested.

Book one in the next duet in the Dirty Universe will be delivered a chapter a month to your inbox starting late May 2018. Sign up for my newsletter now so you don't miss out! Link can be found on my website.

www.laurelinpaige.com

DIRTY SEXY PLAYER
SNEAK PEEK!

A New Duet in the Dirty Filthy Universe from NYT Bestselling Author, Laurelin Paige.

Weston King knows how to play. But wild nights and owning an extensive collection of women's panties don't carry the thrill they once did, so when his business partner Donovan suggests an outrageous plan to allow them to take over their competition, Wes takes him up on the offer. The crazy idea? Marry the competitor.

Elizabeth Dyson, the bride-to-be in question, is on board with the plan. She wants access to her trust fund and can only get it once she marries. Each has something the other wants—all they have to do is pretend to like each other well enough to tie the knot.

Only trouble is, playing fiancé to Elizabeth isn't quite that simple. Wes finds her sexy and brilliant . . . and soon wishes their engagement wasn't fake at all. Not that he'd ever tell her that.

But a lover boy like Wes can only stand an empty bed for so long . . . and even the best of players has to put down his cards eventually.

ONE

WESTON

"Nice rock," I said, admiring the diamond ring Donovan placed on the tabletop. I picked it up and examined the stone in the dimly lit lounge of the The Grand Havana Room, the member's-only cigar lounge we often frequented when we were together. The diamond was a big one, in a platinum setting with at least four carats between the large center jewel and the scattering of smaller diamonds surrounding it. A serious engagement ring. I wouldn't expect anything less from one of the world's most successful young billionaires.

I just had no idea Donovan was even dating anyone.

Of course, we weren't as close as we used to be. Physically, anyway. He'd been managing the Tokyo office with Cade since we'd expanded our advertising firm into that market. He rarely made it stateside, and it had been nearly a year since I'd last seen Donovan in person. When he'd shown up tonight unexpectedly asking Nate and I to meet him at the club, we'd guessed he had serious news but that it was about the business.

An engagement ring was a whole new level of serious. No wonder he wanted to do this in person.

"Who's the lucky girl?" I asked, trying not to sound bothered that this was the first I was hearing about her. A glance at Nate said it was the first he was hearing about her too.

"You're asking the wrong question," Donovan said, and bit off the end of his cigar. "The question is who's the lucky *guy?*"

I raised a brow, confused. But not surprised. Donovan was known to speak in riddles. I'd figure out what he was trying to tell me when he was ready to spill. Might as well play along in the meantime.

"Okay." I pinched the ring between two fingers and lifted it toward the nearest light source so I could see the full effect of its sparkle. "Who's the lucky guy?"

He lit the end of his cigar and puffed a couple of times before taking it out and answering. "You."

"Oh, Donovan. You shouldn't have." I clutched my hand to my chest for dramatic effect. "I don't know that we've ever said it, but I love you too. Still, I don't think I'm ready for this." I handed the ring back to him with a shake of my head.

Nate hid his smirk by taking a large swig of his imported beer.

"Very funny." Donovan carefully placed the ring back in its box. "I'm not proposing *to* you, Weston. I'm proposing *for* you."

"You are, are you?" I chuckled at his attempt at a joke. Inside my jacket pocket my phone buzzed with a text. I pulled it out and quickly skimmed the message.

I need to see you.

Normally I'd be all up for a booty call, but my night belonged to the guys. I deleted the message without reading who it was from, silenced my phone and put it back in my pocket.

I gave my attention back to Donovan, continuing to play along with his hoax. "Just who exactly are you proposing to *for* me?"

He puffed heavily on his cigar before removing it from his mouth to speak. "Her name is Elizabeth Dyson. She's the sole inheritor of the Dyson Empire. She's twenty-five, classy though spirited, well-bred—definitely a suitable bride. Your union is going to take our business to the next level. Once you marry her, Reach, Inc. will be the biggest advertising company in Europe."

All humor drained from my face. He was serious. Donovan never joked about business. But marriage? "You've got to be kidding me."

"Not even a little bit."

I was beginning to regret not looking at the name before I deleted that text. I'd have loved to have a reason to bail right about then.

But it was Donovan's first night back in town, I really couldn't leave him now. Not to mention, I knew him. Once he got an idea in his head, it was nearly impossible to get it out. My best chance was to listen, find the weakness in his scheme, and then propose an alternate strategy.

If that failed, I'd tell him *fuck, no*, and that would be that.

Hopefully.

Saying *fuck, no* to Donovan Kincaid was often a bit harder in reality than it seemed in theory.

If I was going to stay, I was at least going to need a stiffer drink. I signaled the waiter. "Can you bring me a shot of Fireball?" Nate nudged me. "Two shots of Fireball?"

Then I turned to Donovan. "You'd better explain this from the beginning."

He took a puff of his cigar. "It's a short explanation. Dell Dyson, founder, CEO, and majority shareholder of Dyson Media—basically France's version of Time Warner—died about eight months ago, leaving his daughter the sole inheritor to the bulk of his fortune. However, the will states she can't get her hands on any of it until she's 29—with one exception."

"Ah, I think I'm getting the picture," Nate said, taking a pull on his beer.

My brows remained wrinkled, *my* picture still unclear. "Explain it to me then," I said, turning to Nate. "Because I'm not following."

He set his bottle on the table and tilted his head toward me. "Daddy Dell was a traditionalist. The daughter inherits when she puts a ring on it."

"Oh." Understanding settled in. I screwed my face up in disgust. "That's gross."

"Completely terrible and misogynistic," Donovan agreed, not sounding terribly upset at all. "But there's nothing we can do about the unfortunate set-up to her situation, and there is something we can do to get her out of it. Something that works out in our favor. So what we need to do is focus on getting Elizabeth married to our man Weston—"

I started to protest, but Donovan rose a hand to silence me. "*Temporarily* married—a couple of months is all we need for Elizabeth to claim her inheritance of Dyson Media. Once she does, she can push through the merger of Dyson's advertising subsidiary with Reach, and we'll take over as the biggest ad company in the European market."

"Just like that," I said, skeptically.

"Just like that." There was no trace of doubt in Donovan's voice.

"And what makes you think that she'd be interested in this?" I asked. "I mean why would she be interested in giving someone—giving *us*—part of the company? Not why would she be interested in me." I wasn't worried about women being into me. But I certainly wasn't into discussing it with Donovan.

Of course he had an answer for this as well. "I'm in preliminary talks with her already. And she seemed quite interested in the whole arrangement. I didn't specify who her groom would be but told her I had an eligible bachelor. She's thinking about it further. Tomorrow afternoon in the office, all four of us will have a meeting to hammer out the details. I've already cleared your schedule."

It was a good thing the shots arrived then. "You mean I have to have this all thought through and decided by tomorrow afternoon?"

"Oh, you'll agree," Donovan said, confidently.

I threw back the shot. It didn't burn half as much as Donovan's proposal.

I rolled my neck, easing the muscles in my shoulders. "I need a minute to think about this."

"Take two."

I wasn't really considering any of it, but it was an excuse to order another drink and make Donovan pay for it.

I gestured for the waiter to bring two more shots. Then I leaned back against the plush leather upholstery of the bench seat and rubbed my hand across my forehead, pretending to weigh Donovan's offer in my mind.

To be honest, I'd been restless recently. I enjoyed the benefits of my life—my rental apartment in Midtown, my sex life, the view from my office. But my twenty-ninth birthday was looming and that was so close to thirty. A milestone birthday, and what did I have to show for it?

Okay. I was one of five shareholders of Reach,Inc., one of the most successful ad agencies in the world, but everyone knew that was Donovan's brainchild.

What did I have that was purely my own?

A month ago, I'd been so caught up in the desire for clarity that, on a whim, I'd asked a girl to move to New York from LA. It wasn't the first impulsive move I'd ever made, especially not for a girl—a girl I'd been naked with all weekend, no less—but it had been the craziest.

Almost as crazy of an idea as getting married to a stranger in order to improve our business status.

Sabrina, the naked woman, had been a peer that Donovan and I had gone to Harvard with. I'd been fortunate enough to spend a magical reunion weekend with her. There was something about her—a combination of her sexy laugh, serious demeanor, and intelligent brain that struck a chord deep inside me. Our conversation had made me feel warm and interesting and I wanted to capture that. Wanted to make it last.

So much so that right there on the spot, I demanded she take the position of Director of Marketing Strategy. Who cared that there was somebody else who held the position already?

She'd turned me down, wisely, but after she'd left, when the hormones calmed down, I looked into her resume anyway. Turned out she actually deserved the position, and I'd been halfheartedly working on making the transition happen legitimately ever since.

I'd spent good time thinking about making a real go at a relationship with her, too, if I got her to take the job.

I'd even told Donovan about my plans. Had he forgotten?

"But I don't want to get married," I reminded him now. "I want to bring Sabrina Lund to New York City and find out whether or not we fit together."

"Sabrina *Lind*," he corrected, his tone peppered with annoyance.

"Isn't that what I said?" I was starting to feel the alcohol.

"Still bring her here," Nate suggested, always the reasonable one.

"She can take the job, and settle in. By the time she gets the hang of things around here, you'll be through your annulment and then you're free to date her."

"That could work, I suppose." Still wasn't considering it.

"If *she's* interested, that is," Donovan scowled.

"Why would she not be interested?" I asked.

"She'll be interested," Nate assured me. "But it is hard to move into a new city and get into a new relationship all at once. Better to take it in steps. And meanwhile, you can do this thing for the company."

I could hear the subtext in his words. Subtext that said he thought maybe I owed the company a little more *doing*.

Possibly I was reading too much into it.

I slammed back my next shot and considered what other reason there might be for Nate Sinclair to take Donovan's side. He was usually Switzerland.

"You're just saying all that because you don't want to be the one to get married, aren't you?" I eyed Nate accusingly.

He averted his eyes. "I'm old enough to be her father. It's not really appropriate."

I turned my stare to Donovan. There wasn't a band on *his* finger.

"It wouldn't work," he said flatly, guessing my thoughts. "No one would ever believe I'd get married."

"I can't dispute that." It was hard for me to believe the guy had friends. And I was his *best* friend.

"You are the ideal candidate," Donovan insisted.

"Damn right I'm the ideal candidate." I grinned, giving him my full dimpled smile, because hands-down, I was the best looking of all of us. My panty collection proved it. Cade could give me a run for my money with his constant brooding—women seemed to go for that—but he was in Japan. And Dylan Locke's charming British accent only worked on girls outside the UK, and he was never leaving the London office.

So, I wasn't just the ideal candidate—I was the *only* candidate.

But I wasn't doing it. It was crazy. Stupid crazy.

I ran my hand over my face, wondering how much longer I should allow Donovan to think I could be convinced. There was a fine line between hearing him out and becoming roped in.

"Is this Elizabeth person hot?" I asked, my lips numb from the shots.

"Why?" Donovan asked suspiciously.

"If I'm stuck with her I might as well . . . you know."

"You just said that you couldn't marry her because you've found the love of your life with Sabrina . . ." I could practically see steam coming from Donovan's ears.

"I didn't say Sabrina was the love of my life. I said she *might* be the love of my life. It's too early to tell."

"Either way," Donovan said, snarling, "it's probably a good idea if you don't sleep with your fiancée."

I exchanged glances with Nate.

Donovan followed my gaze as he tapped the ash of his cigar into a tray. "That didn't sound right, but I stand behind my recommendation."

Again, Nate and I looked to each other. We maybe had less conventional sexual standards than our business partner.

Correction—we *definitely* had less conventional sexual standards. Especially Nate. Which made him a god in my book. But that was beside the point.

The point was that good ideas were for the office. In the bedroom, I preferred my ideas to be bad.

I was just messing with Donovan, anyway. I didn't need this set-up to get laid, and I most certainly didn't need this set-up to feel like I'd contributed to the company. I'd strung him along far enough.

"Well, Donovan, this is maybe the most strategic and outrageous plan you've ever come up with, also possibly the most brilliant." I patted him on the back. He did deserve credit where credit was due. "But I'm going to have to pass, brother. It's a little too crazy for me."

Donovan sat back and slung out an arm, his elbow resting on the back of the bench. He looked relaxed, far too at ease with my decision, which made *me* uneasy. He was a guy who was used to things happening his way. He didn't like it when his plans were altered. If he wasn't upset now, it meant he had something else up his sleeve.

Which meant I needed to keep my guard up.

Unfortunately, Donovan also had patience. So despite my suspicions, I'd have to wait until he was prepared to move into the next phase of his plan to find out what he was hiding.

I glanced over at Nate who shrugged again before catching the eye of a gentleman at the bar.

"Excuse me," he said, "I know that guy. I need to say hello."

I gave him a wink because there was no telling how Nate knew him—whether it was from his past crazy illegal dealings or from his current wild sexual dealings. Either way, it probably made a good story, and one I'd like to hear.

A good story that I wasn't going to get to hear because I was stuck at the table with Donovan and whatever bullshit scenario he had worked up for me now.

Before he could start in on another one of these brilliant schemes, I started a conversation of my own. "How long are you staying in town, Donovan?"

"Haven't decided yet. A few months. Longer, maybe. Cade's handling Japan for now. Meanwhile, you've been complaining about needing some help up here. So here I am."

"Well." This was awesome. Donovan and I hadn't lived in the same city for years. Our parents owned King-Kincaid Financial, and we'd spent so much time together growing up, we were practically siblings. My only sister was a decade younger, so Donovan had been the one I'd bonded with most. Only four years older than me, he was the one who had mentored me through all my significant firsts. First time drinking, first time smoking, first time sneaking out to meet a girl, first time starting a company.

"Glad to hear it. You should've told me sooner. Are you moving back into—"

"I'll wipe the loan," he said, cutting me off.

And there it was. The bit that would make my jaw drop. The offer that would make me sit up and listen.

"The *entire* loan?" My heart was thumping in my chest now, and I could hear blood gushing in my ears.

"The whole thing. Gone."

Gone. All of it. *Whoosh.* Just like that.

What a fucking relief that would be.

Donovan was the only one who knew that I hadn't put all my own money into the company when we first started up. After nearly draining my inheritance from my grandmother, I'd borrowed the rest of the seed money from him, a sizable amount that I'd slowly been paying him back with the profits earned over our five years in business.

I still owed him a million.

It was quite an amount to just write off, even for him.

The irony of it was that I had more than twenty times that in my trust fund. I could've wiped the loan out myself years ago. If I'd wanted to.

Again, Donovan was the only one who knew why I chose not to borrow from that sizable fund.

And so, since Reach had begun with Donovan and I—and since we had pledged the most start-up money—when he covered my portion, he also got the advantage.

It was one of the reasons why the company always felt like it was more Donovan's than mine.

And it was a reason I often bent to his will, even when I'd rather not.

"Why is this merger so important to you?" I asked, unsure what to make of this offer. It wasn't like Donovan held the loan over me all the time. It wasn't like he wasn't generous. He would give me the shirt off his back if it was the last thing he owned.

But he also knew about integrity, and he understood that I wanted to be a self-made man. And he respected that.

I respected him for getting me.

So if this was that important to him, then I really needed to be listening. Because I would give Donovan the shirt off my back too.

"Number one in Europe, Weston," he said with a gleam in his eye. "We've only been open five years, and it would take a long time to get that title any other way. It's been far more difficult than I'd hoped to crack that market the way we have here."

I always knew the guy was competitive, but this really took the cake. "And it's just a fake marriage then? Just a sham?"

Dammit. I couldn't believe I was actually considering this.

"A complete farce. You'd start right away, fake a whirlwind romance and engagement. Have the whole thing done in four, five months tops. But the benefits to Reach would last a lifetime. Think of it as your legacy, Weston."

I drummed my fingers on the table top. "This is fucking insane."

"You *like* insane," he said, leaning in close, knowing exactly which words would push my buttons.

How did he do this every time? He really was a mastermind. Able to wield the strings of all the puppets, controlling everyone, getting them to do his bidding. Not that I resented him for it. I admired him, truthfully.

And there was that something in my life that was missing.

Not that a fake wedding was going to fix it, but maybe the chance to contribute could make a difference. The chance to leave a legacy.

And to be able to give something back to Donovan after all the things he'd given me—well, that was something I couldn't take lightly.

Plus the end of that loan. To be my own man. Finally.

"Ah, fuck it. I got nothing better to do with my life. Let's be number one in Europe." Actually, that did have a pretty decent ring to it.

The corner of his lip lifted. "You know how to talk dirty to me." He reached into his pocket, where he'd deposited the ring back into its velvet box earlier, and handed it over before taking a long, satisfied sip of his drink.

I dropped it inside my jacket. The small square shape felt like a lead weight against my chest.

I wondered how heavy its contents were going to feel when it was on Elizabeth Dyson's hand.

Want more? Get Dirty Sexy Player now, available on most vendors!

Also by
Laurelin Paige

THE DIRTY UNIVERSE
Dirty Filthy Rich Boys—READ FREE
Dirty Filthy Rich Men (Dirty Duet #1)
Dirty Filthy Rich Love (Dirty Duet #2)
Dirty Filthy Fix (a spinoff novella)
Dirty Sexy Player (Dirty Games Duet #1, July 23, 2018)
Dirty Sexy Games (Dirty Games Duet #2, November 12, 2018)
Sweet Liar (Dirty Sweet #1)
(for newsletter subscribers now! early 2019 everywhere)
Sweet Promises (Dirty Sweet #2) (early 2019)

THE FIXED UNIVERSE
Fixed on You (Fixed #1)
Found in You (Fixed #2)
Forever with You (Fixed #3)
Hudson (Fixed #4)
Fixed Forever (Fixed #5)
Free Me (Found Duet #1)
Find Me (Found Duet #2)
Chandler (a spinoff novel)
Falling Under You (a spinoff novella)
*Dirty Filthy Fix (*a spinoff novella)
Slay 1 (Slay trilogy) (June 10, 2019)
Slay 2 (Slay trilogy) (Fall 2019)
Slay 3 (Slay trilogy) (Winter 2019)

FIRST AND LAST

First Touch

Last Kiss

HOLLYWOOD HEAT

Sex Symbol

Star Struck

SPARK

One More Time

Want (Coming soon!)

Close (Coming soon!)

Written with Kayti McGee

under the name LAURELIN MCGEE

Hot Alphas

Miss Match

Love Struck

MisTaken

Holiday for Hire

Written with SIERRA SIMONE

Porn Star

Hot Cop

Acknowledgments
and
Author's Note

I'm quite familiar with OCD and mental illness.

My first exposure was growing up with a family member who had the disorder. I was about ten or so, and I remember reading The Boy Who Kept Washing His Hands, a book my grandparents owned to help the rest of us understand what my aunt was going through.

It was a fascinating topic.

Later, there were friends I was close to who had it. All of this, I believe, was preparation for me to be mother to three daughters who each have different forms of OCD.

I'd written the first Fixed book before my kids were ever diagnosed with their disorders. I based Alayna's obsessions on my own tendency to fixate and obsess. I was never Alayna—but I knew that I *could* be.

I didn't decide to revisit Hudson and Alayna in order to focus on these issues, but getting the chance to do so, with the added knowledge of what it's like to live with these disorders (as well as depression and anxiety—my house is full of sensitive, empathetic unicorns!) has been exactly the book I needed to write at this time in my life.

I hope this book is also meaningful for some of you. These experiences might not be what you've heard about OCD or what *you* know to be true about it, but they are pieces of my own truth.

I didn't write anything that I didn't understand.

I didn't add anything I hadn't seen or lived.

Beyond resonating with the path that I knew these characters had taken, I was reluctant to write another book for Hudson and Alayna. I loved where I'd left them off—happy and safe and in love. I definitely didn't want to introduce another conflict that would tear them apart— these two have committed to each other. Their struggles are not about staying together or loving each other—they belong to each other and they know that.

But even so, I have a husband I belong to. He's the forever guy for me, and still we have the times we rub against each other. Not just with the "I forgot to go to the store, there's no toilet paper" kind of friction, but with deeper confrontations. Those days where I feel, "Gah! Does this man even know who I am?"

And he does. Sometimes better than I know myself. Always *different* than I know myself.

That was the story I wanted to write for Alayna and Hudson—the story of a marriage. The story of two people who are going to be forever, and in order to be that, they work hard at keeping their magic alive.

I hope that's the story you find in the pages of this book. I hope they're helpful or useful or *validating* or just plain entertaining for the people who read it.

Now onto the gushy part.

This past year has been incredibly tough for me. In just 12 months time I had emergency gall bladder surgery, broke my arm, lost my dog, got a new puppy who broke *his* arm, lost some very significant friendships, discovered two of my children had OCD that I wasn't aware of before, had my estranged dad reappear in my life after 25 years, dealt with my 8-year old having a major nervous breakdown and refusal to continue attending school, watched my 15-year old daughter be diagnosed with a chronic syndrome that has no cure and become a depressed shell of the girl she once was, decided to move out of state for better services and resources for my children, wrote more books in 12 months than

I've ever written in that time period while suffering from chronic pain after my arm break, and am now in the process of both selling a house and buying a house.

With the completion of this book, my grandmother passed away. And that's how this year ended.

It's been hard getting here. And, besides mentioning the usual book supporters, there are definitely people I need to thank for helping me arrive here, because this was not a journey I could have made on my own.

First of all, to my best friend Kayti McGee, the person whom this book is dedicated to—I've already said all my nice words to her this year at this amazing Unicorn summit we attended, and I can't give her more without ruining my grumpy cat reputation. But if I could say more, I'd thank her for never tiring of my bullshit, for reading my mind, for being willing to always drive to my house, for listening when I ruminate over and over, for the visits to my house to get my ass out of bed and keep me focused, for "getting me", and, most especially, for letting me feel at every turn that I wasn't broken. You're my other half. I love you big. (Move to Texas, m'kay?)

To Candi Kane, Melissa Gaston, Rebecca Friedman, Jana Aston, Christine Reiss, Lauren Blakely, Melanie Harlow, Roxie Madar, Michele Ficht, Amy Libris, and Liz Berry—all of you deserve sainthood. These shit storms wouldn't have been weathered without your amazing, incredible, compassion. You've been patient friends who reached out through messages and phone calls, always reminding me you were there. I am humbled and honored to be worthy of your time and love.

To Anthony Colletti for knowing what I needed and pressing me out of my comfort zone. To Chris Yonkers, the guy waiting outside that zone to teach me flow.

To the people who make the stuff happen behind the scenes—Rebecca Friedman my agent and best friend who is going to live near me soon (I. Can't. Wait). Flavia Viotti and Meire Dias for being formidable, intelligent women to work with. Nancy Smay who continues to edit my work IN CHUNKS. (God, you're just too good to me.) Andi Arndt and Marni for always being willing to work with me, for remaining professional and KIND at the same time. Also for producing such amazing audio recordings.

To my earliest readers, Roxie, "Vox", Serena, Candi, and Liz—you all came with me down to the wire on this one. Again, I'm so humbled. So grateful. Thank you, thank you.

To my Snatches (Mel, Sierra, and Kayti; the girls who have been here from the beginning) and The Order and Shop Talkers and Jenn Watson. You're all incredibly inspiring and real and raw with your interactions with me. I'm lucky to have so many amazing, strong women in my tribe.

To my LARCs—I made you wait so long! You're incredibly patient with me, and I thank you for that and for always helping me do what I love to do most—give stories to the world.

To my readers in The Sky Launchers, and to the bloggers and the readers who love these books and share them with others. I will never not be amazed by your love and passion for the silly things in my head. You make my life possible, and I don't forget it.

To my family. My beautiful, crazy, smart and funny and brave and "enough" girls; my steadfast, loyal, strong lobster husband; my two sweet puppies and my cats with personality—you are my reasons, the wind beneath my wings. And you belong to me so you can't get rid of me, even if you want to.

And to my God who brought me through the fire that sloughed off the shame and the rust and found the precious girl underneath. I'm learning. Still. Always. Forever.

About Laurelin Paige

With over 1 million books sold, Laurelin Paige is the *NY Times, Wall Street Journal*, and *USA Today* Bestselling Author of the Fixed Trilogy. She's a sucker for a good romance and gets giddy anytime there's kissing, much to the embarrassment of her three daughters. Her husband doesn't seem to complain, however. When she isn't reading or writing sexy stories, she's probably singing, watching *Game of Thrones* and *the Walking Dead*, or dreaming of Michael Fassbender. She's also a proud member of Mensa International though she doesn't do anything with the organization except use it as material for her bio.

www.laurelinpaige.com

laurelinpaigeauthor@gmail.com

33395455R00165

Printed in Great Britain
by Amazon